# KNOWN UNTO GOD

Best wishes
Bob Bobby

# KNOWN UNTO GOD

## *Bob Bibby*

PIERREPOINT

PRESS

A CIP record for this book is available from the British Library.

ISBN 978 0 9533196 7 1

Cover design by Clare Brayshaw from a photograph by Alex and Chris Painter

Typeset, printed and bound in Great Britain by:

York Publishing Services Ltd.,
64 Hallfield Road,
Layerthorpe,
York,
YO31 7ZQ

Tel: 01904-431213

*To Enid*

# Other books by Bob Bibby

***Crime Fiction***
Be a Falling Leaf
Bird on the Wing
The Liquidator
The Llareggub Experience

***Travel Writing***
Grey Paes and Bacon
Dancing with Sabrina
Special Offa
On the Wall with Hadrian

***Walking Guides***
The Shropshire Cakes and Ale Trail
The Worcestershire Cakes and Ale Trail

Cuánto vive el hombre, por fin?
Vive mil días o uno solo?
Una semana o varios siglos?
Por cuánto tiempo muere el hombre?
Qué quiere decir 'Para siempre'?

PABLO NERUDA

# PART 1

# 1

A time comes when we all have to embark on a mission into our past. To revisit, to re-examine, perhaps to resolve. Besides, she had promised Bert that one day she would go. It was probably too late already, she thought, but, if not now, then when?

The hot stink of donkey was not, however, what Meredith Ennis had anticipated when she had asked for a Mediterranean cruise as a celebration of her ninetieth birthday. And, with her small figure sidesaddle-mounted and clinging to the beast's wooden harness, she was beginning to doubt the wisdom of her decision as the donkey lurched up the rock-strewn path. Above her towered the glistening slab of rock of the cliff face, behind her the richly blue waters of the Libyan Sea reaching towards Africa, ahead of her the black hole of the cave that was her goal. With her free hand, she shielded her face and pushed wisps of white hair back from her eyes.

Forward on the path, loosely holding a rope attached to the donkey's harness and carrying a limp sack over his shoulders, strode the stocky figure of her guide, her messenger from and to the past, her very own Hermes, Nikos Themistocles, though he insisted she call him Themis. Although only a few years younger than her, he still chose to walk while insisting that she ride on the donkey. She had protested but in the end conceded defeat, though the jarring of the beast's movement and the stink of its snorted breath were making her review that decision. She wrapped her linen scarf over her hair and pulled her thin dress down over her legs to protect them from the sun's dying, late-afternoon heat.

What was she hoping to find in that cave? Surely, after all these years – well over sixty now, a lifetime – there would be nothing concrete to see, no evidence from then, no sign of its occupation. Was it just some sense of where it had all happened that she hoped to experience for herself? Did she really think she could recapture those moments from the fragmentary knowledge she had? And what of her guide, the grey-eyed Themis, striding ahead in his baggy trousers and collarless white shirt? What would he bring with him? What would he be feeling now, all these years on?

The finding of him was her grandson Will's doing. He'd called to see her one day and, to satisfy her curiosity, had shown her how his laptop worked. Thoughts of Will now flashed into her mind, replaced immediately by thoughts of his namesake, his great-uncle, her husband Bert's brother whom Will had never known, Bill Ennis, the reason for her visit to this cave just outside the village of Hora Sfakion on the southern coast of Crete.

'Are you sure it was here?' she called out to her companion as he coaxed the donkey over the rocks and through the wiry thorn-bushes, like someone luring a reluctant fish to the river's surface.

'Definitely,' came the reply. 'It's just ahead. You can see? It's just there.'

She nodded to herself, as if giving reassurance, and let him lead the heavy-breathing donkey higher up the cliff face. If anyone had asked her the reason she hadn't come earlier, she would have told them 'Life'. Life, with all its demands, its complexities, its peaks and troughs, had always pushed this journey further and further back in her mind. She had almost forgotten about it. No, that was not true. She had convinced herself she had forgotten about it, though in reality it was always sitting there in the depths of her heart, that ancient wrinkled prune of a heart, awaiting its time.

On her next visit to the Public Library, she had typed 'Themistocles' into the online Greek telephone directory. Of the twenty or so names that she came across, there were only four in Crete but only one in the place she was looking for, a place called Xamoudochori. She had noted the number, then later dialled it and had been relieved when the voice answering admitted to speaking English. Her heart had jumped when this voice turned out to belong to the very man she had been seeking – Nikos Themistocles.

'Of course,' he had said. 'Of course I knew Bill Ennis. He was a good man. He saved my life, you know.'

She had almost dropped the telephone then. Saved his life? How? What did that mean? The telegram had told of Bill's death but nothing of the circumstances surrounding it. Was it then, on hearing Themis's words, that the notion of making this trip had first wriggled into her mind?

She had explained that her late husband had been Bill's brother and that she had promised him that one day she would visit the place where he had died.

'So, you must come to Crete,' Themistocles had said in his guttural voice, tinged with a slight Australasian accent. 'It is never too late. Crete is a beautiful island, especially in May when the spring flowers are out.'

'I'm almost ninety,' she had replied, smiling to herself at the silliness of his suggestion, though, if she allowed herself to be honest – always a difficulty - it had echoed her own thoughts of a few moments earlier.

'So? I am seventy-seven next month. I swim in the sea three times a week. My village is in the hills and I walk in those hills every week. Why not come?'

She had thought the idea preposterous and told him so, but gradually over the coming weeks, especially through the bitterly dark month of February, the notion took hold and, without telling any of her immediate family, certainly not her son Tom or her daughter Nancy, she had formulated a sort of plan. She knew they wouldn't let her travel alone so, when Tom had asked her what she wanted as a special gift for her ninetieth birthday, she had asked for a Mediterranean cruise, knowing that, if they agreed to it, they would insist on her having company. She'd thought of that too. Ellie, her granddaughter from Tom's first marriage, had recently broken up with her long-term boyfriend and had taken extended leave from her work with the Arts Council. She would make the ideal companion, not only because she was the first grandchild and had therefore always had a special place in Meredith's affections but also – and it was terrible of her to admit to knowing this – because Ellie was too trusting. There was a lot to be said for the naivety of Ellie's trustfulness but Meredith Ennis knew she could also use it for her own ends.

So, when the *Ariadne* had eased slowly into the noisy port of Heraklion, where taxi drivers and street vendors vied to attract the attention of curious passengers leaning over the ship's railings, her lips had gone suddenly dry as she realised how close she was to …what? Enough. For now. The passengers had been advised that a guided tour of the city, together with a trip to the fabled ruins of Knossos, was to take place on the following morning. Meredith had been delighted to see Ellie chatting animatedly on deck to that young, smartly-bedecked officer with whom she had been dancing the previous evening. Excusing herself, she had announced that she needed an early night if she was to enjoy the trip on the following day. As soon as she had left Ellie, she had rung Nikos Themistocles and very early next morning, dressed she hoped suitably in a thin green cotton dress, beige cardigan and white trainers and clutching her canvas handbag, she was sitting next to him in his comfortable Honda saloon, where the air-conditioning fought with stale tobacco, heading along the National Road away from Heraklion, away from the *Ariadne*, and away from Ellie, while listening to his story.

*

'I was one lucky fellow. I got off the island just before the Germans took control. Thanks to Bill. Or Skip, as they all called him. My family was not so lucky. After the British soldiers were either evacuated or surrendered, the Germans brought cruelty to Crete. They had expected us to welcome them but found quite the opposite. Many men took to the mountains to join resistance. My Uncle Alexandros was one of the leaders of the resistance movement. It lasted the rest of the war. The Germans rounded up women, old men and children they suspected of hiding resistance fighters or escaped British soldiers and they shot them. Cold-bloodedly they shot them. My grandfather and my mother, God save them, died that way. Lined up beside the wall of our own house in Xamoudochori and shot.'

Themis's voice caught in his throat and Meredith felt a shiver in her stomach. So long ago these matters but still they tugged at the heart. She glanced at him and took in his strong profile – a big man, beside her small frame, with thick white crinkly hair and even thicker moustache, aquiline nose and deep-tanned face. A handsome man in his day. Still was.

'My Uncle Alexandros told me after the war when I came back. He tried to persuade them to flee with him into the mountains but my grandfather thought he could fight them single-handed. He was a very brave man, my grandfather, but he did not understand the cruelty of the German soldiers. When they found the bodies, my uncle told me, they thought my grandfather had thrown himself on top of my mother as the soldiers fired to try to protect her. When he told me about that, I vowed that I would dedicate my life to the memory of my grandfather. I do not know if I could have been as brave as him but I remember him still today and what he did. I remember.'

Their initial telephone conversation had been brief. She had explained to him that she wanted to see the place where Bill Ennis died, because she had promised her late husband that she would. That was all. It must have been dreadful for him to learn about these deaths of his loved ones. But the war was long over. Why was he telling her about this?

She unbuttoned her cardigan, slipped off her shoes and gazed at the rocky inland slopes as he drove westwards. Best to be polite, show an interest. No need for him to know any more. And she was genuinely curious. Here he was – the twelve-year-old boy she had read about now an old man of seventy-seven. He wanted to tell his story and she knew that somehow it all connected.

'So how did you escape?'

A silver taxi flashed past them, ignoring the double white lines in the middle of the road. Themis turned the wheel lightly towards the roadside and she swayed briefly towards him, as if to avoid the rocky outcrop they were passing.

'Let me tell you I was very lucky. We were on the beach at Hora Sfakion - I will take you there and show you. Skip tried to persuade the Royal Navy officer to take me with them on the boat. Then we would be put on the ship sailing to Alexandria. I can remember the night. The sea was dead calm but there was complete pandemonium on the beach. The night before they had taken off only the wounded soldiers. Skip had been told that he and his men would be among the first to be taken off the island. As the day wore on, more soldiers came down from the hills, because the British generals had decided to withdraw from the island. Thousands of men were forced to march from Chania on the north coast, where we are heading now, over the Lefka Ori to this little village of Hora Sfakion to be taken off in the Royal Navy ships. There were so many men waiting to board the ships that the soldiers had cordoned off the beach and threatened to shoot anyone who tried to sneak into the lines.

"Allied soldiers only," said the officer who was standing at the head of the queue to check that the boats were not overloaded.

"The boy's with us," Skip said, looking straight at him. "Without him, we wouldn't be here. If we leave him here, Jerry will shoot him. To them he's a collaborator. He comes with us."

"Sorry," said the officer. "Orders. Military personnel only. No civilians."

Skip tried to argue but there were so many behind us he couldn't continue. So he pushed the others on to the landing craft – Eddie, Jack, Carl and Jim. Not Skip, though. He refused to leave without me. Alec, one of the New Zealanders, insisted on staying behind too. They told the others not to worry, as they'd find a way.'

The pictures in Meredith's head flew back, like the pages of a photograph album, to the time she had last seen Bill, on leave in Birmingham and just about to sail out to what turned out to be Crete, the place where he died. She could see him still – young, callow, uncertain about the future, a little afraid. It was difficult to think of him being so determined – he had always seemed rather unsure of himself. It was harder still to think that he had never got beyond that age, that he would remain forever as that fresh-faced young man with the tiny moustache twisting up to his eye. Unconsciously she touched her upper lip, as if to remind herself.

'The beach was cordoned off, so there was no way we could rejoin the line and try again, so Skip, Alec and me went to look for somewhere to shelter until they could think of some other way of getting me off the island. That's when we came upon the cave. It had been occupied when we had first got there by

Australian troops from the catering corps. Somehow they had managed to get on board one of the boats leaving that night and they'd left behind what seemed to us at the time a treasure-trove of tins of stew, tins of pineapples, dried biscuits, bottles of wine from somewhere, even coffee. There were also cooking pots and blankets. After eating our fill – I can still remember the tastes of that meal sixty years later – I settled down for the night, while Skip and Alec stayed up planning ways of getting me out.'

Meredith tugged impatiently at a crease in her dress. He had obviously been rehearsing his tale in his head ever since she had told him on the phone that she was coming to Crete. But she wanted to know more about Bill than about him.

'So was that when Bill was killed then?'

His eyes flickered briefly as he brushed her inquiry aside. She had to hear the full story.

'No. Not then. Skip and Alec decided there was no point trying to get on to the boats by joining the queues. So the plan they devised was for us on the following night, when the Navy returned, to swim out directly to the big ships and try to climb aboard. They were confident that the sailors wouldn't throw them overboard and they couldn't send me back once I was on a ship. It was a good scheme and it worked. Unfortunately, the next day, while out looking for water, Skip was shot by a German Messerschmitt that strafed the village indiscriminately as it flew over. They couldn't have seen him. He was under cover. But the bullets penetrated the ruined house where he was hiding and he got three in his chest. By the time Alec found him, he was already dead.'

So that was the moment, Meredith realised. Plain, unadorned, sudden. No great act of heroism. No glorious warrior-like deed. Just the sheer bad luck of a moment in time. The moment that precipitated the telegram that had arrived several days later in Birmingham. She was aware of the sound of her heavy breathing momentarily as she remembered, almost as if it was yesterday. She looked out of the window at this foreign land yellow with sunshine, at the pristine blueness of the heavens and at the light ruffling waves of the Aegean Sea. He had died in this idyllic place.

'I was so upset. He had become almost like a father to me.

My own father was missing in northern Greece and my mother was sure he was dead. Skip meant so much to me. I wanted to stay here then. Somehow it felt wrong if I escaped from Crete and Skip was left here. "He would have wanted you to survive," Alec said later in the day, after he had returned and given me the awful news. "That's why we're still here, Nikos. It's why we must go ahead with our plan. There's no going back now." So that's what we did.'

In her mental photograph album, Meredith could see Bill with his brother Bert in wartime Birmingham and she was only half-listening, as her Cretan guide continued his story. Had this been a wise journey? She had always had doubts about taking it but now, as those sixty plus years fled away from her and the images of the two brothers came sharper into focus, her heart beat faster against her ribs.

'Everything had to be decided so quickly then because the Germans were getting closer. We left the cave in darkness and skirted around the cliffs away from Hora Sfakion then waded into the sea. The salt water mixed with my tears as we swam out into the ocean, leaving my homeland, leaving Skip, leaving my family. The ship we reached was called HMS *Perth* and it had nets over its sides for the troops from the landing craft to crawl up. As Skip and Alec had said, the sailors didn't bother to distinguish who we were in the darkness but leaned down to haul us up on deck and, once there, we were safe. There was no question of us being sent back at that stage and, once the ship was full of soldiers brought from the beach, we set off for Alexandria. We were hit by German planes on the journey. Some of the crew and some of the evacuated soldiers died but eventually we reached Alexandria. Alec had to rejoin his unit, of course, but he made sure I had plenty of money and even found me a Greek family living there from before the war to take me in. I was one very lucky boy, believe me.'

She pressed her lips together, determined that no sounds would emerge. She knew it was wrong to think this way but she resented his good fortune. If it hadn't been for Themis, Bill would probably have survived. She clenched her lips even tighter, as if to force the words and the thought behind them back into the deepest recesses of her brain. She had not expected to feel this way.

*

Meredith watched the scenery unfold through the window of the car as they sped westwards towards his home village. The overwhelming impression was one of greenness – a landscape filled with silvergreen olive groves, regimental vineyards and tall cypress trees but behind them the snow-covered rocky mountains loomed in silhouette up towards the sky. At times they were riding parallel with the cobalt blue of the sea, at other times the road cut through the rocks in great curving slices before settling back into the flat plains of the northern coast. Occasionally she was aware of tiny marble shrines beside the road or of a solitary black-robed old woman sitting on a thin wooden chair underneath a shading umbrella with a basket of brightly-coloured oranges at her feet, hoping for customers. And everywhere on the road verges flowers – blousy white and pink oleander blossoms and plump clusters of golden mimosa buds filling the space and breaking the monotony of tarmac. Everywhere the pungent aroma of the maquis overwhelmed the petrol fumes of the busy National Road.

Her first meeting with Bill and Bert was in the winter of 1940. She was driving an ambulance in those days, having signed up with the ARP when the blitzing of Birmingham had begun in August of that year. She had been working as a typist in the town hall, a job secured for her by her father, an architect in the Borough Surveyor's office, when the German bombers started to drop their lethal loads on to the city of her birth. Always a person of sudden enthusiasms, she felt she had to do something to help, so she volunteered for the ARP. She had to take a special driving test before she could drive an ambulance but had been driving her father's car for three years and passed it easily.

It was during one of the worst periods of the blitz in November of that year when she and her team were sent to the factory of E.J. Ennis & Sons in Small Heath. Before the war this factory had manufactured metallic hooks and eyes as clothing fasteners but had switched to producing shell cases for anti-aircraft guns to help the war effort. Virtually every other manufacturer in Birmingham and the surrounding Black Country towns had followed the same route. The factory's redbrick outbuildings had suffered a direct hit from the bombs and the firefighters were already there, the long jets of water dousing the greedy flames, when Meredith and her companions arrived. Luckily, there were only minor injuries to deal with, mostly the result of the women workers being hit by flying shrapnel as the bombs exploded in the outbuildings and there were no lives lost. One of the boss's sons, however, had broken his arm in trying to hold a door open to allow several women to crawl out of the debris and, as the last one had escaped, the door fell on top of him, breaking his left arm. This, as she discovered later, was Bert Ennis, twenty-four years old, the same age as herself, and in charge of production in the bombed factory. His younger brother Bill came in the ambulance with him as she drove them through the fire-ravaged city to the General Hospital in the city centre.

'This is an old Austin, isn't it?' said Bert Ennis, looking around at the inside of the vehicle. 'Dad had one of these before the war. Remember, bruv?'

His younger brother nodded, while Bert felt around the inside of the ambulance with his free hand, fingering the canvas drawn tightly on to the metalwork.

'What have they done? Oh, I can see, they've cut the back of its bodywork off and replaced it with this green canvas cover. Very clever. How long you been driving this old crate?'

'Few months. I work shifts - eight hours on, eight hours on standby, ready if the siren goes, and eight hours off. How come neither of you has been called up?' she shouted above the throaty growl of the engine, as they travelled through the darkened streets, passing burned-out buildings, where flames still licked the debris-strewn ground, and dodging gaping potholes hacked into the tarmac of the roads.

'I wanted to go and fight,' answered Bert, wincing from the pain of his broken arm. 'Still do. But they wouldn't let me. Said I was a 'Reserved Occupation'. Needed here to supervise the war work in the factory.'

She looked over at this tall and vivacious man, with dark flashing eyes and black hair brylcremed back with a right side parting. His clothing was unconventional – brown brogue shoes covered in dust, Oxford bags and a turtleneck sweater, which were torn from the impact of the door and the rubble that had fallen on him. His younger brother was of medium build, with the same dark hair and a little dark pencil moustache, which twitched curiously up towards his right eye when he spoke. He wore a sombre grey suit with white shirt and tie.

Was there something that stood out about them then? Something that stayed with her? Or did it all come later?

'They said the same about our Bill originally, though he's had his call-up papers now,' Bert continued, nodding towards his brother. 'Seems like they needed us to keep the factory going and no-one else could do it. Dad's tied up making sure that we get the raw materials through to make the munitions, so it had to be us two running the shop. D'you know, we're the only men working there now? Every other person in the building is female. Begging your pardon, lady, I'm not insinuating anything. Just saying.'

Bill said nothing, just smoked languidly and looked out of the ambulance window as she drove. She glanced from one to the other and caught the smile that hovered in Bert's eyes.

The bombing was particularly severe that night. It began at seven in the evening and went on for the best part of eleven hours, helped by the clearest November sky imaginable and a nearly full moon. A bomber's moon. A force of two hundred bombers attacked Birmingham throughout the night, arriving in terrifying waves. They dropped landmines, bombs and incendiary devices, their main target being the industrial heartland of the city and the factories where armaments were being manufactured. The BSA factory in Small Heath, which manufactured so many of the precision weapons made in the United Kingdom - aircraft machine guns, Sten guns, rifles and cannon - suffered the greatest damage. That night bombs landing on the factory ripped apart one of its buildings, killing over fifty people who got trapped in there and injuring many more. Other factories were also hit, though less severely, including E.J. Ennis & Sons.

As Meredith drove her ambulance through the burning city, her ears reverberated to the constant bombardment – the whumph of bombs, the creak and crash of falling buildings, the roar of fires licking the skyline. It was a scene that stayed to haunt her memories even now, and it repeated itself many times over that long winter of 1940 and into 1941.

She had to wait for other passing traffic as she reached the city's Bull Ring, where her eyes took in the once-familiar Market Hall that was now a mere shell with only its outer walls remaining.

'Our mum used to love going there,' said Bert Ennis, gazing fiercely at the mass of rubble, charred beams, broken bricks and twisted ironwork. A number of men, in caps and scarves, and boys, in grey gabardine macs, were leaning on a barrier, staring at the fractured building, as if still unbelieving.

'Yes, me too,' she nodded, wanting him to know she shared his sentiments, that she empathised.

'That was when we knew they were serious about hitting Brum,' he added, 'when they got the Market Hall.'

Meredith nodded agreement again then, as traffic cleared, drove on. At the General Hospital Bert Ennis had to wait his turn for treatment as far more serious cases were arriving by the minute. The three of them stood in the main entrance watching the stretchers carrying blood-soaked bodies, some with limbs torn off by the force of an explosion or in the collapse of a building, many with temporarily-bandaged bleeding head wounds, all in states of awful shock.

'Makes my problem seem small, doesn't it?' said Bert, accepting a cigarette from his brother. 'Guess I'll be waiting quite some time. Don't worry, lady, Bill will stay with me. You're needed elsewhere.'

At the time, as she drove away from the hospital and headed back towards Small Heath to assist with further incidents, she had thought only a little of the chance encounter. There was too much activity that busy night for her to dwell on one journey. In the course of the night she must have ferried almost sixty people to the hospital, all rescued from the bombing, all in need of treatment, some more serious than others. And there were often moments when, in those shared moments with people in pain, she felt emotionally close to one or other of them. It was the nature of the work. You shared the grief, you showed yourself sympathetic, you spoke encouragingly, then you moved on to the next incident.

If anyone had asked, she would have been hard pressed to explain it honestly but she got a real thrill out of the ARP work. She felt she was really doing something useful but even more she felt the glow of excitement at driving through the ravaged streets, past the charred and broken buildings, to the rescue of unknown people. It wasn't just the satisfaction of knowing she was doing good. Her heart and her head were themselves on fire at the thought of facing and overcoming danger. When she drove through the blackened city, she often felt for the first time in her life a real sense of power.

A fortnight or so later, on one of the days when the German bombers didn't fly over dropping their deadly litter, she was on standby, expecting the wailing sirens at any moment, and decided to head into the blackened city centre from the family home in Edgbaston. As she strolled, she became aware that more and more people were walking in the same direction as her and there was a buzz of conversation unlike any she had heard for some time now. It was a buzz of hope, of expectation, almost of optimism. She stopped one of the families hurrying past her to enquire what was going on.

'The king's 'ere,' was the jubilant answer. 'King George. He's come to Brum.'

So that was it. She smiled lightly to herself, surprising herself with the satisfaction she felt about the king's visit to her city, so she decided to follow the growing crowds as they moved towards the city centre. As she rounded a corner some way from the Town Hall, however, she was halted in her steps as the crowd had been held back to allow the king's party to pass through. Too small to see over the heads of the crowd, which must have been thirty to forty deep at that point, she stretched her neck to look.

'Here, lady, want a hand up?' said a voice – a voice she recognised. It was Bert Ennis, in brown trilby and gabardine raincoat, standing a few yards from her with his brother Bill, now kitted out in his newly acquired RAF uniform. He grinned at her. 'Come on, lady, we'll push you up on this lamp-post.'

Her face coloured slightly but she moved across to where the two of them stood beside a lamppost. Bert still had the plaster on his left arm but with his right arm he assisted his brother to hoist her up so that her feet were on the ridge of the metallic lamppost a few feet from the cracked pavement. Then they held her there, each with a hand firmly against her backside.

When the royal party arrived, walking, Meredith could see everything clearly, while the brothers, being taller than her, caught only glimpses through the swaying crowd. King George VI appeared at the head of the party, wearing an army greatcoat, buttoned up against the cold, and his military cap. His face was drawn and haggard but he stopped and spoke to members of the crowd, many of whom had been made homeless by the bombing. Children at the front leaned forward to touch him as he passed, a woman told him how she had been dug out of her own Anderson shelter, an adolescent boy was congratulated for his bravery. Suddenly and spontaneously singing broke out.

> *God save our gracious king,*
> *Long live our noble king,*
> *God save the king.*
> *Send him victorious,*
> *Happy and glorious,*
> *Long to reign over us,*
> *God save the king.*

Then there was a tremendous, reverberating cheer as the king acknowledged the crowd with a practised wave and, with the Lord Mayor and other dignitaries a few paces behind, moved on and away from where Meredith and the two Ennis brothers were situated.

All through those few minutes, Meredith was conscious of those male hands clasped to her buttocks. It was the first time any man had touched her there since her father had ridden her on his shoulders as a young child and later as he taught her to ride a bicycle. At first, she had dismissed such thoughts. It was wartime. It was no time to be prim and proper about social proprieties. The bombs had blown away notions of dignity. Hadn't she seen semi-naked men, their clothes burned from their bodies by fire? Hadn't she even helped such men into her ambulance without any inhibitions? But this was slightly different. These two men, these brothers she had met again by chance, were not casualties, they were men. Full-blooded, full-bodied men. Those hands on her buttocks belonged to men with normal feelings. And normal longings.

14

She stopped herself. What had made her think like this?

'Thank you,' she said, as Bert Ennis helped her down from her precarious position.

'It's a pleasure, lady,' answered Bert with a grin that split his face. 'I really should ask your name.'

'Meredith. Meredith Wilson.'

And she gave him her freshest smile. This was no time for coyness. Besides, he interested her – there was something indefinable about him, something she wanted to know about.

'And I'm Bert Ennis. And this is my brother Bill. But you know that already. Why don't you join us for a cup of coffee? Or are you just going on duty?'

No, she wasn't and yes, she would. And yes, she did. And that's how, indirectly, she came to marry Bert less than twelve months later.

Meredith Ennis sat back in the car, sighed at the far-distant memory, and watched the flower-bedecked Cretan roadside speeding past her through the window.

\*

'What did I do in Alexandria? Have you ever been there? No, well let me tell you the city stinks. It has many beautiful buildings but its situation is against it. It's the heat mostly and the mosquitoes and the sewerage. It stinks, trust me, I know. Or it certainly did in 1941 when I got there. Everything seemed to be steaming. The water in the harbour was dull and brown and full of rubbish and had a nasty smell. When you walked along the Corniche in the middle of the day, you could smell the sweat of humans and of animals mixed with the melting tar and the sand blown from the desert. And the slums? Let me tell you about them, because I lived in those slums for four years. They were like rotten teeth, too close together, leaning into each other brokenly. The balconies swarmed with rats, half-naked children with flies on their faces stared through broken shutters, wrinkled old women with unwashed hair held out their hands begging from you all the time. In the centre of the slums the shrieks and calls of fights, of street-sellers, of beasts. It was truly horrible.'

He had resumed his tale, Meredith realised, expecting her to listen. She knew now how Bill had died, so long ago, so abruptly, just as he was about to make his escape. Now the beneficiary of that escape plan needed to tell her more about himself - that twelve-year-old boy who had become this elderly, white-haired man. It was almost as if he was telling her things he would have wished Bill himself to know, explaining what Bill's courage in helping him to be saved had led to. She had overcome her feelings of resentment now. Too late for all that. There were still many miles to travel. She had to let him talk, even though she could feel her eyes half-closing.

'I don't want you to think badly of my adoptive family, the Bazakis. They were good people. Remember, I was a boy of twelve when I was given to them. I had never travelled far from my home in Xamoudochori except when I went on hunting trips with my father and my uncle. I had never been abroad. I had no knowledge then of what had happened to my mother or my grandfather or even my father, though my mother thought he was dead because he was reported missing in the fighting against the Germans in northern Greece. I had learned a few English words but not many and I certainly knew no Arabic. But the Bazakis family was kind to me. They gave me food, they made a bed for me in their kitchen and I could understand them because we spoke Greek together.

I learned that they had been in Alexandria for over six years. Stavros Bazakis, the father, was a big man with a big moustache and dark hair, huge shoulders and arms like a wrestler's. He told me that his family had lived on the same patch of ground in the Peloponnese for centuries but, when for two years in succession, his vines failed to produce enough wine to take to market in order for him to feed himself and his family through the winter, he had bought a ticket on a passenger boat and arrived in Alexandria.

"This is a great city," he told me. "A city like I had never seen before. I got a job working in a bakery at nights but during the day I used to wonder around the city looking at the buildings and the monuments. I love the great Qait Bay fortress at the western end of the harbour. You know, that was where once the Pharos lighthouse stood – one of the Seven Wonders of the World. And the mosque that looks like a huge Easter cake and the big red Pillar of Pompey. I fell in love with this city and, once

I had saved enough money, I sent back for my wife, Maria, to join me. We have been here ever since."

Living in this tiny slum in the most crowded part of Alexandria was success to the Bazakis. I did not understand. In my village in Crete, there was no stink, except when the goats were being driven through. Our houses may have been simple but they were clean – my mother made sure of that; she was always sweeping, sweeping, sweeping. I can picture her now, chasing me out of the house with her twig besom with a "Shu, shu". It makes me weep still to think those German soldiers murdered my lovely mother.'

Meredith glanced sideways at him in his pause, noticed the moistening in his eyes and reached out to touch his sleeve. Someone had told her the Greeks were an emotional race.

'Forgive me. I was telling you what I did in Alexandria for four years. I sold things to make money for myself. I had to earn money to give to the Bazakis for looking after me. I started selling matches. I'd stand outside the Pillar of Pompey and look for people who were pausing to gaze at it, then I'd sidle up to them and, with the saddest face, I'd ask them to buy a box of matches. I didn't earn a lot that way so I tried other things – ribbons, necklaces, bracelets, belts. Then I met a hat-maker who took me as his assistant and taught me how to make the fez - you know what I mean? He wanted me to sell the fezzes on the street because he was busy making them in his shop, so I used the tricks I had previously learned. When I got braver, I'd go down to the harbour and sell fezzes to British soldiers coming off the ships or going on to them. They always had plenty of money and they were always willing to take pity on a poor boy. I followed some of them one day – a group of officers who were laughing and joking all the way through the streets of the city till they reached the very tall Hotel Cecil with its balconies. One of them saw that I'd been following and gave me a five hundred drachma note. You think that's no use in Egypt? Believe me, in a city like Alexandria you can exchange any currency in the world. I got a good deal for that note – it enabled me to buy new shoes, trousers and a jacket for myself and a cake for Mrs Bazakis. Best of all, though, was the realisation that the Hotel Cecil was where a lot of British officers were stationed throughout the war.

17

One day, while I was hanging around outside the Hotel Cecil – it had become a regular haunt of mine by now – one of the British officers stopped to buy a fez from me. I had seen him a number of times before but he had never previously bought anything, so I thought he perhaps didn't like me or didn't approve of what I was doing.

"You make plenty baksheesh like this?" he asked me. He was a tall thin man, very straight-backed and with a sharp-pointed nose.

"Yes, captain." I'd found it easier to call everyone captain, even though I didn't understand any of their ranks.

"You Arab?" he continued, giving me a curious look.

"No, captain, I am Cretan."

"Really? Well, well, there's a coincidence," he laughed. "Some of my best friends are in Crete right now. Well, well. So what brings you to Alex?"

I don't know why but I felt I could trust this man, so I told him the whole story about Skip and Alec and the others. He was shocked.

"So they got you off the island and then left you here? In Alex?"

"The Germans would have killed me," I told him. "Because of my Uncle Alexandros. He is an *andarte*."

He looked at me again with a puzzled expression.

"Your uncle is part of the resistance in Crete? Are you sure?"

I was surprised that he knew the word I had used

"I haven't seen him for a long time." I thought maybe I had said something wrong, something that would cause problems for my uncle.

"What's your name?"

"Nikos Themistocles."

"Listen, young man, I just might be able to find out about your Uncle Alexandros. Come back here tomorrow evening. I'll see what I can dig up."

I went back and told Maria and Stavros what had happened. They made me promise not to say anything to anyone about this.

"They say that the British Secret Service operates from the Hotel Cecil," Stavros told me, looking at me sternly. "You'd best be very careful. You don't know what that officer might want from you. Be careful."

But, of course, I had to go, didn't I? And that's when I learned that my Uncle Alexandros was still leading his band of *andartes* in the mountains. He had helped many British, Australian and New Zealand servicemen to escape from the island over the past two years, finding safe shelter for them on the island and then boats to take them away. You know, perhaps, that not all of them were taken off the island after the surrender? Thousands were marched back across the mountains to where they had started from and were put into German camps. Some of them escaped into the hills, however, to try to escape on their own.

That's how I knew my uncle was still alive. That's how I knew he would still be there when the war ended. I just knew. And that's why I saved enough money to buy a ticket to take me back to Crete when the war ended and found my Uncle Alexandros. That's when I learned about how my mother and my grandfather died.'

All she had known was Bill's death. Now she knew more about Themis, about the chances that had shaped his life, about the German occupation of Crete. It was all more complex than she had thought. She was beginning to gain a perspective on everything. Bill's death had been a terrible shock to Bert and to her but his sacrifice had granted Themis a life. She stared straight ahead through the fly-encrusted windscreen, willing her journey onwards.

*

That winter of 1940 Meredith and the Ennis brothers had made their way on foot through the ravaged centre of Birmingham, where the blackened shells of buildings and the still-smouldering ruins created a strangely eerie emptiness in what had once been a heaving, jostling metropolis. Few people were about – tin-hatted ARP wardens inevitably, firefighters pointing their hoses on to charred woodwork, the occasional housewife with half-empty shopping bag, and small gangs of sooty-faced children scavenging in the wreckage for mementoes.

19

The only place they could find for a coffee was a dingy café opposite Snow Hill Railway Station. There, seated at a table covered with a grease-stained oilcloth, they sipped the thin coffee from stained china cups and began to learn about each other.

'Our grandfather started the family business at the turn of the century. Brum was the workshop of the world then, granddad used to say. Manufacturing was almost a guarantee of a good life for those who were prepared to invest and work hard,' Bert explained as he stirred his coffee. 'Grandfather Jabez worked hard all right. Grandma used to say she never saw him in daylight because of the hours he worked, Monday to Saturday, never stopping. And on Sundays he'd go into the works to deal with the paperwork. He was a slave to hooks and eyes was Granddad Jabez. I bet you've got some in your clothes, haven't you, Meredith? Sorry, it is all right to call you that, isn't it?'

'Yes, of course,' she replied, blushing slightly at the reference to hooks and eyes, for surely he must know that they were the fastenings in most brassières. But there was something about this man that attracted her. She had watched him as he spoke, noting the smile that always played around his lips. She had had dates before the war, of course, and even occasionally during it, though the shortage of young men in the city made that increasingly difficult. Now, out of nowhere, there were two such young men, and sitting with her. She glanced across the greasy tablecloth from one to the other.

'Dad went into the business straight from school,' continued Bert, offering her a cigarette, which she declined. 'He was just like granddad. What am I saying? He is just like granddad. Works all the hours under the sun. Or at least he did when we were growing up. Now it's just us running the factory because he's on this committee they've set up to ensure that the raw materials get to Brum so we can make all the things that are needed. And now it's just me. Bill here, as you can see from his resplendent uniform, is off to fly Spitfires. Aren't you, bruv?'

Bill Ennis smiled lightly and inhaled deeply from his cigarette before replying. She half-turned to give him her full attention. He had not spoken much in their two brief encounters to date and she had found his reserve oddly contrasting to his brother's bonhomie.

20

'I don't know that I'll be flying, Bert. You know that. It depends what they think I'm most suited to. Might be ground crew. Might be flying. Might be anything. Who knows? I've only got my uniform so far.'

Meredith Wilson watched him as he spoke. His voice was softer than Bert's and had an uncertain tone. He was certainly less flamboyant than his elder brother – the hair now given its regulation forces short back and sides cut, though his tiny moustache remained, giving him a slightly sinister look.

'What do you hope to do?' she asked, looking at him and hoping to see into those smoke-wreathed eyes.

'To tell the truth, I really don't mind, though I'm not sure I'd be very good at the fighting side of things,' he answered, avoiding her gaze. 'I told them I was a bit of a radio ham. I did a badge in the scouts about using short-wave radios and I thought they might use me somehow in that capacity. But I don't have any say in the matter, of course. No doubt I'll find out when I get there on Monday.'

He was giving little away about himself, she realised, as she watched him suck on his cigarette. His brother, on the other hand, was much more open.

'We were both in the scouts,' chipped in Bert with a grin in her direction, as he drained his coffee cup. 'It was one of the things dad was keen for us to do. Character building, he said. Learning useful skills. Well, I still haven't found any use for all those knots we learned. Bill enjoyed it more than me, didn't you, bruv?'

He was permanently cheerful, she could see that. It was in his nature to take a positive view of everything. Life for Bert Ennis, and with Bert Ennis, she caught herself momentarily thinking, meant a glass that was always half full.

Bill Ennis nodded agreement with what his brother had said.

'We're like chalk and cheese, Meredith,' explained Bert, leaning slightly forward with his right hand stroking his chin. 'Bill's the brains, I'm the brawn. I left school early, like dad, and I've learned the business from the shop floor up. That's what dad wanted. Bill's cleverer than me – he's had a story published in the *Birmingham Post*, haven't you, bruv? - so he stayed into the sixth form at King Eddie's. We both went there. Dad paid for us to have a proper education. Bill could have gone to university but then the war broke out and he couldn't decide what to do. Dad always wanted him in the business at some point because he says that it will all change after the war and we need to be ready to move with the changing times. Bill's job is to use his brain to find out which way we need to move, how to keep ahead of the trends, so to speak.'

'I'm supposed to lead E.J. Ennis & Sons into the brave new world of post-war capitalism,' laughed Bill sardonically, stubbing out his cigarette on the metal ashtray and straightening his uniform trousers. 'If I survive.'

Maybe he was just being fatalistic, Meredith thought to herself. He certainly seemed more brittle than his brother, despite his education and the company's plans for the future. Maybe he was just anxious about being called up. She certainly didn't feel any warmth from him, any sense that he had noticed her at all really, other than to humour his brother.

'Anyway, Meredith, what about you?' Bert asked. 'How come you're doing ARP duty instead of seeking safety in the country?'

'I would not do that,' she answered tartly, straightening herself up on the wooden chair. 'We all have to make an effort to help out. We're not going to beat Hitler if we don't all stand together, are we?'

'You should be giving Churchill's speeches for him,' mocked Bill, as his brother smiled.

They were laughing at her now, especially the younger one, Bill. She didn't like the way his moustache twitched up towards his eye when he smiled and she didn't like being made fun of.

'Sorry,' Meredith said, looking down at her lap in mild embarrassment. But wasn't that what everyone thought? What was so funny about standing up to Hitler? 'It wasn't meant to come over like that. Only I worked in the typing pool at the Town Hall before the war and I saw a number of girls who jumped at the chance to be evacuated to the country, to look after their younger brothers and sisters. Not for me, though. I wanted to help out. I really believe we all have to stand up to Nazism.'

She couldn't tell them, couldn't tell anybody really, about the buzz she got from driving her ambulance through the bombs. She almost looked forward to hearing the sirens, for they meant action, excitement, engagement. The air you breathed became suddenly hot and vibrant.

'Oh, I'm with you there, Meredith,' said Bert, nodding his head in agreement. 'As I said when you came to the works that day, I wanted and still want to fight but they won't let me. They say I've got to stay and run the factory. Well, they've let our Bill go, so maybe it'll be me next, eh?'

They stayed for a few minutes longer, looking out of the window at the blackened buildings and the pockmarked streets, where bombs had dug round holes in the tarmac. There was no pleasure to be taken in being out in the city and soon after finishing their coffee, she said she had to get home to change into her ARP uniform before her turn of duty. But not before a date had been arranged.

*

'When I found out that my grandfather and my mother had been murdered, I wanted to find the murderers and seize them by the throats and squeeze them until all the life drained out of them and they died. But, of course, this was war. No one knew who these German soldiers were, they were just men in uniform, the cold uniform of Nazi Germany. There was no Cretan person who saw what happened. Everyone in the village they could find was set in front of those walls and shot, because they had helped the British forces. Was it an order from the German High Command? Or were they just murderous troops killing for killing's sake? Who knows? And it doesn't matter now. I see German tourists all over my island now and I do not feel a need to kill them, or even resent them. War brutalises people and makes them do things they would not do in peacetime. The young Germans I see in Chania market may be the grandchildren of those soldiers who killed my family. But can I blame them? They were not even dreamt about then. It was not their fault.

Eventually I came to see this for myself. My Uncle Alexandros was telling me this too. He said he had killed many German boys, though he did not feel any personal hatred for them. But that was the nature of war, he told me. He was a proud Cretan and he would not allow his island to be dominated by those *fascisti*, as he called them. There was freedom from tyranny to be fought for. The British soldiers, especially those that remained on the island after 1941 and worked with the *andartes* under cover, understood that and that was why he had chosen to fight with them. And he was not alone.

"Show me the Cretan who welcomed the Germans and I'll show you a traitor," he said once to me, puffing out his chest and bristling his moustache. "No Cretan loved the Germans." '

Typical man, Meredith thought to herself, always wanting to be brave, always wanting to be the best fighters. Just like Bert. Though, if it hadn't been for the men, the war would not have been won. She had woken up again as the car slowed, caught in a stream of traffic. Curious though that all that time in Crete after the Allied troops had been evacuated, after Bill Ennis's death during that evacuation, there had been British soldiers working alongside the Cretan resistance fighters. She had not known about that either. Her brother-in-law's death was, if she was honest, all she ever knew about Crete. But Themis was telling her something new now. She had thought his post-war return to Crete had reached the end of his tale. Not so.

'The letter I got several months after I had returned to Xamoudochori at the end of the war was a huge shock. I was trying my best to replant the olive grove and the vineyard that had belonged to my family. It was hard work, for so much of the land had been ruined in the war by bombs and by soldiers marching through. For four years the land had been greatly neglected. Some of the olive trees still stood and some were still producing olives but most of the vineyard had been trampled to death. With my uncle's help, I had started to replant, when the letter arrived one day out of the blue.

It was from New Zealand, from an Alec Bryce. Although I didn't recognise the name, I soon realised, as I listened to it being translated for me by a friend in Chania I had taken it to, that this was the Alec who had swum with me to the HMS *Perth* on that fateful day when I had escaped from Crete and who had placed me with the Bazakis family in Alexandria before he rejoined his unit. He told me that he had survived the war unscathed and that he was now back home at his family farm on the South Island in New Zealand. The nearest town, he said, was called Cromwell. He had even included a small photograph of him in front of the farmhouse where he and his family lived. He looked just as I remembered him.

But the biggest surprise came at the end of his letter. He told me that the New Zealand government had a scheme whereby returning soldiers could sponsor a Greek citizen to come and live in New Zealand and Alec wanted to sponsor me. Naturally, he hadn't been able to do anything about it yet because he didn't know if I was still alive, if I was still in Alexandria, if I was back in Crete or if I was anywhere else in the world. So he had trusted his luck and posted this letter to Nikos Themistocles, Xamoudochori, Crete.'

So that explained the slight Australasian tang to his voice, Meredith realised. That explained why his English was so good, not at all like that portrayed in *Zorba the Greek* or *Shirley Valentine*. Tom had taken her to see that second one, she remembered. It must have been after his marriage ended, when he came back to Birmingham. What would Tom think of her now, when he found out what she had done? Too late to worry about that. Best to listen to Themis and his story.

'I was almost seventeen, remember, when I received this letter. I had grown up over four years in a strange city in a country that was not my own. I had returned to my home village to find much of it in ruins and my family all dead. I had started to attempt the restoration of the family olive grove and vineyard but I was living on next to nothing. This out-of-the-blue offer would give me the chance to put everything behind me and start afresh but I would be leaving my homeland, the graves of my mother and grandfather, my village friends, my Uncle Alexandros.

"*Endaksi*," said my uncle when I told him the contents of Alec's letter. "Alec is good man?"

I reminded him of the story I had told too many times already, I thought, about how Skip and Alec helped me to escape from Crete and about what Alec had later done to help me in Alexandria.

"Go!" he said when I had finished. "Alexandros strong. Alexandros see to olives and vines. Go to New Zealand. Make fortune."

So I wrote back to Alec, telling him how excited I was at his offer and about what had happened to my family, and in no time at all it was all arranged. Some weeks later I got an invitation from the New Zealand government, with papers and tickets for my journey. A friend of my uncle's took me in his lorry to Heraklion for the ferry across to Piraeus. And that was where I got on board the ship that was to take me to the new world.'

Tom had once talked of emigrating to New Zealand, Meredith recalled. That was when he was in his unsettled period in between his two marriages. Maybe he should have gone. She had been against it at the time, didn't want to lose him. It had been hard to explain all that to him but he probably felt her negativity more heavily than perhaps she had wanted. He was always too sensitive for his own good, always picking up on her moods. Had done since he was a child. Even when he moved away from home to go to university, she could reach him and affect him by one phone call. She knew it, knew she had that power. Had she been right to hold him back? Who could tell? And he was all right now, wasn't he? It had all turned out for the best in the end. Hadn't it? Tom could cope with anything. She had gifted him that.

'I spent five years with Alec - tough years, making that farm grow. His father had been getting more crippled with arthritis during the war but Alec had known nothing of it. So the farm had started to run down – fences and gates needed repairing, lambing had to be properly organised, all the sheep had to be sheared, not just the ones his father managed to round up. The farmhouse itself was also in need of repair – part of the roof had to be replaced, a new range was installed in the kitchen, outhouses were falling down and so on. We were two young men, though, relieved and delighted to have survived the war and eager to use our strength to rebuild.

By the time I was twenty, Alec's farm was prospering and I was earning good money too. He bought himself a motorbike and sidecar and on Saturday nights we'd ride into Cromwell for a few drinks at the Victoria Arms Hotel. That was where all the boys gathered on Saturday nights for a few beers. Once or twice we ventured as far as Queenstown, which is very beautiful with a big bay and mountains behind – it reminded me very much of Chania. For the first time I began to feel homesick. It was in Queenstown that Alec met Katie. Well, Alec courted her so quickly that she agreed to marry him within three months and within the year she was living at the farm and taking over a lot of the domestic duties from Alec's mother.

That was when I first started thinking about coming home, to Crete. Alec didn't want me to leave but I felt like an extra person there now, what with Katie established at the farm. I wrote to my Uncle Alexandros and he told me that things were improving back home. The post-war shortages had ended and life was getting back to something like normality. So in August of 1951 I set sail from Christchurch.'

'Did you ever see this Alec again?' asked Meredith. Alec would have been the last person to see her brother-in-law. Maybe he too was still alive. For some reason this thought kindled a spark of hope, as if finding the New Zealander might in some strange way be helpful.

'Of course, I stayed in touch with him after all that had passed between us. We wrote regularly. I learned about his children – he had three boys, all growing strong and all in time becoming farmers themselves. One of them, Kevin, played rugby for Otago and had trials for the famous New Zealand All Blacks. Alec's farm prospered and grew in size. I visited him three times and he came over here on a couple of occasions towards the end of his life. He died eight years ago. He was a wonderful man, a brave man, a great man. I still miss him. Without him, and Skip of course, I would not be alive today.'

So there was only Themis remaining. And herself, of course. Bill dead, Bert dead, Eddie dead, Alec dead. Only Themis and herself to bear witness now.

'What about you? Did you marry?'

'Of course. My wife Katerina was from Deres in the mountains. I met her at the feast of Saint Kiriaki in July a couple of years after I returned. Because of his exploits in the war, my uncle was known everywhere and he had an old friend in Deres who had invited him to the traditional feast-day. I was twenty-five then.

I had re-established our vineyard and olive grove. In fact, I had increased the size of the olive grove and had several acres now. I had also rebuilt the family home that had been half-ruined in the war. My uncle thought I needed a wife to start a family. That was still the way of thinking in those days although some of the old ways were already beginning to die out. Remember, I had lived in Alexandria for four years and New Zealand for five and I had seen different customs. So, I did not realise, when my uncle offered to take me to this feast in Deres, that his old friend there had a daughter of marriageable age and they had planned beforehand for us to be introduced!'

'So you still had arranged marriages?'

Would that have been a better way? Would she have been better prepared? Would she have accepted that it was not love that kept a marriage together but something else, something agreed between families, a political settlement, a compromise that did not promise the impossible?

'Listen, I do not regret this. Katerina was lovely. We sat next to each other at the feast and I felt myself to be the luckiest man in the world, sitting next to this beautiful, dark-eyed girl with wonderfully long curling hair that flowed over her shoulders. We were married within the year, in Deres of course.

I will never forget my wedding day, although it was so long ago. My Katerina looked wonderful in her white dress and her red veil. We had the traditional orange blossom crowns placed on our heads and then the priest performed the wedding ceremony. After that, there was a great feast. We Cretans like our feasts, you know, and our wedding feast went on all through the night. There was much dancing, of course, much eating and much drinking. My uncle and Katerina's father fired their rifles into the air at midnight. Everyone got very drunk. It was a wonderful occasion.

Next day, as the sun rose, my uncle drove a cart with Katerina and myself in it along the dirt track from Deres to Xamoudochori and our married life began.'

*

In late June 1941, Bert Ennis had received his papers and was about to join up. Three weeks earlier they had learned by telegram of his brother Bill's death in the Battle of Crete. Although he had been originally told he was in a reserved occupation, after his brother's death Bert was determined that he had to do his bit. So, despite the protestations of his mother and father, he presented himself once again for enlistment and this time, because there had already been too many losses, there was no hesitation from the military authorities. The official papers were sent and Bert was ordered to report to Aldershot barracks for basic training on the morning of Wednesday 9th July. Four days previously he had married Meredith Wilson, despite the misgivings of both sets of parents.

On that Saturday morning Meredith Wilson left her parents' home for the last time as a single woman. There had been little time for much by way of preparation. Once Bert Ennis had decided he was going to enlist, he wasted no time in proposing to her and, when she accepted, he quickly made the necessary arrangements. What else could they do? Her parents had wanted a proper church wedding at the very least but that had proved impossible to arrange so quickly and neither prospective bride nor groom wanted to wait for his first leave. So it had to be at the Birmingham Register Office in the city centre. Meredith's mother bowed reluctantly to this inevitability but insisted that her daughter, their only child, should be dressed properly for the occasion. Family and friends rallied round and, despite the wartime restrictions, enough clothing coupons were collected for Meredith to be able to purchase a length of white velvet for her dress. Her mother had to conjure this dress up so quickly her feet hardly left the heavy treadle of the sewing machine from under the stairs. Everyone was utterly amazed at the speed and ingenuity of the operation. A gold-trimmed veil and an orange blossom headdress complemented the dress while an aunt gave her an old pair of blue topaz earrings. Bert's mother, although still grieving the death of her younger son, persuaded a local florist to give her entire month's ration of red roses for the bride's bouquet. Bert himself had his best grey suit pressed and bought a new pair of black shoes.

Bert had to walk to the Register Office, because there were no buses running, petrol was strictly rationed and cars could only be used in emergencies. Meredith's ambulance crew ensured that she did not have to suffer the same indignity, delivering her and her parents to the city centre in a ribbon-bedecked ambulance. As she stepped from the makeshift vehicle, helped by Bert's outstretched hand, there were cheers and spontaneous applause from the assembled friends, family and passers-by, for after the misery and deprivation caused in the city over recent months, all were desperate for glimpses of happiness and brief moments of optimism.

'Are we doing the right thing?' she whispered to Bert as they paused briefly at the Register Office steps to acknowledge the enthusiastic but unexpected reception. It had all happened so quickly – Bill's death, Bert's call-up, his proposal, the wedding arrangements. She had hardly had time to catch her breath. She was caught up in this movement that drove her on she knew not where. For the first time in her life she felt out of control, driven by other narratives, incapable of imposing her will on events. It was as if it was all happening to someone else.

'You look like a queen,' he answered, smiling encouragingly at her from his deep blue eyes.

Meredith blushed and looked down at her feet. It was not meant to be like this, she thought.

The ceremony itself was a blur. She could remember standing in front of the Registrar – a short, chubby man in a morning suit who spoke in a kind of high-pitched whine – and she could recall making her vows:

'I call upon these persons here present to witness that I take thee, Albert Frederick Ennis, to be my lawful wedded husband.'

How had she felt at the time? She reached back into her memory. Uncertain, yes. Were they doing the right thing? Weren't there any other choices? Or was she just trying to make him happy before he joined up? What if he was killed, like his brother? Certainly she was confused because it was all happening so quickly, but how could she refuse him?

And then when Bert's Uncle George, who had had to act as best man because all his friends were serving overseas and his brother Bill…..Meredith shut out the thought. She recalled that embarrassing moment when Bert's uncle dropped the ring and it rolled under the Registrar's desk. Everyone in the room stifled gasps of anxiety, which turned rapidly into muffled sounds of amusement as the fat Registrar bent down to retrieve the ring leaving his large backside on view beyond his desk. When normality was finally restored, the service was completed and there they were – man and wife. The ancient rituals performed again. The ancient gods appeased. Or almost.

After the simple ceremony, they stood outside the Register Office while photographs were taken by Uncle George using a Brownie Box camera because it had been impossible to find a professional photographer on the day in question.

'Say Cheddar,' called Bert's uncle, a stout man with a pronounced limp, and all duly smiled. Because of the price and availability of film, there were only eight photographs, so it didn't take long for the carefully posed but artless shots of bride and groom, bride, groom and sets of parents, plus the assembled guests. She could remember the false smile she wore for each photograph – it was what was expected after all.

Then all the wedding guests – only twenty-four in all, because so many were serving in the forces or had been evacuated to the country – went back to Edgbaston and Meredith's parents' large Edwardian house. Again through the generosity of friends and family, a proper wedding breakfast was served. Two pounds of cooked ham was allowed for a wedding and nothing else but friends and neighbours had contributed tea and sugar and precious rations of butter. Others had given hoarded bottles of pickled cabbage and onions, while those with allotments had raided their winter stores for potatoes, beetroot and hothouse salads. Meredith's mother had even managed to make a wedding cake using mostly donated ingredients and this was displayed in the middle of the dining table.

As family and guests tucked into this welcome and, for its time, sumptuous repast and as the barrel of beer and the case of champagne provided by her father began to empty, Meredith sensed the volume of conversation begin to increase, noticed faces become hotter and redder, and realised people had begun to forget this was the middle of the war. There had not been any bombing from the Luftwaffe for several days now. In fact, the significant raids had ceased around Easter time of that year. The radio news told how the German High Command had opened a new offensive against Russia.

Bert's Uncle George, the one who had acted as best man and taken the photographs, made a short speech.

'It 'as fallen upon me to say a few words at this point. You all know that it shouldn't 'ave been me 'ere now; it should be Bert's younger brother Bill, who we all miss terribly. But I 'ave to say, if we're going to beat this 'itler feller, there's going to 'ave to be sacrifices and that's going to 'urt us all. We all miss Bill but we 'ave to look forward now to a brighter future. Adolf seems to 'ave stopped trying to destroy Brum, thank God, so maybe we can get back to something like normality again. Today, 'owever, I'm proud to be launching my nephew on the first stages of 'is married life but I 'ave to offer him some advice. People say that in ancient China, a man doesn't know 'is wife until 'e marries. Well, Bert, take it from me, that 'appens everywhere, son, everywhere!'

Meredith's heart felt as if it was shrinking inside her body. Bert leaned over, took her hand and smiled cheerfully at her. She tried to smile back. There was guffawing around the room, at first nervous but then, as all saw from careful sideways glances that no one was upset by these remarks, increasing in volume. Uncle George decided to ride his luck.

'A man placed an advert in the newspaper. "Wife wanted". Next day 'e received an 'undred letters. They all said the same thing: "You can 'ave mine".'

The assembled gathering laughed again, temporary relief from the strains of war and from grief for the recent death of Bill Ennis.

'Anyway, I'd like you all to raise your glasses to this 'andsome couple,' Uncle George continued, raising his newly charged glass of champagne in front of him. 'To Meredith and Bert. 'Ere's to an 'appy first night, ho, ho. And long may their love last.'

Meredith managed her wan smile once again. She was not being appreciative enough of all that was being done for them – the ceremony, the wedding breakfast, the attempt to send the couple into a happy marriage in spite of the war, in spite of the deprivations, in spite of the loss of Bert's brother. Somehow, though, she knew she was only acting a part.

Afterwards, as the long evening light began to fade at last, friends and family began to drift away from the Edgbaston house until the only ones left were the two sets of parents, Bert and Meredith. By midnight there were only the two of them, still up to their elbows in dishwater washing up. When they got upstairs to their wedding bed and pulled back the top sheet, they found what Uncle George had been amused by. Too tired to bother, Meredith pulled the flour-covered sheet off the bed and they fell asleep on the bare mattress.

Four months later on 3$^{rd}$ November 1941, in a nursing home in Bromsgrove to which she had been taken by ambulance because of worries about new bombing threats to Birmingham, Meredith gave birth to Thomas William Ennis.

## 2

By mid-morning they had reached the entrance to the Allied War Cemetery in Souda Bay. Themis parked his car in the dusty olive grove near the entrance and close to an old caravan where a group of other old men in waistcoats and baggy trousers was playing *tavli* at a wooden table. He had nodded to them as he opened the car door to let Meredith alight.

'Do not build your hopes too high,' he had said, as he escorted her through the olive trees to the cemetery. 'Many soldiers died and were buried without names. Although I am sure he is buried here, there is no named grave for your brother-in-law.'

She had stumbled slightly as they were walking. The heat was overbearing now, its strength hitting her unexpectedly.

'Are you okay?' he had asked.

'Yes, fine,' Meredith replied, taking a deep breath to compose herself again and pulling her scarf over her head.

As they walked through the gate into the cemetery itself, she stopped to read the marble plaque set into the wall:

1939 -1945


THE LAND ON WHICH THIS CEMETERY
STANDS IS THE GIFT OF THE GREEK PEOPLE
FOR THE PERPETUAL RESTING PLACE OF
THE SAILORS SOLDIERS AND AIRMEN
WHO ARE HONOURED HERE

'Are you sure there is no grave? Might somebody have got his name spelled wrong?'

He had shrugged his shoulders, as he took her arm and led her on into the graveyard with its array of brightly coloured flowerbeds and its ranks of stiff white headstones stretching out left and right, as if for inspection by some heavenly field-marshal, towards the glittering expanse of the Aegean Sea.

She had gulped again, partly at the curious beauty of the spectacle and partly at the thought that she was as close as she had been for over sixty years to her brother-in-law.

'The Cemetery Register is in that shelter there,' he had pointed out, 'where you can look for Skip's name. They have a record in there of who is buried in each grave and where they died. You can then easily find the tomb you want. Except, as I say, there is no separate tomb for Skip.'

'Why is that?'

'The Germans moved all the dead bodies into four large burial grounds, which they called British Military Cemeteries. That's when the identities of many were lost,' he had explained. 'After the war, the Australian War Graves Commission moved all the remains from burial grounds and other places on Crete into this cemetery. There are special memorials for those they know were buried in particular places but they could not identify individuals at that stage.'

The black book of the Cemetery Register confirmed what Themis had said. Sadly, there was no grave of a William Ennis. She had looked in the book, hoping for a name that was similar, that perhaps might have been Bill's but there was nothing – no Ellis, Ellison, Innes or any of the other variations she played with in her head. Themis had explained how unlikely such an error would have been, as bodies would have been identified by their tags. She had leaned into his arm as they walked slowly over the soft grass down the lines of immaculately tended graves, each with a froth of red roses softening the pristine white headstone with its engraved name. British. Australians. New Zealanders. All so young. And so many unnamed dead with merely the phrase 'KNOWN UNTO GOD' at the base of the headstone. They reached one that read:

# AN AIRMAN
## OF THE
## 1939 -1945
## WAR

## ROYAL AIR FORCE

and Meredith paused.

'It could be any of these,' she had said and then, with a hint of hope, 'maybe this one.'

'Perhaps,' he had said sighing. 'But we cannot know. That is why I said to you beforehand when you telephoned that the cave at Hora Sfakion is better. That was where I last saw Skip. I will take you there.'

But she was not ready yet to leave the cemetery. Somewhere in this hallowed ground were the remains of Bill Ennis. She had last seen him in February 1941, his last leave. And yet she remembered him now as then. A fresh-faced young man with a small moustache and wavy black hair, shaved at the back and sides at that time, of course, in line with military custom, who, smartly dressed in his RAF uniform, had opened the door to the family's home after she had rung the bell. Although she hadn't been able to say when her shift would end because of the relentless German bombing, she had promised she would get there when she could.

'Bill will be pleased to see you,' Bert had said a couple of days earlier. 'He thinks he's going overseas soon and won't get any leave for quite some time.'

How could she have known that would be the last occasion she would ever see him? Troubled thoughts began to course through her brain. She looked over at her companion.

'I lost my husband twenty years ago,' she said flatly. 'And you think you've dealt with it all, got over it, as we used to say. But you never forget. You tell yourself you have but you never do.'

Themis took hold of her arm again and steered her towards a stone bench in the shelter that housed the Cemetery Register and they both sat down, glad of the cool shade there.

'No, you do not forget,' he sighed, gazing out to the silent sea. 'I still think of my poor mother every day. I was only twelve

36

when I last saw her. My Uncle Alexandros said I had to help these English to get across the mountains to escape from the Germans. He said I would only have to be away from home for a few days, so I never said goodbye properly to my mother. Then, as we were crossing the mountains, he changed his mind and told Skip that they had to take me with them when they disembarked because otherwise the Germans would shoot me as a collaborator. Even then I did not think it would be forever. I thought maybe, you know, a few months at most and then I could come back. I did not think I would be in Egypt for four more years. And especially I did not think that the Germans would murder my poor mother. What had she done? She had not killed any Germans. She had not given information to the Allied troops. How could she? She knew nothing. But, because she had cooked food for Skip and the others, they said she was a collaborator and, when my grandfather protested and tried to protect her, they took his life too. Every day I see that moment when they aimed their rifles at my mother and my grandfather threw himself on top of her as the bullets flew from their guns. Every day I see it. Every day I weep.'

Meredith sat in silence as Themis talked. She stared at the pure white gravestone immediately in front of her, with its 'KNOWN UNTO GOD' message, and tried to think of that young man she had known so long ago. Might that grave contain his bones? Curiously it was memories of his brother, her late husband, that came most vividly to mind.

'Bert was Bill's elder brother,' she began, knitting her hands together, as if to prevent those precious memories from slipping away. 'We married in the war. A few weeks after Bill died in Crete. I was pregnant, you see, Bert had decided he wanted to join up and did the honourable thing, as we used to call it in those days. I had only met him a few months previously but that was what happened in wartime. Everything speeded up. You took chances with life because life seemed so brittle, so mercurial, so uncertain. I didn't plan to marry like that but then I didn't plan to get pregnant either.'

There was a silence between them, as they both reflected on that long distant yet freshly remembered time in their lives. To any watcher, they looked like two old people, sitting side by side in a military graveyard, reminiscing perhaps on loved ones lost. To themselves, they were twelve and twenty-four again, wishing they had the opportunity to start the story all again and write it differently.

'I think I should like a coffee,' he said eventually, getting up. 'Will you join me?'

She looked up at him from her twenty-four-year-old self but saw only a white-haired old man.

'No, I think I would like some time to myself, if you don't mind. Will you give me half an hour? I shall never be here again. It is important to me.'

'Of course. I will be at the tables just outside the cemetery. Join me when you are ready. Are you sure you're all right?'

She nodded and pulled her cardigan loosely over her shoulders where she sat, as he walked stiffly away from her.

'Yes, thank you. I will not be long.'

*

Tommy was four when Bert Ennis returned from prisoner-of-war camp at the end of the war. Captured at the Salerno landings in 1943 he had ended up in Stalag XVII camp in southern Austria. After a time in the camp, the prisoners were given the opportunity to go to work on local farms in the area, instead of being interned in the camp where living conditions were dreadful. Bert decided that working on a farm might be marginally better, so he volunteered for that detail. As it turned out, the farm where Bert went was run by a family whose son had been conscripted into the German Vermacht and who had no real love for the Nazi rule. Here he was treated fairly and helped the elderly farmer with his business. In return he was well fed once a day before he had to return to the Stalag. He stayed there until sometime before Germany capitulated in May 1945. Near to the time of the German surrender, Bert and a couple of other prisoners-of-war simply walked out of the farm and began to make their journey back to England. Meredith's first inkling that he was alive and well came in a letter written on the special 'V for Victory' paper telling her that he was safe and coming home.

The promise of great happiness when he did finally reach Birmingham turned out to be transitory. He was a changed man, she had realised. No longer the brashly confident young man who had gone away to war determined to avenge his brother's death but a quieter, more withdrawn person, a man with an interior she could not for a long time penetrate. He was physically desperate for her love, for her body, for sex. Four lonely years made that an inevitability and she had experienced a similar but different loneliness, especially after she received news of his capture. The passion of their first few weeks together after his return was intense, perhaps too intense. His scrawny body, weakened by the poor diet of his time in capture and by the lengthy journey across Europe in the final weeks of the war when the whole continent seemed to be on the move, bore into hers when they made love. The frustration of those missing years made their couplings ferocious but unsatisfying and it wasn't long before he withdrew even further into sullen silences, sitting in an armchair smoking.

Throughout his time away Meredith had lived with her parents in the Edgbaston house. She and Bert had never had the time to find somewhere to live after the wedding. It seemed sensible for her to stay with her parents until the war ended. The aerial bombardment of Birmingham had ceased for the time being and the residential area of Edgbaston had never seen much of the bombing anyway. Her parents' house was spacious enough for her and, from November, her baby Tommy. Bert had seen the baby only once. He had been given forty-eight hours leave to visit home on the birth of the baby. Tommy barely knew him and, when Bert returned in 1945, his four-year-old son was frightened of this tall thin stranger with the black hair. The first time Bert bent down to lift Tommy up off the ground, ready to whirl him round in laughter, the boy screamed the house down.

'Don't worry,' Meredith had said, as her mother and father had looked on in embarrassment, not knowing whether to offer help as they had been doing for four years or to stand back to allow the relationship to settle. 'He hardly knows you, you know. Remember that little bundle you saw five years ago couldn't see you. He has no memory of you really.'

'But my photograph?' Bert had said.

'Yes, I showed him your photo every day. But it's not the same. He's just a child, Bert. He doesn't know that a photo is different from the real thing. You're a stranger to him really. It will take time. Be patient.'

But time didn't heal. Oh yes, Meredith thought, to the outside world all was well. They were a family again and there were lots who would never be able to say that because their men hadn't returned and lots whose men had suffered terrible wounds that would render them incapable of full lives. But all wasn't well in the Ennis family. Tommy never really took to Bert. To him the important male in the family was still his grandfather, Meredith's father, the architect, who had dandled the baby on his knee, who had minded him while his mother went out to shop and occasionally to the cinema, who, as the child grew, had shown him how to kick and throw a ball, how to make a tower with dominoes, and how to press wild flowers. It was Meredith's father who had read to him stories of Robin Hood, of the Arabian Nights, and of the Pied Piper.

The same situation was being repeated in thousands of homes throughout the country, Meredith realised later, much later, too much later to be of help. Returning heroes they might be, these soldiers coming back from war, but they were all strangers to their children, strangers too to their wives often. But there was not time to dwell on this nor was this a time when people wanted to talk about these matters. A war had been won, a country had to be rebuilt, fractured families had to re-embark on civilian life in conditions of great shortages. Everything, including love, was still rationed.

Bert Ennis returned to the factory in Small Heath and immediately threw himself into the rebuilding and restructuring that were necessary. Bombed buildings had been temporarily patched up but there were government grants now to help businesses get back on their feet, especially businesses like E.J. Ennis & Sons which had contributed so much to the war effort. After Bert had joined up, his father had had to resume hands-on management of the factory with its complement of women workers, which had meant he rarely worked less than a seven-day week. By 1945 he was weary from the effort and was happy to entrust the redevelopment to his newly returned son. Bert for his part had spent many long nights in Stalag XVII thinking about what they might make of the business. His brother Bill should have been the one to come up with all the bright ideas – that was why his dad had wanted him to go to university – but Bill was dead. It was up to him now to think of the way forward.

It was not until the middle of 1947 that Bert Ennis had the brainwave. By this time he, Meredith and young Tommy had moved into a house of their own, an older Edwardian property in Moseley, and he had been sitting in the kitchen smoking, his feet up on the top of the grange as had become his custom, and idly glancing through the *Daily Mail* one Saturday, when his eyes paused on the photograph of an attractive model on the Paris catwalk, showing off one of the first bikinis. That was it, he had thought, not just hooks and eyes but complete brassières. Why hadn't he thought of it sooner? And if these new bikinis took off, then they could branch into swimwear too. Thanks to those government grants, new machinery had been purchased for the hook and eye manufacture but there was still an empty shell of a building not yet completed. His father had thought to put more machinery for hook and eye making but Bert realised he should fill this with different machinery, machinery to make brassières. This was it!

'We could make a fortune with this, Meredith,' he had said, as he triumphantly explained his plans to his heavily pregnant wife over mid-morning coffee that same day. 'I can see these being the future, can't you?'

Meredith had puffed out her breath as she lifted her stomach into a comfortable position.

'Could be,' she admitted. 'I'm not much of a fashion expert, I have to say, but bras are a hell of a lot more comfortable than the old corsets my granny used to have to lace herself into. But won't you need a designer? You've never made anything like this before.'

'Listen,' he had said, urgently pressing her hand. 'Yes, I'm sure you're right and of course I haven't thought it all through yet but, trust me, this is it, Meredith. This is the big one. I can feel it in my bones. I don't often have brainwaves. I'm more of the steady plodder, you know that. But everything feels right about this.'

She had smiled at his boyish enthusiasm, so typical of the old him at last reappearing, as she was beginning to realise. There would be other such moments over the years but none so central to the financial well being of their lives as that Saturday morning flight of fancy.

By the time Nancy was born in September of that year, E.J. Ennis & Sons was well on the way to being transformed into a manufacturer of ladies brassières. New machinery was being installed, a designer with knowledge of current fashions and of the new synthetic materials beginning to appear in America had been employed. Bert Ennis was like a man possessed as he strove, just like his grandfather and father before him, every hour of the day and night to transform E.J. Ennis & Sons into a power in the world of fashion.

Nancy was a great solace to Bert. Tommy was still remote from him, just started school and out playing every night with his pals on the bombsites of Birmingham. Bert did manage to play with the boy occasionally. Tommy liked the green-liveried Hornby train Bert had saved up to buy and was happy to indulge his father's childlike pleasure in winding up the engine, connecting the carriages to it then releasing it on to the silvery circular track. But it was Nancy that Bert loved most. He couldn't help it. He was there from the start. Well, at least, thought Meredith, he was when he wasn't working, for he really was spending every hour he possibly could to get his new enterprise up and running. And she hadn't really minded. It was more peaceful at home when he wasn't there. Once she'd got Nancy fed and Tommy off to bed she often had some precious time to herself, when she'd sew while listening to the radio. *Twenty Questions* was one of her favourites and, if Bert was at the factory on a Sunday afternoon as he often was in those days, *The Brains Trust*. But she liked the plays they put on too, as well as the occasional light orchestral music.

It wasn't all good but it was better than it had been in the war. At least they were a family, they had a home and Bert's factory was beginning to prosper. But there was something missing.

*

42

Meredith Ennis shielded her eyes from the orange sun that was climbing beyond the olive trees that up till then had guarded her from its raw power. She shifted her gaze to the still waters of the Aegean then back to the unknown soldier's headstone that stared blankly back at her. Thoughts of the brother who had died and of the brother she had married coursed around her brain.

The first time it had happened was on a Wednesday in June of 1952. Meredith could picture it vividly still. Tom had just come home and opened the letter that she had carefully placed beside his usual glass of milk and Penguin biscuit. It was the official confirmation that he had passed his eleven-plus examination and had been offered a place at King Edward's Boys Grammar School in Camp Hill. She knew as soon as she saw the official-looking, Birmingham-franked, brown envelope what it was – the pinnacle of all her aspirations for young Tommy, or Tom as he now insisted on being addressed. And she knew in her bones that he had passed. She hadn't needed the words of his junior school headmaster nor the meagre comments on his school report. She just knew her boy was, if not a genius, at least the next best thing. Had he not already taught himself some rudimentary French after one weekend's summer trip to Calais? Had he not come consistently top of the class in his junior school, even skipping a year at one point because he was so far ahead of his contemporaries? Had he not been chosen to represent his junior school in a citywide version of one of her favourite radio quiz shows, *Top of the Form*?

When Tom had finally returned, carefully wheeling his bike down the side passage to the wooden shed where it was kept overnight, and entered the kitchen through the back door as he always did, he had not seen the envelope at first.

'Hi mum,' he had called, casting around in the cake-smelling kitchen. 'What've you been baking? Have you seen my *Eagle*?'

'There's a letter for you,' she had pointed to the table, where the brown envelope stood upright against the cool glass of milk. Her body was tensed, her eyes ablaze.

'Oh,' he had said. He too knew what it was and something of the importance of it. If he had failed, it would be the grim

Secondary Modern at the bottom of the road with its metal fencing and its air of menace.

Silently he slit the letter open and, standing as still as a statue, read its contents.

'Well?'

'I've passed. I'm going to King Edward's, Camp Hill.'

She leaned over and kissed his cheek. It embarrassed him, she knew that, but she couldn't help it. After all those years when there were just the two of them, she had prayed for this day. She hadn't wanted him to get stuck in that family factory. She had wanted him to have a proper career – a professor, a lawyer, a doctor, whatever he shone at. Her own opportunities had shrunk with his birth. Her hopes and aspirations had been transferred on to him. And now he had taken the first step. She grabbed him and swung him, big as he now was and small as she was, around in a huge celebratory whirl.

In doing so, she knocked some papers off one of the work surfaces and one of the papers became detached from the others, floating to a corner of the room. She laughingly let go of her son, bent to retrieve the errant piece of paper and glanced cursorily at it. It was a hand-written note on works notepaper. She saw E.J. Ennis & Sons in its bold black lettering at the top and then beneath, in a semi-illegible scribble, a message:

'Bert, sorry. Can't make it Sunday. Mum's acting suspicious. Will explain. Rita xxx'

What was that all about, she had wondered. And then, as she took in the meaning of the note, her brain flooded with anger. She looked at her son, sipping his milk and munching his biscuit contentedly now at the kitchen table with the *Eagle* comic spread out before him. She remembered his news and the euphoria of just a few minutes earlier. This would wait. Tom mattered most at this point. Bert's sordid affair, if that was what it was and it certainly looked like it, would wait.

He was late back, as usual. Tom was in his upstairs bedroom reading. Eight o'clock had become standard for Bert, as he had taken to calling in at the pub on his way home. He was never drunk, she had to give him that, but he liked his couple of pints. Said it relaxed him after a busy day oiling the wheels of industry.

'Hello, love, anything new?' he had asked, reaching into the oven for his evening meal as always. 'Hm, smells good. Steak and kidney? Brilliant. My favourite.'

Taking her for granted, as usual. To him she was often just part of the furniture, she felt, almost invisible as a person. She had become accustomed, even accepting, of this, for she understood his need to build the business. But now there was this. She had to get him to see her properly.

'There's good news and bad news,' she had answered grimly, standing away from him by the sink. 'Which would you like first?'

'Oh, bring me the good news, of course? What is it? Have we won the pools?'

She paused for a moment, her eyes glinting with suppressed anger.

'Tom's passed his eleven-plus. He's starting at King Edward's in Camp Hill in September.'

'Great!' he had said, genuinely pleased for the boy whom he had never understood and not noticing his wife's look. 'I knew he'd do it. Just what the firm needs, someone with a brain to look at where we go next. Since Bill died in Crete.....'

'That's enough!' she had cut across his words, as she had heard Tom's footsteps coming down the stairs to retrieve something from his coat then ascending again to his bedroom.

He had started tucking into his pie and mashed potatoes.

'Don't you want to know the rest?' she had continued between gritted teeth.

'What's that then?'

'This.' She had held the piece of notepaper out to him, slamming it on to the table beside his plate. 'And don't lie. I know when you're lying. Tell me the truth. Who's this Rita? How long has it been going on?'

Bert Ennis had blanched. He had set aside his knife and fork and read again the telling note he had stupidly left under some papers in the kitchen.

'It's nothing,' he had said finally and feebly. 'It was just a bit of silliness. It meant nothing. Honest, Meredith. It was nothing.'

'Who is she?'

'She was just one of the models we'd been using for our advertising.'

'Did you sleep with her?'

'What do you think I am?'

'Did you sleep with her?' she pressed angrily.

'It wasn't like that, Meredith, honest. She turned up at the office one Sunday afternoon when I was doing the paperwork. Said she'd forgotten something earlier in the week and saw the light on as she was passing, so she came in. She threw herself at me, I couldn't help it. Nothing serious happened. Honest, it was nothing, just a bit of silliness.'

The fingers of his right hand played nervously underneath his chin.

'So why the note? You'd arranged to meet her again, hadn't you? And she got cold feet?'

'No, I told her never to come again. I told her it was stupid, she was only in her twenties. There was a misunderstanding.'

Meredith Ennis drew herself up to her full five feet two inches and jabbed her finger into his ribs.

'Bert Ennis,' she said, her voice low and insistent, 'Whoever this Rita girl is you'd better get rid of her straightaway, sack her if she's on the payroll. I have my ways of finding out about what goes on in the factory, mark my words. Don't let anything like this happen again. Ever. All right?'

He had nodded numbly, aware he had been found out, determined never to let it happen again, genuinely contrite and deeply embarrassed at being found out in this way. He was telling the truth. Nothing had happened. Well, nothing much. But enough, if Meredith ever did find out, to bring severe grief on himself.

\*

The second time was even more troubling. It was a year or so before Tom's wedding to Julia. Meredith had not exactly taken against her but had been disappointed that Tom, after winning a scholarship at Oxford and embarking on the first rungs of the brilliant career she had always planned for him, had fallen for this very pretty but empty-headed primary schoolteacher who was the sister of one of his best pals at Merton, Danny Thomas. It would never have happened if they hadn't started work at the Atomic Energy Research Establishment at Harwell at the same time. Tom had told her how one evening he had gone for a drink at the village pub when Danny appeared with his sister Julia. He knew her slightly from the June Ball in their final year at Oxford. Danny had taken her, because he had no girl friend of his own and, not wanting to be a wallflower, had invited his sister along as his partner. Tom had his own partner that evening but he had enjoyed one dance with Julia.

She was just visiting, she had told him, from Didcot where the school she worked at was situated. He'd tried explaining to her about the dangers of nuclear fission, of possible leakages, of possible explosions even. Then she had teased him by saying he was too serious and why didn't he come with her to see *Goldfinger* in Oxford the following week. Danny had tried to discourage him by telling him it was only his sister but Tom was flattered by her attention and attracted to her. So he'd gone to the cinema with her.

Meredith realised Julia's attractions the first time she met her some time later. She had caught a train to Oxford one Saturday to see her son because he hadn't been back to Birmingham for some time and during his last phone call he had admitted that he was having doubts about working at Harwell, because all this nuclear power stuff was too dangerous, and he was considering a career as a physics teacher. Meredith could see her hopes for him draining away. Tom took his mother for lunch in The Wheatsheaf in the town centre and then afterwards, as they strolled along the grassy banks of the Isis, suggested that they might have afternoon tea before her train back to Birmingham. In the selected tearoom was Julia, sitting at a small table, dressed demurely in a knee-length black skirt and mauve sweater but not so modestly that her figure wasn't emphasised.

'Hello! Fancy seeing you,' said Tom, not very convincingly. 'This is my mum. Mum, this is Julia, Danny's sister.'

Meredith knew immediately as Julia rose to peck Tom on the cheek that this was no accidental meeting and she knew what the attraction was for Tom.

'Are you at university?' she asked, through narrowed eyes.

'No, I teach in a small church primary school in Didcot,' said Julia in her gurgling voice, like that of a young child. 'I'm coming to the end of my first year.'

'That's nice,' said Meredith without meaning it. Tom could do better than a primary school teacher, she thought.

'I've saved enough to buy a second-hand car in the summer holidays,' said Julia. 'Tom's going to help me choose it.'

'Oh yes,' said Meredith, but she also noticed the looks that passed between the two young people, noticed the way Julia's hand reached for Tom's, noticed the way his arm settled on the back of her chair.

Meredith Ennis had returned home on the train to Birmingham deeply troubled. Not only had she failed to convince her son that he should concentrate on his career at Harwell and forget about notions of schoolteaching, but she had also realised that Julia's physical attractions were proving too much for her son. When he rang a few months later to say that they were getting engaged, she was bothered but not surprised. Her husband, however, was all in favour, especially after he had met the intended bride.

'It's what he needs,' Bert had said, settling down in his armchair after his usual late dinner and lighting a cigarette. 'Settle the boy down. He's had too many fancy ideas all his life, if you ask me. It's time he realised the world doesn't owe him a free ride. Anyway, she's a nice enough lass. I was quite taken with her.'

She knew about Bert's gullibility, so wasn't surprised at his reaction to Julia, though she hadn't expected him to slip from the straight and narrow again. Her mind had been taken up for several weeks now with her son and his intended future. What had happened to that bright-eyed scholar she had waved off to Oxford only five years previously, armed with his scholarship and his books and her ambitions? They had no knowledge of university, neither Bert nor herself, and they had been surprised the first Christmas he had returned home with his hair down to his shoulders and a wispy beard. Subsequent returns had seen a succession of different costumes – that was all she could call them: variations of corduroy trousers or denim jeans, leather jackets or tweed coats, cravats or bootleg ties, brown leather brogues or suede desert boots. His final degree, a high second class, was adequate but not what she had hoped for when he first went there, although it did get him the offer of work at Harwell. She had been reasonably happy at that. Even though his status there was low initially, there would be opportunities for promotion. But now he was threatening to throw it all away, talking about becoming a schoolteacher and marrying this vacuous girl with her casual ways and her provocative body.

It was at this time she discovered that Bert had a mistress. This was no casual, one-off stand, as she had realised eventually that the brief affair with that young model had been thirteen or fourteen years previously. No, this was something much worse. This had been going on under her nose for the best part of five years before she found out. Her name was Dorothy Garbett and she had been working at the factory as the chief designer for the brassières for all of those five years. She had come straight from her training at the London College of Fashion and had revolutionised the designs and styles of the bras E.J. Ennis & Sons had been making for the past few years. Meredith had had no doubts about her. Although her creations were flamboyant and in some ways often outrageous, Dorothy Garbett was very plain herself. She wore no make-up, because of a dermatological problem, preferred loose-fitting men's cardigans and denim jeans to conventional women's wear and was singularly tall. She towered over Meredith. She smoked hand-rolled cheroots all the time and Meredith always afterwards associated that strong tobacco smell with her.

So, when her daughter Nancy, home for the weekend from her nurses' hostel, appeared at the house one day with red, tear-stained eyes and she asked her what was wrong, she was taken aback when she found out.

'It's dad,' came the sobbed reply. 'I think he's having an affair with Dorothy at work.'

'What?'

Nancy had been to visit her father's factory to advise him about his first-aid materials.

'I know I shouldn't say but I caught her with his arm around her waist when I went into the main office. I didn't believe what I'd seen but I kept my eyes on them both whenever they were together and it's true. They kept touching each other and giving each other secret smiles. I overheard then planning a trip to London for a fashion show. They're sharing a room in the hotel. Oh, mum, why's he doing this?'

Meredith's fingers dug into her palms in anger but then she sought to calm her daughter and assure her that there must have been a mistake and she would sort it out with her father. But there was no mistake, and she knew it. There were the usual denials, of course, the usual excuses, but she knew he was lying. On this occasion she had had time to resolve her strategy however. This time would be the last time. From now on, she would never let him out of her sight. Dorothy Garbett was sacked and Meredith installed herself as chief designer to the newly named Enniswear. She knew the business inside out and, though she had never been to Fashion College or any college for that matter, she was a quick learner. There were others in the factory, too, who advised her and showed her the plans for the following season's bras that Dorothy had been working on. Those plans could be effected – Dorothy wouldn't dare complain that someone was using her ideas – and then Meredith could think creatively about future ideas.

On a sunny July Saturday in 1966, Tom and Julia were wed in the lovely eleventh century Norman church of St Helen's in Abingdon where Julia's family lived. Her brother Danny was best man and two of Julia's cousins were bridesmaids. It was the best day of her life, she always said afterwards – she looked like someone out of the wedding magazines, bedecked in glistening white chiffon with a long train held delicately by the two bridesmaids. Tom and Danny wore morning dress, as did most of the other male guests, and all the middle-aged women sported huge hats.

Later that day, as she waved bride and groom off in their tin-can festooned Ford Cortina on the first journey of their married life to their honeymoon destination in the Lake District, Meredith could not help thinking of her own wedding and hoping against hope that Tom's marriage would prove stronger than hers had. The seeds of doubt, however, had already implanted themselves in her mind.

*

Why had she allowed it to happen? Why hadn't she put an end to the sham of their marriage earlier? Meredith often asked herself. And she was asking herself again now as she sat on the wooden bench in the Souda Bay cemetery, the sunlight dazzling her eyes. It just wasn't done in those days, at least not among the people she knew in Sutton Coldfield. Yes, divorce happened but it tended to be among the poorer types. In her circle, it was looked on as a social stigma, as if somehow a woman had failed. That was how it was and no amount of legislation could change that. Nor could she confide in anyone of her friends. She was fairly sure that some of them too might be part of dysfunctional marriages but none could admit it. It was like during the war – you just got on with it, for the sake of the children if nothing else.

But the children had gone. Tom and Julia were still in Oxfordshire at that point, where he had gone through with his intention to become a teacher and was teaching physics in a local grammar school. They had moved into an old cottage out in a tiny hamlet in the country beyond Didcot. The house had been half-modernised but had no central heating until Bert was persuaded by his wife that the young couple couldn't possibly bring a baby up in those conditions and he had paid for radiators and an oil boiler to be installed. It was some years, however, before Julia succeeded in getting pregnant and their first child, Eleanor, was born.

Nancy too had left home. After leaving school, she had enrolled to train as a nurse at the Queen Elizabeth Hospital in Birmingham and was living in a nurses' hostel near the hospital. She had applied to do further training as a mental health nurse in north Staffordshire and was awaiting the outcome of her application.

So why had she stubbornly clung to this notion of marriage? Why had she stuck with Bert? It didn't make sense then and it didn't make any more sense at this point in time, just after her ninetieth birthday in this foreign landscape.

There had been someone else for her too, however, someone she had met through taking on the chief designer role at Enniswear. Part of her work required her to travel occasionally to fashion shows in Paris and that was where they met. Pierre was a couturier, just starting up and hoping to break through into one of the bigger fashion houses. At first she thought he was a homosexual with his loose handclasp, his quick walk and his immaculately styled curly hair. That was probably why she agreed to go out to a restaurant with him. It was the second time they had met, the first being the previous year when there had been no more than a casual introduction at a pre-show party. On this occasion, at the same pre-show party, Pierre had launched himself at her as soon as he saw her, clasping her in a too-tight embrace and kissing her on both cheeks effusively. It was all terribly over the top but she had liked it and when he asked her later if she would care to join him for a meal, she had accepted gracefully. He promised entertainment and it was time she forgot the restraints she had placed on her own restless spirit.

They went to a small restaurant in Montmartre where he bought champagne, insisted she should eat *pâté de foie gras* and *confit de canard*, which he said were specialities of the house. Throughout the meal he kept her entertained with stories of some of the characters in the French fashion business he had come across – their scandalous behaviour, the spats, the tears, the incredible creations. When a gipsy woman entered the restaurant selling red roses, he bought her one and insisted on presenting it to her from between his clenched teeth as he knelt on the floor. It was all completely outrageous, especially for Meredith, still living in the conventional *mores* of Middle England but she loved every minute of it. When later, after walking her back to her hotel, he suggested they finish the evening off with a good Napoleon brandy in her room, she consented readily, still under the impression that he was safe to be with.

She was very surprised when later he reached across for her glass, placed it on the side table, then stood and lifted her on to the bed. But she did not stop him. When it was over, he leaned on his back and lit a cigarette.

'You are a very good lover,' she said eventually. 'I thought you were a queer, you know.'

He laughed.

'It is how you have to appear in the fashion business in France,' he said. 'But, as you see it is a front, it is a pretence. It has led me into problems in the past. But now, I think, most people know what I am.'

After that, she saw Pierre twice a year, at the Paris Show and at the London week and more rarely on other occasions when it was convenient for them to escape from their daily routines and lives for nights of delight. It was never any more than that. He made her laugh. There was never any talk of living together permanently. This suited them.

*

And then Bert had died.

It had all started very suddenly. One morning he had complained of feeling slightly woozy and she could see from the way he was moving that he was stumbling a little.

'I think you ought to book an appointment with the doctor,' she had said, as she put away their greasy breakfast plates into the dishwasher.

'I'll be all right,' he had said, brushing aside her suggestion as he had so frequently done and reaching for his suit jacket from the back of his chair.

But he wasn't. The next day he came home with a blinding headache in the middle of the day and took to his bed. Unheard of from this captain of industry, this scion of manufacturing, this holder of the Queen's Award for Enterprise. Unheard of from Bert Ennis who had never had a day's illness in his life, or none that stopped him going to work.

That evening Meredith found him spreadeagled on the floor in their bedroom when she took him up a mug of Horlicks to help him sleep. He had climbed out of bed but stumbled against the side of the wooden bedstead, losing the use of his right leg. She had helped him back and driven him the following morning for an emergency appointment with their doctor. Bert himself had insisted they join BUPA a couple of years earlier in 1982, because he said the National Health Service was falling apart. He was kept in for observation and tests then sent home to rest while the results of the tests were analysed. They were invited back for a full consultation the following Tuesday.

'So what's the news, doc?' asked Bert, back now in his *faux*-cheery mode, though he still looked pale. 'Are you going to tell me I picked up some lurgy back in Austria all those years ago and it's just worked its way into my system?'

'I'm afraid not,' replied the doctor, whose clean-cut features were emphasised by the sharply pressed pin-stripe suit he wore. 'Nothing so rare, I'm afraid.'

Meredith placed her hand on Bert's. She could sense this was serious. Whatever had happened between them in the past, they were still husband and wife, still parents to Tom and Nancy. And this was serious. He needed her.

'So what is it then?' continued Bert, still trying to joke his way through. 'You're going to tell me I'm working too hard. Need to take a rest. Cut back a bit, eh?'

'Mr Ennis,' interrupted Dr Sykes sternly, 'I'm sorry to say that you have cancerous growths in your liver and in your stomach.'

Meredith held her breath.

'Can't you deal with that sort of thing nowadays?' asked Bert. His voice had suddenly become feebler now.

'I'm afraid the cancer is at a very advanced stage. The growths are too large to be surgically removed without causing significant damage to the rest of your internal organs. I'm going to arrange for a course of chemotherapy immediately.'

Bert Ennis gulped. She watched that familiar stroking of the chin, as the colour drained from his cheeks and his forehead.

'Will that get rid of them, these growths?' she asked, aware that her husband was sinking into a trough, as he absorbed the news and aware too that she would have to give him full-time care for however long it took.

'No, I'm afraid the cancer is too well established,' said Dr Sykes. 'All we can do is seek to slow its progress.'

'How long have I got then, doc?' asked Bert weakly.

'I would say six weeks at most. I'm sorry. It may be longer. But you need to know.'

In the end he had lasted ten weeks. The chemotherapy certainly slowed the cancer's progress briefly but no more, as Dr Sykes had forecast, than temporarily. In March of 1985, as a cruel wind blew from the north, gusting the litter and dust from the paving slabs, Meredith Ennis, supported on either side by her son Tom and her daughter Nancy, followed the coffin containing Bert Ennis's body into the Sutton Coldfield crematorium building. Although neither of them were churchgoers, she had acceded to his final wishes and had a Church of England ceremony, complete with *The Lord's My Shepherd* and *Abide with Me*. A vicar they didn't know had spoken a few words in tribute. And then the final organ chords echoed around the chapel as the coffin rolled out of sight behind a dark blue velvet curtain and Bert Ennis's remains were confined to the fire. And that was that.

She had kept her composure throughout. Tears had come but later, when the numbness had worn off, when friends and neighbours had stopped phoning or calling round to check she was okay, when she had done with comforting Tom, Nancy and the grandchildren.

But they were tears of regret for what might have been as much as tears of grief for him. Near the end he had made her promise to visit his brother's grave. And she had meant to but somehow it had never happened.

Later, she had briefly toyed with the notion of a more permanent relationship but she was already almost seventy and Pierre the same age. They had not been seeing as much of each other for five to six years. He had suffered a heart attack and, although now fully recovered, had reduced his commitment to the business. His firm was an established brand by now and he had others who could run the business for him, including his son Jacques.

And Meredith had her own concerns. Tom's first marriage had ended in divorce, as she had known it would, and his teaching career was not going so well. Meredith had been trying to persuade him for some time to return to Birmingham and take on the family business, long before Bert was taken ill and eventually she succeeded. She hadn't wanted to be working all the hours under the sun at her age, for what had become a secure and stable business in the nineteen seventies was beginning to feel the pinch of Far Eastern competition in the nineteen eighties. If Tom hadn't taken on the business, she would have had to sell.

One day, without warning, she had a letter from Jacques to say that his father had collapsed one evening and suffered a massive heart attack. Pierre had died before the doctors could reach him. Jacques knew of his father's friendship with Meredith, though how much he really knew she was never sure. So that was that too.

She stretched out her arms in front of her and clasped them around her own shoulders, embracing the empty air as she thought of the wonderful moments of passion they had shared. What right had she to find love in that way? She had castigated Bert for his affairs but then found happiness in the same fashion. She had thought to have given all her love to her children, to her family, to have substituted matriarchy for physical love and sexual pleasure. And then Pierre had happened. And she hadn't denied him. Or it. And now he too was gone. The great sadness of reaching an old age, she reflected, is measured by all those who die before you.

*

Suddenly she remembered Ellie. By now her granddaughter would almost certainly have realised she was missing. It was approaching mid-morning and, even allowing for Ellie's normal late awakening, she would be up and about by now and would have realised that her ancient grandmother, whom she had sworn to look after on this Mediterranean cruise, was not to be found. She would have hunted on all the decks, in the lounges and in the restaurants. She would have persuaded that young officer she had been clinging to the previous evening – and quite possibly spent the night with – to instigate a hunt for her grandmother. She would have checked that no tours of Heraklion had gone off with her in them, no visits to Knossos. She would have discovered that an early morning sightseeing tour had embarked but no one of her grandmother's description was on it. She would have discovered that Meredith's handbag and passport were missing too, so it would be obvious that she had chosen to go somewhere. But why hadn't she left a message? And where had she gone? How could she find her?

Meredith Ennis stood up from the bench she had been sitting on and made her way slowly from the martial rows of graves to the cemetery exit and out to the caravan where Themis was sitting in conversation with another elderly man.

'My friend Georgios,' he said, standing and pulling a plastic chair out from beneath the table for her to sit on. 'We have known each other many years. My daughter married his nephew.

56

Please, would you like a Greek coffee? Fresh orange juice? Something to eat?'

'Fresh orange sounds just fine,' she said, sitting on the proffered chair and looking around her.

Georgios was much taller than Themis. Although the hair was very thin on the top of his head, the bristling moustache that buried his upper lip was definitely of a brownish colour. He wore an unfastened black waistcoat over his shirt. There was a *tavli* set on the table.

The place was non-descript, little more than a few formica-topped tables spread loosely about outside underneath tired canvas parasols.

'I am worried about my granddaughter,' Meredith said. 'I left her on the *Ariadne* without saying where I was going. She'll be going crazy by now.'

'Why did you not tell her?'

'Because I wanted to do this on my own. Ellie's a lovely girl but she would have insisted on coming with me. Her father got her to swear she wouldn't let me out of her sight on this trip. And I needed to do this on my own. She has no knowledge of my contacts with you. Nor does her father. You might think me crazy but this is my adventure, my mission, if you like, and it had to be kept secret. I have my reasons.'

She smoothed her skirt and fanned her face with the end of her scarf. She noticed the look that passed between the two men – a look that suggested they had been talking about her while she had been sitting in the cemetery. What had they said? That she was a crazy old woman? Well, maybe they were right.

'So why are you fretting now? Young people always make too much fuss but they calm down eventually. She will see sense sooner or later,' said Themis

'Maybe I should leave a message for her.'

'You want pigeon?' joked Georgios, who had been listening in to the conversation. 'I have at home!'

They all laughed.

'No, I thought I might sent her a text message,' she said. 'The problem is that, if I use my mobile phone, she'll ring back and start nagging me.'

'You have a mobile phone?' asked Themis surprised.

'Yes,' she answered, reaching into her canvas bag and rescuing the shiny black phone. 'Don't you?'

'For the young maybe. But for me?' He shrugged and looked up to the skies. 'How quickly can you send this text message? I mean, how quickly will your granddaughter receive it?'

'It's instant, I think.'

Themis scratched his thick white hair as he contemplated this, then suddenly sat forward, turning his face away from her.

'Manolis! Let this lady use your mobile phone,' he called over to the skinny waiter who was at the counter pouring out orange juice for Meredith and fresh Greek coffees for the two old men.

When the waiter had brought the drinks and the phone to them and Meredith had replaced her own phone in her handbag, Themis spoke again.

'Don't send your message yet. Wait till we've had our drinks and then send it just before we leave. That way, if she calls back, she'll only get Manolis and I'll swear him to silence. Trust me.'

He was right. She was unsure but, when she thought about it, it seemed a good plan. By the time Ellie received the message, they would be long gone and she wouldn't have to deal with her own guilt when her granddaughter, as she surely would, tried to reply. What difference would a few minutes make? Meredith slowly typed out her message:

*DONT worry. Am OK. Will contact later.*

Just before they left, she pressed the SEND button. Then, saying goodbye to Georgios and with Manolis's promise he would say that someone must have used his phone while he was away from it, they drove away from Souda Bay.

*

When Ellie, or Eleanor Rose as she was christened, was growing up, she used to come to stay with Meredith and Bert for weekends when her parents needed time for their own business. Meredith always loved having her. She was a pretty child, with a dimpled cherubic face, blonde curls and the most irrepressible laughter imaginable. When she was old enough, Meredith used to take her by train into Birmingham itself, exploring the recently revamped Bull Ring, shopping in Lewis's and – their favourite – picnicking at the Botanical Gardens in Harborne.

Meredith loved it there, wondering around in the safe steamy environment of the glass-roofed Tropical House with its rubber trees, its tall green sugar cane plants, its leafy banana trees and its ornamental plants with their multi-coloured leaves. Ellie loved especially the ones that were called flamingo flowers that she called 'famindo ploughers'. They would always stop and sit on the edge of the pool in there and Ellie would gaze down into the depths of the dark green water while her grandmother skimmed its surface gently and stroked the smooth leaves of the water lilies. In the Subtropical House they would marvel at the variety of emerald-green ferns stretching up to the glass roof and then gape at the extraordinary carnivorous plants – butterworts, bladderworts and, most amazing of all, the Venus flytraps. As they passed the orchid beds, Ellie called out one day:

'I want to have those white ones when I get married. Do you think they will let me have some from here, Granny?'

Meredith had smiled at the childish simplicity.

'Why not?' she had replied. 'I'll tell the manager today, shall I? To get some ready for you? How many years do you think it will be till you get married, Ellie?'

'Oh, I think about two hundred,' came the eight-year-old's studied reply.

You might wish that indeed, thought Meredith, as she thought of the grief that she had endured twice in her own marriage. But how could she advise an innocent child of all that?

'Let's go out into the gardens for our picnic, shall we?' she said, taking her granddaughter's hand and steering her out of the moist heat of the Subtropical House and into the real warmth of the late summer sun.

They found a place on the grass in front of the bandstand but only after Ellie had insisted on visiting the curious sundial and trying to tell the time by standing on the stone strip below it in the space marked 'August'.

'What time does my shadow say, Granny?' she called out.

'I think I should do that,' Meredith replied. 'You come over here and let me stand there. Then you can tell me the time.'

They swapped positions.

'It's two o'clock,' said Ellie, dancing excitedly on the grass. 'I think that's time for you, me and Gladly to have our picnic, don't you? Come on, let's sit down here.'

'Ooh, good, is Gladly coming too?' cooed Ellie.

Gladly the cross-eyed bear, named after the famous hymn whose proper lyric was 'Gladly my cross I'd bear', had once been one of three brown bears kept at the Botanical Gardens in the early part of the twentieth century. Meredith had read about him in a guidebook and had told Ellie that Gladly's spirit still lived in the Gardens and, if she was very well behaved and ate up all her picnic food, she might find a treat left for her at the counter as they left.

Meredith took off her small knapsack, pulled out a blue check tablecloth and spread it on the grass, then proceeded to empty the rest of the contents on to it – a tupperware box of fish-paste sandwiches, a bag of crisps, two cans of Coca Cola, another tupperware box with grapes in it and a plastic bag for the litter.

'Come on then, young lady,' said Meredith. 'Eat up or Gladly won't give you a special treat.'

The innocence of childhood. It never failed to lift her spirits. Even the memory of it as they drove away from Souda Bay and through the outskirts of Chania before returning to the National Road was enough to give her that warm glow. Reminders flashed through her mind – Tom returning from his primary school with the letter from his headteacher about his selection to be in the *Top of the Form* team, Tom swimming his first length after weeks of trying, Ellie peeping over the shoulders of the tall girl stupidly placed in front of her in the church for the school Carol Service and giving her little smile, Will coming last in the sack race in the school sports but laughing his head off at the sheer fun of it all, Tom again in his cap and gown approaching the Vice Chancellor's throne in Oxford to have his head tapped with an ancient copy of the Bible as he was awarded his degree. The memories came flooding back now – Nancy's first solo bicycle ride and the bloody knees that followed when she fell off, Ellie as a Munchkin in *The Wizard of Oz* in her first year at secondary school wearing that hooped costume she had made for her, Tom's excitement on learning that Bert had managed to get two tickets for the Cup Final at Wembley in 1957 and the look on his face when he returned home after Aston Villa's victory, Nancy coming home with the news that she had been made a Sixer in the Brownies, Ellie coming to visit her over twenty years later with the same news, Will at four pronouncing 'supercalifragilisticexpialidocious', Nancy in hospital holding her newly-born baby, Ben, in her arms and crying with delight.

Meredith was crying herself now but still the memories came – memories of her bloodline, the fruits of her body, her family. Will coming to her house a few years previously to help clear out her attic, losing his footing so that his right leg crashed through the plasterboard of the ceiling and left his leg dangling helplessly there. Nancy on her first visit home from the nurses' hostel in her starched cap and her big blue cape, so proud of her new uniform and excited at the job she had started to learn. Tom carrying Will on his shoulders all the way to the top of The Wrekin in Shropshire on a day out. Memories above all of Ellie, her beloved Ellie, always memories of the child who, unbeknown to her, was the recipient of all her grandmother's secret love. She was the one to whose sleeping head she would whisper, she was the one who received the secrets, she was the one who, if only she had been able to hear and understand, might have helped her to a resolution. And she was the one who, unwittingly, was now helping her to a resolution.

# 3

They had left the coast behind now and were climbing steadily on a narrow tarmaced road through acres of bottle-green olive groves and past occasional new villas that leapt suddenly from the hillside, all white paint, shiny orange-tiled roofs, wooden shutters and exposed balconies. As they rounded a sharp bend, Themis slowed to park his car beside a white stone wall with a peeling blue-shuttered window and a wooden door badly in need of paint. Next to the wall was a more modern construction, a *kafeneion* with metal railings around it and green vine branches dangling from its roof, where a solitary man sat with a glass of water placed on the table before him.

'This is my village,' explained Themis. 'Xamoudochori.'

He helped her out of the car and she wandered briefly around in the sparkling sunlight, taking in the sight. It was nothing exceptional, merely a collection of houses, some in states of considerable disrepair, surrounding what might loosely be called a square. Beyond the metal railings of the *kafeneion* she could see more olive groves stretching into the distance and beyond them the blueness of the Aegean Sea.

'This was my family's house,' Themis continued, pointing not at the wall where he had parked the car but at a taller building next to it that was in a better state of repair. 'And this is where my mother and my grandfather were killed.'

By now he was indicating the white-painted wall, taller and plainer with no windows, right next to where they were standing. Meredith stared at this wall long and hard, trying to imagine what those two poor people must have felt as they stared in terror at the German soldiers pointing their rifles at them.

'I'm so sorry,' she said, turning to watch his expression.

'It was a long time ago,' he said, nodding to himself. 'I have grieved. I still grieve. But my tears are almost dry now. Thank you. I had to show you. Now come, get back in the car. I will show you where Skip and his men were based in 1941.'

They drove a short distance through the old village and back towards the coast, passing a glistening pink church that looked as if it were newly built.

'Can you stop a moment?' she asked.

She climbed out of the car again to look and peered up at the inscription on a stone let into a wall that indicated it had been built in 1955, though there was obviously building work still going on as she could see a yellow mechanical digger around the side of the building and there were piles of grey tiles near a fence. She walked around the freshly painted pale pink building with its orange pantiled dome, its lattice-like windows and its tall, rectangular bell tower. Was this where Bill had left his few coins and lit a candle? she wondered. Not in this particular building, certainly, but in its predecessor?

'You want to know about this church?' asked Themis, leaning out of the car window and twirling his worry beads as she returned.

'No, it's all right. It was just something my brother-in-law mentioned in a letter, about a chapel or a church near where he was stationed. I wondered if this was it.'

There was a small oblong cemetery just beyond the church, cutting into the olive trees. Themis noticed her looking at it.

'That is where my mother and grandfather are buried. And my dear wife Katerina. And my Uncle Alexandros,' he said, gazing intently at the cemetery walls. 'He was a very brave man. He was all of my family that was left. He gave me everything.'

She said nothing. This was his private grief. She watched him narrow his eyes to keep back the wash of tears. Then he turned back to her and gestured to his car. As she climbed back in, Themis pointed ahead through the windscreen.

'See those? Radar masts.'

She peered through the windscreen beyond the church wall, past the plane trees bounding the road and over the olive groves. Where the road bent left there was another white-walled house, still in the process of construction, and beyond it she saw the tall, red and white, metallic masts that rose like silver rockets from the ridge above.

'For the Greek Air Force. At Maleme. That is where the British had their radar base too. On that same ridge.'

So. That was where Bill had been stationed. That was where his flight had begun. She swallowed hard. He had definitely been here, walked this road, maybe visited this church.

'Can we get up there?'

'No, it is forbidden. We can drive closer but really there is nothing more to see.'

Meredith gazed around her at the acres of olive trees. Just to her left the ground fell away into a deep valley then rose gradually again before levelling off. The view in the opposite direction was not much different, except that it included the village of Xamoudochori. This was fertile land. This was farming land. This was the land where the olive was king. It was hard to imagine a time when this peaceful countryside was riven with bombs dropping, the rattle of rifle fire and the marching boots of troops of soldiers.

'Where were they billeted?'

'There was a house just over the hillside. But it is gone now. There is nothing there to see.'

She was disappointed but not overly so. She knew she had walked on ground he had walked on. That was enough for the moment.

They wound their way in the car back to the village square then turned right and headed towards the White Mountains and, as Meredith thought, away from the village. What she hadn't anticipated was the huge amount of new housing that had arisen at the edge of the village.

'That is my house,' Themis said, inclining his head to the left towards a long drive to a large newly-built property, whose front balcony gazed out to the Aegean Sea. 'And those are my houses too.'

She looked where he pointed at the row of villas on the opposite side of the road, facing over the olive groves towards the sea. Each villa was painted pure white, each had ocean-blue window shutters, each had a vine-clad balcony facing over the green valley and each had its own swimming pool on a terrace in front of the villa.

'You own all of those?' she queried, surprised at this.

'Yes. I owned four thousand olive trees once but, since Greece joined the European Community, we have had much house building on Crete and many more tourists. I was becoming an old man, my son is a doctor in America and my two daughters live in Athens. What did I want with working four thousand olive trees? So I sold nearly all of them and I built those six holiday villas and a new home for Katerina and myself. Then, two years after we moved into our new house, she died. There is just me now.'

There were several moments of silence between them.

'Who has won? Who has lost? It is not easy,' said Themis.

She could not look at him but stared instead out towards the sea and the hilly peninsula that bounded one side of her view. So many deaths. So many memories. When would all end?

'No. Old age is not the privilege some people think.'

*

It wasn't just the letter from Bill that had mentioned the chapel. It was also in his diary.

It was in 1995 that she received the unexpected call. She had been working her way through *The Telegraph* quick crossword, as she frequently did mid-afternoon, when the doorbell had rung. When she went to answer the door, she found herself confronted by a very large young woman, with a stud in her nose and a safety pin piercing her eyebrow. She wore all black clothing and what Meredith could only describe to her daughter Nancy later that evening on the phone as lurid make-up – green lipstick, purple blusher, heavily-stenciled black eyeliner. She was chewing gum.

'You Mrs Ennis, eh?' said the woman in her deep voice.

'I might be. It depends who's asking,' replied Meredith cautiously.

'Well, either you are or you ain't,' said the plump young woman. 'You are, ain't you? I ain't come on a wild goose chase, I hope. It's took me long enough to find you anyway.'

'And who exactly are you?' demanded Meredith, worried that this was someone trying to sell her something. She'd read about such people in the local paper. They preyed on elderly folk apparently.

'Oh, don't worry, you don't know me,' came the reply. 'But I've got something you'd like to see, I'm betting. My name, for what it's worth is Jessie. Jessie Martin.'

'Well, Jessie, what can I do for you?'

'I'm Eddie Martin's granddaughter. He was in Crete in the war.'

Meredith had caught her breath then. Bill had mentioned someone called Eddie in his very last letter home. She decided to take a chance.

'You'd better come in,' she said. 'I don't know if there's been some mistake but....'

'Oh, I don't think there's been any mistake,' said Jessie Martin, chewing furiously now and hoisting her black trousers up on her stomach. 'If I'm not mistaken, you're Mrs Ennis and your husband's brother was Bill Ennis. My granddad served with him in Crete in the war. That's why I'm here.'

Over tea Jessie explained the reason for her visit. She had barely known her granddad as he had died in the East End when she was only three, while her family had moved out to Romford, so they didn't see him and her Nan that much. Her Nan had lived another twenty years, staying in the same terraced house that they were all 'doing up now in London and asking a fortune for'. When her Nan died, Jessie and her dad had had to clear out the house and in the attic they had found this writing pad with faded writing, like it had been there for a long time. Her dad had said they should chuck it away but Jessie had taken it home and started reading it.

'That's what this is.'

She reached into the voluminous leather bag she was carrying, pulled out a thick and discolored Basildon Bond letter-writing pad and passed it over.

'It's took me three years to find you but here I am. This is Bill Ennis's diary of the last days in Crete that he and my granddad and several other blokes spent. It's about how they escaped from the Germans and got rescued by the Royal Navy. Some of it's just letters to somebody. I don't think my granddad was your brother-in-law's sort really but they got on okay. But I expect you know all about what happened from when he got back home at the end of the war.'

Letters? And never seen for fifty years? His last letters. Finally she might know the story of those final days. Meredith Ennis looked up at the plump young woman and she could sense a moistness threatening the left side of her face.

'My brother-in-law didn't return,' she said simply. 'He died on Crete.'

'Ooh, I'm sorry. I didn't know.'

Meredith composed herself, pulling a stray hair out of her eyes and at the same time wiping one eye.

'It was a long long time ago, Jessie. But how did your grandfather come into possession of this diary?'

She explained that she had wondered about that too because it had struck her as very weird, him having someone else's diary. Her dad had said that her granddad used to talk about when they were getting on the boat to take them off Crete how Skip – that was what he had called him – had stayed behind because the Navy wouldn't take this Greek kid on board and he had promised to take him with them. Just before they had separated, Skip had given this package to her granddad and asked him to look after it. He said he would get it back from him when they met up in Alex. Of course, they never had met up and her granddad must have carried this thing round with him for the rest of the war and then afterwards she supposed he had just forgotten about it.

As she talked, Meredith was reading the tiny, faded, spidery writing. It was Bill's writing, sure enough. She recognised the odd way he write his 'b' as if it was a Greek *beta*.

'All I knew was that he was called Bill Ennis,' continued Jessie Martin, slurping from her cup of tea. 'Didn't know where he'd come from or nothing like that. I went to the library in Romford and asked them if they could tell me how to find out about someone who'd been involved in the war. They told me to contact the Imperial War Museum, but they had no record of him there. Then I was watching that programme on the telly about family history. You know, that one with him out of *Blackadder* on? Well, he said that you could find out about people's family history on the Internet. So, I went back to the library and looked up one of them Ancestry sites and there he was – William Ennis, son of James Ennis of Birmingham and brother of Albert Ennis. Then I found there was this company called Enniswear making bras based in Birmingham and that you was the owner and then I found your name in the phone directory. So here I am.'

Meredith could feel her heart bursting out of her skin. There was so much she wanted to know but couldn't ask. This Jessie could only know so much.

'Are you here for some money?' she asked eventually, looking across at the plump body that was balanced precariously on the edge of her sofa.

'No, nothing like that,' came the reply. 'I just thought you ought to have it. That's all.'

'But you've come such a long way,' said Meredith, reaching for her handbag. 'You must let me pay your rail fare. It's so kind of you. I'm really very grateful, though it is all a bit of a shock. Bill died such a long time ago. I had no idea about this.'

Jessie Martin had protested but in the end accepted the fifty pounds that she was offered – all the cash that Meredith had in the house. She had left soon afterwards, leaving her telephone number and address. Meredith had insisted on this in case she wanted to contact her again about anything. In the shock of receiving this writing pad she was sure there were things she hadn't asked that she might later want to know. But for the life of her she couldn't think of anything. All she wanted at that moment was to read everything from cover to cover.

And it was then she decided that one day she would do what Bert had asked her to do – to see the place where his brother had died.

*

Themis had pulled the car off the road under the shade of a row of plane trees, the lower part of whose trunks had been painted white. Behind them was a white marble war memorial and on the opposite side of the road, up a few steps, was a *kafeneion* where two hugely flowering red *bougainvilleas* garlanded the roof.

'This is Deres,' announced Themis, climbing out of the car and opening the door for Meredith to do the same.

'This is where you got married?' Meredith said, remembering his story about meeting his wife for the first time.

'Yes, I have happy memories of this place. But I think we should have something to eat here. There is still some way to go before we reach Hora Sfakion and you left Heraklion very early this morning. Did you have breakfast?'

She shook her head. She had had a biscuit and a glass of orange juice. It was all she had needed. She did not eat much nowadays. But yes, she was hungry now.

They were greeted by a tall, handsome man wearing a startlingly white shirt and black trousers, in his mid-twenties she guessed, with dark black hair swept back from his forehead and an open, welcoming smile.

'Please,' he said, guiding them to a wooden table near the top of the steps where the *bougainvillea* flowers were at their most profuse. 'I have reserved this table just for you. Would you like something to drink? I have very good orange juice my mama makes herself. Or we have our own very nice red wine.'

Meredith smiled up at him from her chair. How could she refuse, she thought. His manners were impeccable, his manner was a delight. This was what service really meant. He made it feel as if he was welcoming you into his home and giving you refreshments, rather than being engaged in the sordid business of selling food. How quickly sadness can be dissipated, she thought, by the kindliness of another. Even if only for the moment.

'Your own orange juice sounds very nice,' she said, smiling at him. 'I'll have a glass of that please.'

'The oranges are from our own orange grove over on the other side of the river. We are farmers and everything we give you we grow ourselves.'

'What is your name?' she asked for no reason in particular. She had already grown to like this young man.

'My name is Antonis.'

Themis leaned forward, tapping the table with his left hand.

'We should order some food too. It is still quite a journey.'

'Well, what do you recommend?' she asked, looking up at Antonis.

'The Greek salad is very good. Everything we grow ourselves.

The tomatoes, the peppers, the olives, the cucumber, the onions, everything. And the cheese my mama makes also. It is not *feta*, it is like *feta* but it is called *mizithra*. It is from the milk of our own goats. My mama she makes it. Ten kilos of milk makes two kilos of cheese. Yes.'

'That sounds wonderful. I'll have that please,' said Meredith, quite overwhelmed by the amount of information she was getting about the food and drink she was about to receive.

Themis ordered the same meal.

'So, two Greek salads and two orange juices. Very good,' said Antonis, heading for the kitchen indoors.

'Do you know him?' she asked Themis.

He laughed.

'I knew his grandfather well. But I haven't been here since my wife died. There is something else I needed to tell you about this place, though. This was not only the place I married my Katerina. It was also the place where my Uncle Alexandros brought me to guide Skip and his men across the White Mountains. When the German paratroopers landed at Maleme airfield, they had to get away as quickly as they could. Somehow my uncle found that they had reached Deres in the middle of the night. My uncle was very important in the *andartes*. He knew everything that was going on. When he heard that Skip and his men were at Deres, he came to fetch me to act as their guide across the island to the south coast. This was where we found them. A shepherd had let them sleep in his hut and the shepherd's wife had given them food.'

Yes, she remembered from the diary, and a priest with a shotgun had accompanied Alexandros and the boy Nikos Themistocles to meet them as they sat eating outside the shepherd's hut. She looked out into the village and back up the road on which they had entered. Silly idea, she realised, the village had probably changed immeasurably since that time. The hut could be anywhere, in fact, was probably no longer there at all. Besides, what did it matter? Somewhere around here, Bill and his men had spent a night in their flight from the German advance. It was enough. It was more than enough. She was beginning to sense the journey he had undertaken, his last, fateful journey. Why had she left it so long to come?

There was a sudden 'Toot, toot' as if of a train. Out of the blue from the village appeared a red train engine, mounted on the chassis of a tractor, which moved slowly past the *kafeneion* pulling three carriages, each packed with laughing tourists calling out to each other in German.

'What on earth is that?' Meredith asked.

Antonis had reappeared with their drinks and a basket of bread.

'It comes every day,' he explained as he placed the drinks in front of them. 'From Platanias. Every day it arrives at twelve thirty and leaves at one thirty. The people come to see the river or to visit our church and they usually have something to eat and drink. It is good for us.'

'Germans?' she said, raising her eyebrows quizzically, thinking about the war memorial she had spied on the other side of the road, thinking about the Messerchmitts and Junkers planes he had written about, thinking about their escape.

'It is not always Germans,' Antonis laughed. 'And anyway, that was all a long time ago. There is no point. We are all Europeans now. Please, I will get your salads.'

'Is that really so?' Meredith asked Themis, as she took her first sip of the deliciously cold fresh juice. 'Mm, this is exquisite.'

'Of course,' he answered, breaking bread. 'It is better this way. As Antonis says, it was a long time ago.'

'But you still remember?'

'Of course. How could I not? But the young people think differently.'

Antonis returned with their salads.

'Those *bougainvilleas* are wonderful,' she said. 'How old are they?'

'Twenty six years,' he replied. 'The same as me. My father planted them when I was born. This *kafeneion* has been in our family for one hundred years.'

'You speak very good English.'

'I was on the ferry boats for five years. I saved much money. When I came back to Deres, I already had one thousand olive trees on the hillside and I bought another one thousand olive trees, so now I have two thousand olive trees. I gather three thousand kilos of olives each year. We start to gather them in

November. We make all our own olive oil and sell it in Chania. We also make four types of honey and our own red wine. And I make a very special *raki*. It is a secret recipe, made with honey. I listened to the old men's talk and that's where I learned the secret. It is very special. It cures everything. It clears out the inside, yes?'

He demonstrated with his hand the flow from mouth through throat to stomach.

'Later, I give you, yes?'

The Greek salads were huge but neither had eaten for several hours and the produce was, as Antonis had promised, incredibly fresh and tasty, so they munched their way through it with vigour. As they were finishing, Antonis appeared with two small glasses of his honey *raki*, a bowl of black grapes and two plates with cake on.

'Please. For you.'

She looked up at his smiling, handsome face and across at the wrinkled, warm face of her companion and thought of all those things Bill had written about the Cretans he had met and their friendliness. Nothing had changed, she thought. Yet everything had changed.

*

She had told Nancy about Jessie Martin's visit and later she had told Tom but she hadn't mentioned the diary, merely stating that it was someone whose grandfather had served with their father's brother in the war and had come hunting information about her dead grandfather. It was the curiosity of the visit and the visitor that she talked most about, not the substance of the visitor's reason for calling. Why hadn't she told them about the diary? Why hadn't she shown them the diary then?

Meredith was pondering these matters as Themis drove his car on the upward stretch of road, zigzagging sometimes through ninety-degree hairpin bends, up towards the gap in the White Mountains where the road would start to descend towards the southern coast. This would have been the route they had taken almost certainly, Bill and his group, as they headed for what they thought would be the safe refuge of the south. Leading them would have been the fearless Alexandros and young Nikos, whose aged self now drove. The road would have probably been only a dirt track then.

Nancy had reached a secure middle age without any traumas or serious difficulties. She and her husband Len had settled in the north Staffordshire area where the hospital was that they both worked in. Maybe it was working in mental health that kept them incredibly sane and sensible. They didn't often talk to her about their work but when they did, Meredith was horrified at some of the things they had experienced and still did experience frequently.

Tom, however, had had difficulties in his relationships. First of all, he had married the wrong girl, as Meredith still thought of Julia after all these years and despite the fondness she still felt for the offspring of that marriage, Ellie and Will. He had married out of physical desire, so it was no surprise when the same thing led to the end of the marriage. Tom had had an affair with a younger woman who was teaching biology at the comprehensive school in Oxfordshire where they both worked at the stage when he himself was beginning to question his long-term suitability as a teacher, dealing with troublesome youngsters who had no desire to learn about physics or about anything as far as he could tell. And, as tends to happen, what began as a friendship, a mutual sympathy, a sharing of woes, slipped inexorably into a physical relationship.

Julia had become suspicious because of his more frequent late return from work but then she had intercepted a phone call from this woman and challenged Tom about it. She had forgiven him, of course. What else could she do? She had two young children and a part-time job in the local primary school. How could she possibly manage without his income? He had promised that it would never happen again.

But it did. His wandering eye had not ceased its journeys. True, he did not stray physically from the marital embrace for quite some time but there were plenty of mild flirtations and opportunities, as the children grew up and could be left at home with babysitters, for parties where he could dance too close to someone else's wife or whisper sweet blandishments in strange ears. Emotionally, he had left Julia. It wasn't obvious to most of their friends, who were reaching similar stages of their own marriages, when children were heading for adolescence with their incessant demands, when couples had become inured to each other's vagaries, when work was often preferable to home life, and when that home life largely comprised repeated habits that had become tolerated by and then acceptable to all concerned.

Meredith sensed most of this and had seen it coming from the beginning, so she chose her moment for pressing Tom to rejoin the family business carefully.

'We can't continue running Enniswear the way we've been doing these past few years,' she told him one day, when he had come to visit.

The divorce was going through by this stage. Tom had had another affair, Julia had found out about it and said she wanted a divorce with a proper settlement. They had explained to the children what was happening, Tom had moved out into a flat in Oxford and the wheels had been set in motion. Julia had given up hopes of getting at the Enniswear money now but she held out for the best deal she could get, which for her meant holding on to the Oxfordshire cottage, extensively refurbished and extended over the years.

'But I know nothing about the business,' he had protested. 'I never wanted to go into the firm anyway, you know that.'

'So what happens when your father gets too old, eh? Or if he dies? Nancy can't come and run it, so, if you don't take it on, we'd have to sell it. I haven't worked all these years to let it go just like that. Come on, Tom. You hate what you're doing at present. You've never really used that brain of yours properly. You can apply it to business, I know you can. Please.'

He had blustered and argued but in the end had given in.

'But I can't do it till the divorce is sorted,' he had said. 'Otherwise Julia will want a share of the business.'

'What does she want now?'

'She just really wants the house and maintenance money for the kids.'

'Well, just agree to it. I'll help you out if you need it. Just get it sorted and then we can talk about the future of Enniswear.'

So a settlement with Julia was agreed and the divorce concluded. Tom resigned from his teaching post and came to work at Enniswear with Bert and Meredith. It was understood from the beginning that he was there to learn the business as thoroughly and as quickly as possible, so that his parents could reduce their time commitment and he could in effect take over. Meredith, in particular, was glad to have him back under her wing. She had missed him when he was in Oxfordshire and, though he and the children visited frequently, he was not as close as he had been. Now he was back, she could gradually hand over the reins of Enniswear, knowing that it would provide him with the intellectual challenge he needed and her with the knowledge that the business was safely in family hands.

And it was through Enniswear that Tom, some years later, met his second wife. Chantal was a barrister working in central Birmingham. She lived in Handsworth with her family who had migrated from St Kitts to Britain some thirty years previously. Those parents had been determined that their only daughter should receive a proper education and be able to enter a respectable profession. Chantal had attended King Edward's Grammar School in Handsworth and gone on to gain a first-class law degree at Birmingham University. She had then taken her pupillage in chambers in London before returning to Birmingham to work for the Crown Prosecution Service. They met, however, not through her professional background but through her involvement with the Handsworth Festival, of which she was Treasurer. Her secretary had phoned for an appointment at Enniswear, explaining that she was looking to commission the making of some sequined brassière costume tops for a troupe of dancers.

When she walked into the main office of Enniswear, Tom had been stunned. He had not expected this tall, lithe woman, with black hair swept back in a tight bun, with a light brown face made captivating by her high cheek bones, with her immaculate black suit and sharp-pointed matching shoes.

'Good afternoon, Mr Ennis,' she had begun, coolly extending her hand to him as he rose from his seat behind the desk. 'I am Chantal Solomons. Thank you for seeing me.'

'My pleasure,' he replied, and he meant it. 'Please, call me Tom. Take a seat. I understand you want us to make some costume tops for the Handsworth Festival. I've got some samples you might find interesting. Or do you have a more specific design in mind? Would you like coffee?'

'Thank you.'

She smiled lightly at him, as she sat elegantly in the chair proffered, and he grinned back.

'Perhaps you would have a look at those designs on my desk while I rustle up some coffee then.'

He left her in the room, perusing the designs that he had selected for her. On his return, he noticed that she was sitting straight-backed in her seat, apparently uninterested in the samples he had left.

'Not what you were looking for?'

'I want something that is really going to knock people's eyes out. Not the sort of lurid thing that you expect from Handsworth. I want something classy. Something like this.'

She reached into her handbag and pulled out a photograph of a peacock.

'Can you make something with these textures and these colours? This would remind me so much of my parents' home country.'

'Where is that?'

'St Kitts. In the West Indies. I was born in England but my parents came from St Kitts. I have been there a few times with them to visit my grandparents. It is a beautiful island. Have you ever been to the Caribbean?'

'No, I'm afraid not.'

'You should go. It is beautiful.'

'You'll have to take me.'

He laughed lightly and she responded in a similar fashion. And that was where it all began. Tom agreed to come up with some possible designs along the lines that she had suggested, Chantal gave him her mobile phone number, explaining that, as she was frequently in court, he would be best advised to leave messages about possible meetings. That, of course, entailed her explaining what her job was and he responded by telling her of his background at Harwell and in teaching.

He told Meredith all about this first meeting and she knew he had fallen in love again. This time, however, she felt he was making a better choice.

Two weeks later he left a message for Chantal that he had some possible designs for her to look at and suggested they meet early evening in the bar of the Birmingham Repertory Theatre. When, after surveying the designs and agreeing the one to be used for the costumes, he had suggested they go for dinner, she had agreed and so they had spent the evening dining in Shimla Pinks Indian restaurant. There he explained about his previous marriage, his children and his divorce, while she told him of the string of short-term and unsatisfactory relationships she had had in her younger days and how she had been on her own, by choice, for the past five years as she built up her career.

They did not make love that night. She discouraged him from going back to her flat in the centre of the city and he was wary also of too-soon commitment. He fancied her like crazy but they could wait a little longer. She was much more attractive to him than his first wife, Julia, whose looks had faded with age, but it wasn't just the physical attraction. It was the intellectual playfulness, the fierce determination to demonstrate that she as a black woman could achieve as much as or more than her contemporaries and the spark in her eyes when she looked at him. For her, he was what she had been seeking these many years – an intellectual equal who was not competing with her, from outside her working life and, almost as importantly, from outside Afro-Caribbean life. She had dedicated herself to using her talents to support her fellow Afro-Caribbeans in whatever way she could. Her strong sense of social justice led her to take on a disproportionate number of cases involving black and Asian people and she had no regrets about that. But there was a price to be paid for being seen as the black people's champion and that price was that no one ever saw her as herself. Tom did and she loved him for it. The twelve years between them didn't seem to matter. Nor did his children. She had decided long ago she didn't want to have children herself. Her career was all demanding and all fulfilling. She would not have made a good mother, she knew that. But she could learn to be a good stepmother.

Meredith and Chantal took to each other at their first meeting. Strong women sometimes rub sparks off each other, like strong men can do. But they immediately recognised each other as sisters under the skin, even though that skin colour was so different and even though Meredith was a good eight inches smaller than the woman who was to become her new daughter-in-law in time. Tom's children, Ellie and Will, also embraced her quickly enough. Through their adolescence now and heading for university, they had come to realise that their parents led separate lives and, when they thought about it, which wasn't often, had been leading separate lives when they shared the same family home.

In 1990, five years after Bert had died, Tom and Chantal were married. They bought a house in Sutton Coldfield, not far from where Meredith lived because they both felt an obligation to be near to her in case anything happened, though she herself continued to flourish. Tom was by now in sole charge of Enniswear, which under his direction had gone away from mass production to seek niche markets for high-fashion bras.

Meredith let a small smile play on her lips as she recalled those days. They were climbing more steeply now, she realised, and into low cloud cover, which saved her from seeing the steep unprotected drops at the sides of the road as they continued uphill.

Suddenly they were out of the cloud and in a clear space at the summit of the road. On either side of them, huge wind turbines ascended the mountainsides and beyond them she could see the magnificent sight of those fabled White Mountain tops, still with pockets of marble-like snow.

'This is Seli,' said Themis, as he slowed the car to a halt. 'Down there the Libyan Sea and Sougia, where we will get a boat.'

Such beauty. And Bill would have stopped here and seen this too. Even in their flight, he must have noticed the breathtaking views.

*

After a zigzagging descent they stopped at a *taverna* in the small settlement of Agia Ireni by the entrance to the Ireni Gorge, which a signpost told was part of the E4 walkers' route. The *taverna* was down from the road in a dry, rock-strewn area beside the dried-up riverbed. Meredith ordered another fresh orange juice while Themis asked for a Greek coffee.

'Three hours walk Sougia,' the *taverna* owner told them, a stocky man in a checked shirt, as he brought their drinks. 'Very famous walk. Is better than Samaria. No so many peoples.'

'I don't think it's for us,' laughed Meredith. 'What d'you say, Themis? Would your old legs let you walk for three hours in this heat?'

'I can still walk some distance,' he answered proudly. 'But no, not for three hours I think. And not for you, no. We will drive to Sougia. *Efharisto poli.*'

The *taverna* proprietor shrugged his shoulders and returned to his stool behind the bar where he was talking to another customer.

'I know of this place,' she said, after they had sat at a table beside the huge, twisted and gnarled trunks of ancient olive trees. 'This must be Aiyarini. This was where Bill and you and the others spent the night, wasn't it? You weren't very well received, were you?'

'You know?' he said. His eyebrows rose slightly in astonishment.

'I have not been completely open with you,' she explained. 'Bill kept a diary of his journey. I knew nothing about it until a few years ago when I had a surprise visit from the granddaughter of one of his companions, a man called Eddie Martin. She gave me the diary. You remember him?'

Themis's Adam's apple contracted.

'Eddie? Yes, of course I remember Eddie. He was quite fat and he had difficulties when we were walking, especially going uphill.'

'And he wanted you all to leave him when you were on the cliffs, didn't he?'

'You know about that too?' Themis's mind instantly went back to his twelve-year old self and the fateful journey across the mountains. 'How did this diary come to Eddie's granddaughter then? I know Skip used to write things every day but I never thought about what he was writing or what happened to it. I suppose I thought he was just keeping a record for the RAF I was only a boy then.'

She took a long sip of the cold orange juice before replying.

'You remember you told me that Bill had pushed Eddie and the others on to the landing craft in Hora Sfakion so that they could be evacuated to Alexandria? Well, from what this young woman, Eddie's grandchild, told me, Bill must have given his diary to Eddie then. Maybe he had a premonition he wasn't going to survive. Or maybe he already had this idea of swimming out to the Navy ships and knew the diary would get soaked. Who knows?'

'So you know about the journey? About Sougia, about the cliff walk and all the rest of it?' Themis's bottom lip quivered slightly in disappointment , as if a favourite possession had been taken away from him. 'I did not know. I brought you this way to show you our journey. I am sorry. We could have reached Hora Sfakion more directly. You should have told me.'

'Themis, I am really most grateful.' She reached across the table to clutch his hand. 'I realised that's what you were doing and I could not have asked for more. I am getting a real insight into my brother-in-law's last journey. Thank you so much.'

He drank the glass of cold water that had accompanied his coffee and sat back on the wooden chair, playing with his worry beads.

'You were married to his brother, no?'

'Yes.'

Something was troubling him, something that had been troubling him for some time, something he had been building up to asking about.

'It is strange that you did not think to come on this journey before,' he said, scratching his left ear. 'Why did you leave it till now, when you are old? Forgive me, I do not mean to be rude.'

She gave a dry, rasping laugh

'Themis, it's only the young who take offence easily. When you are nearing the end of your life, the words of others do not cause distress. Besides, you are right, I am old. No one in my family has ever reached this age before. Both my parents died in their late seventies. The oldest relative I know of is a maiden aunt who reached seventy-nine. I have lived a very long time, longer than I should perhaps, but I have kept busy all the time.'

There had been the family business. She told him how she had been a brassière designer for many years at Enniswear and, while he was alive, how her husband had run the business with her as his chief designer. Then there had been the grandchildren, of course, especially when they were younger. She had had a lot to do with all of them. After her husband had died, she had let Tom take over all of the business but couldn't sit there doing nothing, so had volunteered to help out in the local Red Cross shop two days a week and took up music again. She had taken piano lessons when she was younger but had given it up when she was twelve, so she had found a piano teacher and resumed where she'd left off.

'I play the *lyra*,' Themis cut in. 'It is a special Cretan instrument. I have it in my car. I too learned as a child but in Crete there is always a call for music.'

'You are lucky. I play for myself only,' she continued. 'But that wasn't enough either. I had this tremendous need for something physical. I tried ballroom dancing classes but all I got there were the gropings of elderly men and suggestive remarks about possible liaisons. Then I discovered yoga. There was a class one morning a week in a local school and I found it enormously helpful. It kept my body lithe but it also helped my mind to relax. Do you know yoga? Do you have it in Crete?'

'Why do I need yoga? Here in Crete we live the healthy life. I eat well, always fresh food. I look after my olives. I swim. I walk in my village and in the hills,' he said, bristling at the implications as he perceived them. 'There are some Dutch people who have yoga classes but it is not Cretans who go there. It is foreigners.'

Meredith smiled at his defensiveness. She realised there was no point in telling him about the *asanas* that she was taught to help to strengthen her body and improve her energy. The *asanas* and the breathing techniques had also calmed her mind so she could meditate. Once she had learned them, she had started to do these exercises every night for half an hour before she went to bed. They also helped her to sleep well.

'In Crete we have *raki*,' he smiled.

She smiled back at him, recognising his little joke.

'I have not answered your question very well. You wanted to know why I hadn't come on this journey beforehand, why I have waited until I am so old. I have thought about it often, believe me. For sixty years in fact. Ever since I read the telegram. He was given a medal, you know. Posthumously. Distinguished Service Order. I presume those men who got away from Crete, Eddie and company, it must have been their report to the powers that be. I have the medal with me.'

'May I see?'

She reached into her canvas bag for the blue box in which the medal had always been kept and passed it across the table.

Themis took out the medal, a gold cross overlaid in white enamel with a gold crown in its centre over the letters GR, which hung from a short ribbon that was deep crimson with dark blue stripes on either edge.

'This is what you get for bravery?' He nodded as if to answer his own question. 'This is what you get for sacrificing your life for other people? This is all you get?'

'Yes,' she replied, sensing his emotion and sharing it. 'I tried to come earlier. Believe me, I wanted to. But there was always something that was more pressing. The business. Tom's divorce. Bert's illness and then his death. And then every time I took out that medal, my heart stopped me. I just couldn't deal with the emotion. That was one of the reasons for taking up the yoga. I thought it would give me some calm. Silly, isn't it? It's taken me to reach ninety before I think I can deal with it all.'

'I have cried all my life. In Crete we cry. I cried for my family when I was in Alexandria and did not know if I would see them again. I cried for my father when he never came back from the war in Greece. I cried for my grandfather and my mother murdered by those German soldiers. I cried for my Uncle Alexandros, that mighty man who fought so many battles but could not win the last one against cancer. I cry for my wife who died two years ago just when we should have been looking to enjoy our last years together. It is all right to cry. You should have come here sooner.'

Both their eyes were moistening by now. She gazed across at his sun-tanned face. There was a silence.

'I know,' she said at last. 'It's time now.'

*

Sougia is an attractively sited village that nestles in a broad bay of the Libyan Sea, where the road from the mountains and the path beside the dried-up Ireni Gorge lead down to the pebbly seashore. Themis drove his car straight past the *tavernas* and small hotels and signs for 'Rooms to let' all along the seafront to reach the concrete jetty at the western end of the bay that sheltered under a grey cliff face.

'This is where the ferry calls every morning,' he explained, holding his hand out to Meredith as she stepped out of the car. 'Unfortunately, it only comes once a day, so I have arranged for a private boat to collect us and take us to Agia Roumeli. We will catch a ferry from there to Hora Sfakion. Please.'

She took his arm and walked beside him to a place where they could wait in the shade, remembering the description of Sougia and the attempts to get a boat in Bill's diary.

'I hope your boat has more luck than the one you caught in 1941.' She smiled at him, as she wiped the perspiration from her brow.

'Of course, you know of that from Skip's diary,' he chuckled to himself. 'It is easy to smile now but it was no laughing matter at the time, believe me. The storm got up so quickly. I was terrified.'

'I'm sorry. It was thoughtless of me. It must be the sun.'

The private boat Themis had arranged was a small motorboat, driven by a swarthy, middle-aged man in sunglasses and baseball cap. It pulled up to the jetty shortly after they had parked.

'Help the lady, Stelios,' insisted Themis, passing her hand down to the boat's skipper. 'We shall not be long now. Stelios lives here in Sougia but he has to be back to cook dinner for his *taverna* tonight. Otherwise he would have taken us all the way. But it is no problem. There is a ferryboat in Agia Roumeli. We have plenty of time.'

Stelios was clearly in a hurry to get back to his kitchen. When his passengers were safely on board, he revved his engine and roared out to sea, a churn of white water following. Once out of the bay, he steadied the motor and they cruised at a more comfortable speed eastwards towards Agia Roumeli. The cliff face looked all but impassable, rising sheer from the depths of the ocean, with only the occasional pine tree clinging to its grey rocky surface. Even when the cliffs gave way to ravines, Meredith could see the sharp drops from the rocks to the shingle below and then almost immediately a further grey cliff rising remorselessly to the sky. She could understand why Bill and his men had had so much difficulty in crossing this difficult terrain.

'See!' said the hitherto-silent Stelios, pointing to the top of the cliff face with his left hand, while steering with his right. 'Chapel of Prophet Elias. Look!'

She looked where he pointed, shading her eyes against the strong sun. What she saw was a small whitewashed building with curiously inverted indentations on its roof. Hadn't Bill mentioned coming across some such building in his diary?

'They say there is one of the finest views in Crete from there,' explained Themis.

She remembered something from the writings, something about a curious chapel.

'Didn't you stop there?'

'I think so, yes, but it was a long time ago and we were not looking at beautiful scenery then you know. We did not know if any of us would survive.'

In just over half an hour they were disembarking in Agia Roumeli, where a large number of people in hiking gear were already queuing for the ferryboat. The one-time fishing village with its white-painted buildings stretches up either side of the lower part of the Samaria Gorge, which nowadays provides its reason for existence.

'They have been walking Crete's most famous gorge,' Themis explained. 'It attracts thousands of visitors every year. They catch the early morning bus from Chania over the Omalos plain to reach the wooden stairway that leads steeply down to the start of the gorge walk and then several hours later come to Agia Roumeli to catch the ferryboat to Hora Sfakion. This is the only way out. There is no road to Agia Roumeli. From Hora Sfakion, the walkers have to take buses back to Chania.'

And it was those weary walkers who filled the incoming triple-decked ferry *Samaria* that Meredith and Themis climbed aboard. This was strange, thought Meredith. For the first time since she had left her cruise ship, the *Ariadne*, in Heraklion early that morning she was among a crowd. And a crowd of tourists, just as she herself had been before Themis came and took her off in his car. A large part of her wanted nothing to do with these people, resented their intrusion. She wanted to return to the peacefulness that she had enjoyed all day long, but she knew she could not. The presence of all these people, jostling for seats, drinking beer and wine and munching sandwiches brought to mind again her granddaughter Ellie. How long had it been since she left Heraklion? Over eight hours. And several hours since she had sent her a text on that waiter's mobile phone. What would she be thinking? What would she be doing?

It was safe enough now to send another text. Ellie would be relieved to know she was okay and, if she switched the phone off immediately afterwards, she wouldn't receive Ellie's answer. She clicked open her phone and there was an instant beeping, informing her there were six messages awaiting her along with innumerable missed calls. She read the messages quickly, five from Ellie, all asking the same question – 'Where are you, Granny?', with accompanying words asking her to call back, and one from Tom in England, asking the same question, though with a barbed criticism of her for escaping from Ellie. She decided to send the same message to both.

*Don't worry. Nearly there now. Love you.*

*

Themis had insisted on the donkey.

'It is a difficult journey over the rocks to reach the cave. You will be better this way. Please trust me.'

She had argued but eventually accepted. It had been a long day already and it was drawing towards twilight. She really needed to see this cave that day. They had ways of tracing mobile phone calls, didn't they? Even here in Crete probably. By the following day, they would have found her. It had to be that evening.

So, mounted sidesaddle on the evil-smelling, snorting donkey, she had allowed Themis to lead her forward towards the cave where Bill Ennis, the New Zealander Alec Bryce and the younger version of Nikos Themistocles had spent their final night before Bill was killed and the other two swam out to sea and safety.

What was she hoping to find in that cave? She could not put it into words but it was some sense of the *pneuma* of Bill that she craved, some sense that, even after all this time, she could feel his spirit, could sense him again somehow.

'Are you sure it was here?' she called out to her companion as he coaxed the donkey over the rocks and through the thorn-bushes.

'Definitely,' came the reply. 'It's just ahead. You can see? It's just there.'

And then they were there. Themis helped her to dismount then secured the snorting donkey with rope to a bush. The cave was big, seeming to go back some way into the cliff face. It was also deserted. There were no signs of it having been used for many years, not even by goats or seabirds. Inside there was an echoing silence. Outside the soft plash of the sea on to the cliffs below and the occasional snort of the donkey were all that could be heard. Two huge boulders formed a sort of ledge on which they could sit comfortably and gaze out to sea.

'This is what you came to see,' he said, his eyes beginning to moisten. 'This was where I last saw Skip. This is where we waited to escape from Crete.'

She looked at him, this wiry veteran, her last contact with Bill.

'It is the part I did not know until you told me,' she said eventually, stroking her left arm absent-mindedly. 'I always wondered how and where he died. Now I know. It is a blessing.'

There was another longer silence. Themis too was feeling the griefs of the past, the times when tears had welled up and taken control.

'You missed him?'

'Yes, I missed him,' she replied then sighed deeply. It was time. 'I miss him still.'

Themis stared out to the depths of the blue sea, his eyes narrowing as he sought to control his emotions.

'I loved Skip like a father. He was very kind to me. I have thought about him often over the years. When Alec came back from the village and told me he had been shot, I could not believe it. I thought it must have been a mistake. After we had travelled all that way over the mountains and then along the cliffs, after we had nearly collapsed from dehydration, for him to die like that seemed so unjust. I was only a boy, remember. I was trying to make sense of things. I did not know at that point what had happened to my missing father, I did not know what was going to happen to my mother and my grandfather. I did not know what was going to happen to me. But I trusted Skip. He was like a father to me.'

Meredith looked at his face then back out to sea. Sometimes it gives perspective, she thought. There was another long silence, interspersed by the sound of gently lapping waves.

'He used to call me Merry,' she said softly at last, her voice no more than a clear whisper. 'No one else has ever called me Merry. It was because it was the Christmas season when we met and, when I told him my name was Meredith, he said he would call me Merry to remind him.'

Birmingham, December 1940. They had gone to the cinema to see *Pride and Prejudice* with Laurence Olivier as Mr Darcy and Greer Garson as Elizabeth Bennett. Jane Austen's book had long been one of her favourites and the film was no disappointment. As they came out of the cinema, they saw that it was very bright outdoors, unusually so given the blackout restrictions then in force throughout the city. The silver stars sparkled in the cold night sky and the moon cast an eerie glow on everything. For once the German bombers were not wreaking their nightly havoc.

Already a sharp frost sparkled on the pavements and, as she slipped slightly on a particularly shiny paving stone, he reached for her hand to steady her. She looked up at those deep-set eyes and the dark wavy hair and smiled her thanks. He did not let go all the way back to her parents' home in Edgbaston. There were no buses, of course, at that time of night and the streets were almost empty of people. They would not have noticed them anyway. That strong hand she had first felt clasped to her buttock now held and warmed her own tiny hand.

He only had two days' leave, the first since he had joined up, but it was enough. They both knew by the end of that first evening that they were in love. 'I shall call you Merry,' he had said. 'You will always be my beautiful Merry. Wherever this war takes me, I shall think of you. Always.'

Themis was staring intently at her, waiting for her to continue.

'We were lovers,' she explained finally, exhaling loudly as if in relief at finally sharing this information buried so long in her heart. 'We were going to get married. On his last leave, in February of 1941, he wanted us to get a special dispensation and get married immediately but I said I wanted it to be done properly, when he next came home. We thought our love would last forever. I never believed he wouldn't come home.'

Every moment of that last leave was etched forever on her brain. How she had rushed from her ARP duties round to his family home to be there as soon as he got back. How he had held her so tight for those first few minutes of re-acquaintance. How he had escorted her back to Edgbaston, after calling in at one of the city public houses for drinks. How her parents, having welcomed him, had judiciously disappeared to leave them alone. How she had put the Glenn Miller record on the turntable and switched it on. How they had danced seemingly forever around the drawing room of her parents' house, before collapsing on to a sofa. How he had kissed her, his fleshy lips passionately pressed against hers. How his hands had pushed her skirt up. And how, to avoid disturbing her parents, she had stifled the blissful moment of pain and rapture as their passion brought their first and only lovemaking to its conclusion.

Themis looked at her face, still gazing impassively out to sea.

'But you married his brother?'

'Yes.' She sighed. 'You see, I was pregnant. I was fond of Bert too and he thought he was doing the right thing and, after the telegram arrived, I was so confused I didn't know what to think. I was in a state of shock. I just went along with it all. It was a mistake but I have a family from that mistake – a son, a daughter, three grandchildren and no doubt great-grandchildren to come.'

'Skip was your son Tom's father?'

'Yes.'

'Does he know?'

'No.'

The tears had started to flow now. There was nothing to staunch them now. Only the old man sitting beside her. Only the Libyan Sea that they would wash into.

Themis reached into the small blue sack he had slung over his shoulders and pulled out a small wooden instrument shaped a little like a mandolin. It had a pear-shaped body and a short stubby neck from where the three metallic strings stretched taut against the body. He placed the instrument on his knee, reaching again into his sack for a long thin bow.

'My *lyra*,' he explained. 'It is time for music.'

'Wait,' she said, holding up a hand momentarily to stay him and reaching into her handbag, whence she produced a Basildon Bond writing pad and an envelope.

'This is Bill's diary and his last letter to me. If anything happens to me, Themis, promise you will give these to my Tom. To no one else. Promise?'

He nodded and prepared again to play the *lyra*, as she replaced the papers in her handbag.

He bent his bow and started to play. As the first notes wafted into the clear air of the gathering evening, Meredith realised that she knew the tune he was playing. It was a tune familiar from his time around the docks in Alexandria, a tune sung or played by countless soldiers, sailors and airmen from the British Armed Forces.

And through the evening air, from a cave in southern Crete, on a mid-May day, came the curiously blended sounds of a *lyra* playing the haunting, grief-soaked, wailing melody of *We'll Meet Again*.

# PART 2

# AMES, RAF Z Force, Middle East

**12<sup>th</sup> May 1941**

Dearest Sweetheart Merry,

I could be in heaven. This really is the most beautiful place I've ever been in and I promise I'll bring you here when this business is all over. You know I didn't ask to be here but this place is paradise on earth. Spring comes early here and the blossom from the flowers is overwhelming – orange blossom, lemon blossom, may blossom, wild mountain thyme, lavender, honeysuckle, asphodel. There's a beautiful *bougainvillea* that winds around the front door of our billet, its glorious pink flowers wide open now and turning to a deep red hue in the evening. Its sweet aroma clings to my clothes every time I cross the threshold. It reminds me of your perfume.

I think of you all the time. I guess you are still driving that ambulance around Birmingham. Are you still having as many bombing raids? Is it getting any better now? We get no news of home here except when someone new arrives and often they come from some other part of the war – north Africa usually. When I look at this simple house we are based in, I think of my last leave with you at your parents' house and how happy we both were then. But I must tell you more about this place or I will go crazy thinking of just you.

Our billet was requisitioned from a local villager who revels in the name of Themistocles – Mr Themistocles, to be precise. Can you imagine? The hero of the Battle of Salamis alive and kicking here! And more than happy to let us use his house for the duration. He wears the traditional Cretan costume – big black beard, black waistcoat, baggy trousers tucked into his knee-length leather boots, and pushed into his leather belt the most frightening dagger you've ever seen. He's moved into his daughter's house in the village and sent her to be our housekeeper. Her name is Eleni – how these names reverberate! – and she has become very attached to us. Her husband Georgiou is missing in action and she prays daily for his return, though I think from the way she carries herself that she fears he is dead. So she keeps her stocky self busy, cooking for the four of us who are billeted here, washing our flea-infested clothes, fetching bottles of the acrid red wine they all drink here, deliciously-sweet local honey, fresh bread and new-laid eggs from her village, and generally looking out for us in ways that only a woman can.

My Greek has not been much use in talking to Themistocles and Eleni. The way it's all pronounced now is nothing like the stuff I did at King Edward's and anyway they tell me that the Cretan dialect is very different from the way they speak on the mainland. I can read things, of course, but there's little to read. Eleni has taught me to say '*kalimera*' for 'good morning', '*kalispera*' for 'good evening' and '*kalinikta*' for 'goodnight'. Otherwise we get by in the usual mixture of gestures, pidgin and misunderstandings! The Cretans are a very expressive race – their faces do a lot of talking for them and they move quickly between emotions. One day, I thought Eleni was looking especially peaky and I tried to ask her if I could help in any way.

'No, mister,' she began. 'I no eggs. *Poli* chickens, no eggs.'

I'd worked out that *poli* means many but couldn't make sense of this conundrum.

'Chickens not lay eggs?' I tried.

'No, mister. *Adelfos* take eggs. No for you.'

'Your brother?' I guessed, correctly as it turned out.

'Yes, *adelfos* fighter. Take eggs for *andartes*.'

Eventually I gathered that her brother Alexandros – these names! – leads a small band of what I can only call guerillas but that Eleni calls *andartes*, who are stationed up in the mountains. They have some loose affiliation to the Greek Army but they seem to operate entirely at their own discretion and wherever they wish. It seems that they have been asked to work underground and to prepare Cretans for resistance, should the Germans ever get here. I told Eleni that would never happen – what else could I say? Alexandros had left his group somewhere in caves in the mountains and come down to his home village to gather food. Hence, no eggs for us that day.

From the bedroom of this house, there are the most wondrous views. Straight ahead as you look, there are acres and acres of olive groves, at night filled with the gloriously slow 'pieu-pieu-pieu' and then the explosive 'chock-chock-chock' of nightingales and in the day glistening green and yellow as the blossom spreads. And beyond the olives is Maleme airfield and then the sea – not wine-dark, as Homer called it, but the most vivid blue all day long. This is an amazingly fertile land – a surprise to me. I had expected barer and rockier countryside. And the reason for the greenness is what you can see when you look from the back room window – the mountains, *Lefka Ori*, the White Mountains, still in May covered in pure white snow. Hard to believe in the heat of the day down here that the snow can last so long but it does, because these are truly mountains, the highest point being over 8000 feet, so you can see why everything is so fertile.

There are huge birds of prey up in those mountains too. Through my binoculars I've seen eagles, buzzards and falcons sailing through the clear blue sky. I'd like to climb higher from our base to see them more clearly but that's not possible, so I have to be satisfied with looking out for the smaller birds that are so many here. I've already mentioned the nightingales but there are also regular visits from crested larks, ringed plovers, swifts, and dazzling yellow wagtails. Can you see why I love it all so? You would love it too, I know.

Things have been generally quiet here – only the occasional Messerschmitt passing overhead, presumably just reconnoitring because there were no bombs or shooting. So I've been able, when not on duty, to do some exploring. There's a little church on the hillside some quarter of a mile from where we're based and I climbed up there on my own a few evenings ago. It's a simple place, like all such churches here I'm told. I went in and I did experience something curious there. Hard to explain, I know. Maybe it's just the strangeness of this whole wartime experience, the sense of being outside time on occasions, the ever-impending danger and then this place of calm, a place where people have come over the centuries to make their peace with their God. I don't know why but anyway something struck me and I chucked a few coins on to a plate and lit a candle in front of the brightly painted wooden panels of – would you believe it? – St George and the dragon! Then I sat down on a rock just outside and looked out to sea and thought of you. I can't stop my brain seeing your lovely face. I just can't. And I worry about you.

The others in this billet are good chaps generally and we get on fine. Living here in such circumstances has made it so that it's not as formal as usual in the Forces, so the billet is shared between four of us, two of us lowly officers and two NCOs. Since they found out I'd been in the Scouts, they've started calling me Skip. Eddie is the oldest of us, I'd put him at about twenty-five, and he's also the bulkiest. He's obviously always liked his grub because he's already carrying quite a bit of extra weight round his belly and his chin and cheeks are distinctly wobbly. And you should see him in the kitchen when Eleni prepares some food! It's hard for us to get our share because he piles his plate as high as possible. 'You never know when it's your last meal,' he always says, his mouth already chomping on whatever he's shovelled into it, while Eleni is still serving us. He was a Post Office engineer back home but volunteered right at the start and has served all over the place. He was made Flight Sergeant just before this trip but I don't think he'd behave any different if he was just in the ranks. He's never short of a quip either, a real joker is our Eddie. He keeps our spirits up with his stories of his exploits in some of the shadier bits of east London where he lives.

Then there's Ronald, who's the other Flying Officer. He's a bit younger than me so technically I outrank him, though that's never been an issue. Ronald is a lot quieter than Eddie. He's tall and thin, wears spectacles and is trying to grow a moustache. He's from Norfolk and was due to go to Cambridge University. He'd even got sponsorship from an electrical manufacturing company in Norwich, which guaranteed him a job once he'd got his degree. Of course, when the war broke out, the company had to switch to wartime production and his opportunity disappeared. He volunteered too, though he had to wait a year until he was old enough to be accepted. He worked as a service mechanic for a radio dealer which gave him some useful experience in electrics. I like Ronald best of all of them. He's like me in lots of ways, studious, interested in the flora and fauna of this place, curious about the people who live here and their lifestyle, prefers reading to card-playing, which is what occupies Eddie and Jack particularly.

Jack, the other Flight Sergeant, is a bit of a rum cove. On the surface, he's all outgoing and confident, ever ready to join in the banter with Eddie, loves his card games – we play poker mostly, for matches – and is always talking about his 'Lancashire lass' back home. He's from Oldham and used to work in the mills there before the war. He was some kind of a trouble-shooter, as far as I can make out, whose job was to keep the machines in good working order and to fix them whenever anything went wrong. Jenny, his 'Lancashire lass', worked in the mill too, though he says she's now in the Land Army out on the moors somewhere or other. He's got the muckiest tongue – every other word is an obscenity and what he and Jenny get up to is beyond description. Until, that is, Eleni appears and then our Jack becomes the meekest and mildest of persons you might wish to see. He's all bluff, I suspect. 'All teeth and no trousers' is how Eddie would describe him, but he's okay. As I say, we get along fine. You have to, don't you? 'Grin and bear it,' as Eddie says.

We're not the only ones here, of course. We've got a whole platoon of New Zealanders stationed with us to provide cover if we are ever attacked. They are a lively bunch, though we don't spend too much time with them, as they have their own daily drills and we have ours. Still, I've learned to say '*Kia ora*', which is the Maori welcome, and I've been told about this curious war-chant that the Maoris do as they advance into battle. It's called a *haka* and the regular Kiwis say it's very frightening.

Yesterday evening, after we'd eaten a good lamb dinner, prepared by the wonderful Eleni, Ronald and I went for a walk down the old mule-path that leads past the front of our billet. I'd never gone far down it previously, so this was new territory. It's not much of a track, going between earthy banks covered with pink-headed thyme and purple lavender down to the dry bed of a stream. I guess in the winter this is gushing with water but now it is quite dry. We followed it downhill further, past ancient twisted olive trees, drinking in the pungent smell of the blossom, till we reached a road. I guess we must have been no more than half a mile from the sea there and we were just about to head back when we were challenged to identify ourselves. A New Zealand patrol had been sent to hunt around the area because there were rumours of German agents infiltrating the local population. Of course, we had our ID cards with us and were quickly able to reassure them, but it did set us wondering as we set off back. We knew from the radio signals that Greece had fallen, that all the Allied troops had been evacuated to Crete and there was a strong rumour that the Greek royal family had been evacuated here, though we knew no more than that. We all suspect that Hitler has his eye on this island next.

When we got back, Ronald relieved Eddie on duty and I played poker with the latter for a couple of hours, aided I have to say by a bottle of *raki* – a very strong firewater they drink here – that Eleni had brought with her earlier in the day. We talked desultorily about the rumours and about our position in all of this. Eddie's view was that they would get us off the island before the Hun arrived, because of the sensitive nature of our work and because of our precious equipment. I thought we might be needed to help provide cover for incoming flights. I went to bed at midnight and had a troubled night, worrying about all this and wishing I wasn't here but back home with you.

One day, all this will be over, Merry, and we will be together again. I think of you constantly and wish this war had never happened. Who would have believed two years ago that we would still be fighting? And still no sign of an end. I love you so much.

### 13th May 1941

Thank God, we've had a signal to prepare for evacuation, presumably back to Cairo. There's talk too of some leave back home, so maybe we can get married as we planned. We may be heading off the island as soon as tomorrow, so I've been taking long looks at this place again to cherish them in my memory.

Mind you, it's not been quite as peaceful today. The first air attack on the airfield took place today, mid-afternoon. Half a dozen Messerschmitts suddenly appeared over the mountains behind us, strafing the area near where we're situated then dropping bombs on the airfield. No damage to us – they missed by a long way but it shows the recce planes had spotted where to attack, so it's time we were moving. Reports from the airfield say there was no damage there either, despite the black smoke.

Eleni got very frightened by the attacks and we had to comfort her a lot. Eddie was particularly good, putting his arm around her, making her drink tea from his cup, that sort of thing. He surprised me. After the planes had gone and she'd calmed down, she set about preparing dinner for us. We told her it was okay, we'd sort ourselves out but she insisted. I suppose activity takes your mind off things, doesn't it?

We had started to pack up some of the stuff when Ronald stopped us, asking how definite had the signal been about our evacuation. I had to say it was not very definite at all, so we decided to wait until we had something more concrete by way of orders. After dinner – a sort of meat kebab Eleni calls *souvlaki* with salad, then yoghurt – the three of us played poker till midnight, while Ronald read. There were no more raids from Jerry.

This is the closest I've been so far to any action. I'm not scared, though the tracer bullets skidding into the olive groves this afternoon were not far from us. I suppose I feel confident that, if we are to evacuate, it will all be done in an orderly fashion. We're not front-line troops after all, we're part of the back up for the airfield and any planes that the RAF decide to send in to help deter Jerry. I shouldn't feel this confidence, I know. God knows, the speed with which I was promoted because of an elementary understanding of radio, then the incredibly lengthy and hazardous journey to get here. Seven weeks at sea! Can you believe it? Seven weeks in a converted pleasure boat sailing half way round the world to get to this island, so we could avoid minefields and submarines and God knows what else! And then, when we got here, we were told we had to set up base in one village, where we set about requisitioning the necessary accommodation and hiring support, only to be told one week later that we were to move ten miles further west to the foothills of these mountains.

Still, there's something undeniably optimistic and trusting in me. I just know I'll be okay and that we'll be together again in the not too distant future. I'm writing this letter today because tomorrow I might just be too busy to write. I think of you constantly. I love you so much.

All my love,
Bill
x

# CRETAN DIARY
# FLYING OFFICER BILL ENNIS

**19th May**

Supposed to be being evacuated today. At long last! The original plan was for us to destroy everything – files, papers, anything that might indicate to the Germans what we had been doing. We'd been told they didn't know about radar yet, so it was important that, if they did land and find this site, there shouldn't be any clues as to our activities. Once we had destroyed everything by burning it or breaking it up, we were to bury it in a pit in the ground and ensure that there were no signs of our having done so. Then we were to take the W/T and RDF gear with us and drive down to Suda Bay for disembarkation on one of the navy's freighters.

But that didn't happen, so nothing much to do except write a record of events. First of all, the signals came through from Canea that the German invasion was planned for today, by sea from the north it was expected, with an airborne landing to follow, so Suda Bay would be no use to us. If the signal was correct, then Suda Bay would be at the heart of the action. So Plan B came into operation. This was to send us by motorised vehicle with our gear on the road over the White Mountains to liaise with a navy submarine off the southern coast of Crete.

That never happened either. We had destroyed all that we could, we had prepared ourselves to leave, but the orders never came through. We tried making contact with HQ in Canea but couldn't get an answer one way or the other. I think they were busy expecting the German navy and didn't have time for us.

Besides this, there was a lot of traffic in the skies over Maleme airfield today. The first raid, round about 7 am, woke me up and there were three more attacks before 9 am. I got my binoculars and watched from the upstairs window of our billet. Scores of Messerschmitts dived on the aerodrome or the airfield, each of them dropping one huge bomb. The sky was filled with these black blobs, like huge raindrops. Then there was a pall of black smoke over the whole area – you could barely see what was left after they'd gone. The AA guns stuttered back at them but they didn't seem to hit any planes.

During the day, after the bombers left and the smoke had cleared a bit, I could see the movement of troops on the road below me. I guess they were NZ boys, because Ronald and I had learned from our excursion that way some days ago that it was NZ troops who were stationed in that area and the captain of the platoon that was providing cover for us confirmed that it was members of his battalion that were based closest to the airfield. Don't know what damage was done or whether the NZ troops managed to rescue any personnel. No radio communications from the airfield. It was just as well all the RAF planes, the Blenheims and Hurricanes of 30 Squadron, had taken off back to Egypt days earlier. That's when we should have gone too.

Tried to find out from HQ in Canea if any orders had come through for our evacuation and was told that someone would get back to me but they never did. Talked to Eddie about whether it might be worth one of us going down there to beard someone and get a straight answer but Eddie said it would be a waste of time. He'd been in campaigns in North Africa and Egypt.

'The one thing I learned,' he grinned, 'is that the top brass haven't got a clue. They're still fighting the First World War most of them. They sit in their rooms planning battles as if we were all little lead soldiers. They haven't realised that this war is different. It's fast moving. It's not stationary. It's not trenches in northern France. It's all over the place. Hitler knows that and that's why he's doing so well. What he hasn't got, though, is the British spunk. I've seen some of the Jerries that were captured in North Africa. They're all scared silly, believe me. You compare them with your average Tommy, they're nothing like. Trust me, we'll win this thing in the end because of that spunk. You mark my words.'

'So what do you think has happened to our orders?' I said as we lit cigarettes.

'Have you seen some of the equipment they're using for wireless. It's useless. It was out of date when it was made ten years ago, never mind now. The stuff we've got is okay, naturally, but then it has to be, doesn't it? The stuff the boys down there have got is rubbish. Half the time it doesn't work. And, even when it does work, it's at a time when there's no messages to be sent because they're already out of date. If you add in the fact that the top brass haven't got a clue half the time, then what do you expect?'

'So haven't we got any hope of getting orders?'

'Oh, don't worry, Skip, orders always come through at some stage.' He raised his eyes to the sky and gave a little grin. 'I've seen it before. But they usually come through days later than they should have done, so then you have to work a lot of things out for yourself. You'll see. Tomorrow we'll be told to report to Suda Bay for evacuation, while we know that it's been bombarded steadily the last few days by Jerry and there's no way that any ship of the Royal Navy will be waiting to take us on board there.'

He's a bit of an old hand is Eddie and a part of me doesn't want to believe his gloomy prognosis but another part of me suspects that he may be right.

In the evening Ronald and I sat outside the white-painted church just behind our billet, smoking Abdullah Turkish cigarettes that he'd been given as a birthday present and had been keeping for a special occasion, and watched the next lot of German planes – nine huge Junkers bombers dropping whole sticks of bombs on to the airfield. Again black smoke and clouds of dust. Again the AA guns firing back. Hard to tell what success Jerry had had.

I think Ronald is getting the heebie-jeebies now. I asked him why he'd kept these Abdullahs so long and brought them out now. Didn't he think we'd be getting out of all this? He admitted that it was the first time he'd felt really scared. He'd never been this close to battle before and it worried him that our orders kept changing or being downgraded. Even more that we now seemed to have been forgotten about. I assured him that this wasn't necessarily so and that there was probably just a temporary breakdown in communications with HQ.

'Remember,' I told him. 'We're the jewel in the crown, Churchill's secret weapon. If the Germans get hold of this radar gear, we're finished. Until then, we'll always be a long way ahead of them. They won't leave us here. The War Office won't allow it. Mark my words, we'll be out of here tomorrow sharpish, as soon as HQ has sorted itself out. Buck up, Ronald. You'll get to Cambridge yet, old chap.'

We went back down to the billet to find Eleni hiding under a table in the kitchen. Eddie was bending over, trying to coax her out of hiding and to reassure her that the bombs were nowhere near us, that we weren't the target and that we'd be leaving the next day at the latest and we'd take her with us.

'No go,' she was saying in her pidgin tongue, shaking her head vigorously to indicate her determination to stay where she was, even under the table if necessary. 'No go. Eleni stay.'

'But what if the Germans invade and find you?' pleaded Jack, who was also in the kitchen I realised, hidden from Ronald and me initially by the wooden door. 'They'll interrogate you and find you've been sheltering British soldiers. Then what?'

Eleni drew her forefinger sharply across her throat, then pointed to the kitchen knife she'd dropped on to the floor as she had sought refuge under the table.

'Germans, pah!'

'Eleni,' I said, seeking to drop the temperature a little. 'Come out. The planes have gone now. They never come in the dark, you know that, so you're safe to come out. Come on, we need to talk about what's going to happen.'

Just at that moment there was a bit of a commotion outside the door. Eddie reached for his pistol but I steadied his arm and gave him a look that stopped him. Which was just as well, for next minute the door opened and there stood Themistocles, resplendent in his black Cretan outfit, accompanied by a boy we had not seen before, who looked to be about eleven or twelve years old.

'Nikos,' announced the bearded patriarch. 'Eleni *yos*.'

'What's he say?' asked Jack.

'I think he's telling us this is Eleni's son,' I answered, though I was guessing.

'Nikos, good *yos*,' Themistocles continued. 'Nikos take you *spilia*.'

My Greek wasn't up to that, I'm afraid, but fortunately Themistocles summoned us outside the house and, taking my arm, pointed up to the mountainside.

'*Spilia*. You. Eleni. Nikos take.'

'I think he's saying that there's a cave or caves up in the mountains,' I said, realising that the area he was pointing in did have dark indentations in the rocks that might have been caves. 'He's volunteering Eleni's son to lead us up there so we can hide in safety. And take Eleni with us.'

'*Endaksi*,' he said, nodding his head, as he saw from my gestures that I had got the gist of what he was saying.

Eddie gave Jack a look that was reciprocated, then turned back to Themistocles.

'No way, me old china. We ain't leaving here till we're told to leave. And, if that means we have to kill a few Jerries first, then so be it. Tell him thanks but no thanks, Skip.'

Jack vigorously nodded his agreement, while Ronald looked down at his feet.

'Mr Themistocles,' I began, searching for language that he might understand. 'No *efharisto*. We stay here. In this house.' I pointed to our billet. 'You take Eleni and Nikos to *spilia*. We stay.'

Eleni by now had crept out from under the table and was facing her father, hands on hips, an indignant look on her face

'No scared Germans. Scared bombs, no scared Germans.'

And she repeated the throat-cutting gesture she had made a little while back, this time with even more force. Her son Nikos laughed and repeated the gesture.

'No scared Germans,' he shouted, with a delighted grin. 'No scared Germans.'

And he disappeared in the night down the hill to Xamoudochori, calling out these sounds of whose meaning he had only the vaguest of notions, followed more stiffly by Themistocles, who first shook us each by the hand and bowed to each in turn as he bade his farewells.

'*Kalinikta*,' he called after him as he strode off, his head held high and his leather boots thudding into the earthy track.

Told the others to get some sleep, for it was still likely that we would be told to move off the next day. Then I sat up writing this.

When I was in the sixth form at King Edward's, I was convinced that I could establish myself in the world successfully and I don't just mean in the family business. I didn't know how or what I was going to do to gain this success but I knew it would happen. That, I presume, is what grammar school education is all about. I got carried along with all the rhetoric, seeing myself as the sort of person who would effortlessly rise to the top. Now I see that I'm actually the sort of person who just gets carried along. I don't impose myself on any situation. I fail lamentably in my attempts to impose a sense of direction on myself. I just get carried along.

Look at me here. I joined up because I wanted to, although I could have deferred by going to university. Then, because I showed some interest in radio, I was posted into the RAF Signals Training Wing. And what training did I have? Very little. Within weeks of being there, I was made a Flying Officer and sent on this mission. So, here I am, drifting again, getting carried along as ever.

The rest of the chaps here look up to me as if I had something that they don't, some superior sense of what's happening, some better understanding of what might happen. But I don't. I only wish I did, but I really don't. And yet, despite the fact that we get on okay and don't bother too much about rank, they all expect me to make the final decisions about anything, to pass judgement.

Take tonight. Eddie and Jack automatically turned to me to sort out matters with Themistocles and Eleni and it's not just because I've picked up a bit more of the lingo than they have. They just expect me to do it. And Ronald does, maybe even more than they do. And he's the same rank as me, though you wouldn't know it from the way he behaves.

Why am I thinking like this? I guess it's because I am becoming anxious about what is going to happen. It's almost a week since we were first led to believe that we would be evacuated, almost

106

a week in which we've been on edge awaiting the signal to pack up and go. And that signal hasn't come. And the German naval invasion was supposed to happen today but didn't, though their bombers must have done serious damage to Maleme airfield. So what is going on? Does HQ really have a grip on the situation? There have already been some serious errors of judgement by our forces in different theatres of this war. We were told that Crete was a safe venue because Greece was where the battle lines would be drawn. But Greece has fallen and this island is the obvious next place for Hitler to seek control of the Eastern Mediterranean sector. If I can see that, why can't the top brass down at Canea HQ and in Iraklion see it? Why have they withdrawn all air cover from the island? Why haven't they mined Maleme airfield to stop Jerry landing safely there?

I'm feeling weary of it all. I just want to get away from this place. If we don't get any instructions tomorrow, I may just make the decision myself. I can't quite describe my emotions. It's not fear I feel. It's something quite different. It's more a sense of foreboding. As if this isn't going to turn out at all well. Think of Merry constantly – she's the only thing that makes sense. So good to have her photograph to remind me.

## 20th May

06.00. Early morning raids – 'the daily hate', as the Kiwis call it – on the aerodrome again, earlier than usual. Was woken up by them. Looked out of the top window and saw them approaching out of a cloudless sky, no wind, visibility brilliant – you could see the rocky outcrops on the mountains twenty miles to the south-east. Had some fruit and yoghurt for breakfast that Eleni had prepared for us.

Asked Eddie, who had been manning the wireless for the dawn shift, if there was any news but he said there was nothing other than the same talk of an invasion but nobody knew when or how. Maybe today, maybe tomorrow, maybe next week. Who knew?

More attacks on the aerodrome as we're eating but also some strafing of the hillside with machine-guns. Seems more concentrated than previously. Is this it?

Ronald called through from the technical area that there was something big on the radar. Some distance away but looked to be coming towards us.

'Better tell HQ,' I said. 'At least that will give them some warning of more bombs.'

08.00. It wasn't more bombs. It was something altogether different. It was Jack who spotted them first. He'd been outside checking on the W/T when he heard the noise first of all.

'Look!' he shouted back into the billet. 'Get out here and look at this bleeding lot!'

Rushed out and saw Jack pointing agitatedly out to sea. Could hear the heavy droning and first reaction was to look up to the sky but then realised Jack was pointing far out to the sea on the western horizon. My initial fear was of a seaborne invasion but what I saw was almost certainly unlike anything I'd seen before. They came crawling like evil giants towards us, their undercarriages appearing almost to be sweeping the tranquil sea. They were coming in waves, the blackness of them adding the sinister to the fantastic. Easily the largest planes that I had ever seen. Obviously troop carriers. The invasion was beginning but it was airborne. Sent frantic signals to Canea HQ, though they must have been able to hear the droning engines themselves by now.

At the same time as we heard the ground alarm ringing from Maleme aerodrome, we saw the gliders – strangely silent, with long tapering wings, stealthy as they approached. There must have been twenty to twenty-five of them in all, though we didn't realise that was what they were until they got closer and the absence of engine noise caught us by surprise. They circled and turned slowly down to Maleme airfield, looking like giant flies about to land, though most of them went past the airfield towards the dry bed of the Tavronitis river. The Bofors guns and machine guns took a lot of them out of action as they landed – they were easy targets. I saw one that crash-landed about half a mile from us but didn't see anyone get out of it – presumably crew killed on landing.

08.30. Magnesium flares suddenly in bright morning sky. Clearly some kind of signal, because almost immediately mushroom-shaped parachutes all over the sky – white, red, green and yellow. Men and equipment falling everywhere. Sky alive with the descending attackers, as they jumped out of the huge Junkers troop carriers. Never seen anything like it. Lots of them must have died in mid-air – easy targets for NZ battalions stationed around perimeter of Maleme. Others reached ground but shot there, struggling to get out of parachute harnesses. AA guns brought down Jerry planes that crashed on airfield alongside some gliders crash-landed earlier.

Some paratroopers landed well away from Maleme, out in olive groves. Through binoculars from upper window of billet, could see puffs of smoke rising in asymmetric patches above olive groves, where stray paratroopers had landed and been hunted down, and odd patches of white or green where parachutes caught up in trees. Where they landed was just luck really. Good luck took them away from Allied guns and over to west of airfield; bad luck took them right into midst of guns. And almost certain death. Some simply fell into the sea and drowned.

All morning troop-planes arriving, side doors open to disgorge up to ten men at a time in grey camouflage jumpsuits with submachine guns between knees. Sometimes only about 400 feet above ground when they jumped; other times higher, maybe 1000 feet. But kept coming all morning. And all morning killing continued.

11.00. With Eddie and Jack, burned all records and documents not burned previously in pit then covered with earth and trod down so didn't look as if soil recently disturbed. Put cypher books and codes in Receiver Van ready for destruction if necessary. Radar watch still being kept, though not much use now. Made contact on W/T with Iraklion and Rethymnon but found main Operations Room destroyed by bombing. Finally made contact with Canea HQ and received orders to evacuate tomorrow. Orders to liaise with NZ battalion and use them for cover, but, if that impossible, to make direct for Canea and await further instructions.

14.00. Had meeting with Ronald, plus Eddie and Jack as senior NCOs, plus Robin, captain of NZ platoon protecting us, and his sergeant, Carl. Agreed how we should dispose defences until instructions to move off, since clear that German paratroopers landing in the olive groves and likely, maybe probable, that some would head in our direction. Three posts set up, each manned by NZ personnel and each with Lewis gun, to east, west and directly behind, as we could all see area immediately in front of us clearly enough. But no firing unless fired on – didn't want to draw attention to our position. Also agreed to send Jack to Canea to check out what was happening there and find possible route for us tomorrow.

As we finished meeting, NZ patrol came past our billet. Told us they'd flushed out couple of parachutists from Eleni's village and village now clear, though some dead Greeks there. Rumours of Germans wearing NZ battledress. If we left post, needed to remember to use passwords – names of two Derby winners. Told Eleni about what had happened in her village – started wailing at once about father and son Nikos. Said she must go and find out but asked Robin to send an escort, just in case.

16.00. More paratroopers throughout the afternoon and more parachutes carrying equipment. Sky still full of planes, blotting out sun. Still very hot. Paratroopers who survive rifle fire must be baking inside grey suits. From top window through binoculars saw number of German parachute troops managed to join together in field about mile from us and digging in just where field met olive grove. Within easy reach of Maleme airfield, less than half mile from perimeter. Not there long, however, because concentrated fire from NZ battalions well dug in to east forced them back over ridge and away from airfield. Later saw troopships landing on beach at Maleme and large numbers of German soldiers disembarking. Looks like Maleme about to be captured, even after all that killing this morning. Just too many German troops and lack of air cover proving disastrous.

19.00. At dusk further attacks on aerodrome from Messerschmitts and Stukas. Not much resistance from AA guns. Probably all knocked out by now. Sporadic firing of rifles and trench mortars as light faded but hard to see where coming from. Darkness deceptive.

Jack returned with news that Max Schmelling, German heavyweight boxer who'd knocked out Joe Louis before war, one of parachutists captured by British troops further down coast towards Rethymnon. Cheered us up. Don't know why. Just another trooper like us, caught up in war. Suppose some sort of symbol for us. Certainly was for NZ platoon, who got very excited when they heard.

Jack said main road to Canea still controlled by our troops but places where Germans had landed behind our lines and occupied small pockets. Luckily hadn't come across any, though had one close encounter. Apparently found RAOC cookhouse that had been vacated, presumably because of need for troops to operate somewhere else. Went to look for provisions for our journey next day.

'I got in there and there were tins of bully beef, biscuits, all sorts of bleeding stuff,' Jack said. 'And then on a table I saw an opened tin of pears. They'd been left when the paratroopers dropped, so I scoffed the bloody lot. They were scrumptious. I was just about to load up with the other stuff when, out of the corner of my left eye, I saw a movement. It were a bleeding bayonet inching into the doorway, followed by the rifle muzzle. I recognised it straightway as a Lee Enfield 303 but it could have been a bloody German with a captured weapon. I were ready to do or die. I could have hit whoever were behind that British rifle. The bloody wooden door wouldn't have stopped my bullets 'cos I could rapid-fire from my hip much quicker than from the prone position. Then the body appeared. Bleeding British, yes, not a German in our uniform. He gave me the password, 'Sansavino'. Bloody hell! I forgot the name of the other Derby winner momentarily. Then it came. 'Cameronian,' I answered. He quizzed me as to what I were doing and I told him I were here from the AMES post back in the foothills, looking for a route to Canea for tomorrow. He told me there were bloody Jerries all over the place between Maleme and Canea and doubted that we'd get through there tomorrow. His platoon had been sent to flush out as many as they could but he reckoned the word were that there'd been thousands who had landed during the day and, although a lot had been killed or wounded, there were still too many of the buggers out there for comfort.'

That decided me. Little or no point trying the Canea road it seemed. So had to be the southern route. Occasional Very lights flared eerily in the night sky. Sound of rifle fire and machine-gun fire continued into darkness. Left Ronald on duty and went to room we shared.

*

My Darling Merry,

I don't know if you'll ever get this letter but I have to try to tell you about everything, as I promised. This has been the weirdest day I can ever remember in my life. And I hope never to see another one like it. Jerry has staged a paratroop landing here. The drone of the huge planes approaching us this morning, the silent stealth of those gliders swooping through the air towards the Tavronitis river bed, the sight of those thousands and thousands of grey-uniformed paratroopers leaping out of their planes and floating to earth under their billowing parachutes, and then the mounting frenzy of the guns that cut them down in flight or that answered ours. It is difficult to sleep after all that.

For the first time I wonder whether we are going to get out of all this. It's funny, you know you're in a war and you know that people get killed in war. But there is something indomitable in the human spirit that tells you it won't be you. What did those young German paratroopers think as they jumped out of their planes and realised they were open targets for the soldiers dug in below? Did they know that so many would die? Did the German High Command deliberately sacrifice so many men in order to get control of this little bit of Crete? Or were they, as Eddie would say, 'sitting in their rooms planning battles as if we were all little lead soldiers'?

For weeks now I've been looking at the pockets of snow in the White Mountains behind us, never imagining until tonight that we would have to make our way over them in order to make good our flight. Did I tell you I went mountaineering once while I was in the sixth Form at King Edward's? One of our masters, Mr Sherdley, was a keen rock climber and he took us on a climbing holiday in the Cairngorms. Strenuous, yes. Hard work, yes. But tremendously invigorating. I remember reaching the top of one particular mountain, Ben Macdui, the highest of the lot Mr Sherdley told us, and just marvelling at being there. The sheer exhilaration of climbing really does take you into an elevated state. But climbing Ben Macdui in proper climbing gear and climbing over those White Mountains in our battledress and carrying rifles, rations, ammunition, and water bottles are two different activities altogether. Besides which, on

Macdui, there were just five of us, including the master, all of us keen sportsmen, all of us young, active, and fit. While tomorrow it will be a different story. I don't know about the physical fitness of our potential party, though I doubt Eddie's ability to move at speed, given his bulkiness, and Ronald doesn't seem to me to be a physically strong specimen.

And what shall we do about Eleni and her family, indeed everyone in her village? We have received nothing but kindness from the people we have met but I understand from the semi-conversations that I had with Eleni and her father, Mr Themistocles, that their people wouldn't take as kindly to the Germans. Too many of the islanders have died in Greece already. Everyone has a relative or knows someone who has died. Rumours of German barbarity on the battlefields are legion and, even though most of the villages are now only inhabited by women, children and the elderly, it would be a mistake to underestimate the ferocity of their reactions to the idea that the Germans would take over their island. Already there are Greeks killed in Eleni's village because they resisted the German paratroopers.

It's time to try for some sleep, despite the sporadic rifle fire and the occasional Very flare in the night sky. I can still smell the thyme in the night air. I think constantly of you and the last time we were together when you became truly mine. How much I miss you and wish I was with you. Tomorrow will be a long day.

All my love,

Bill

x

### 21st May

04.00. Up early for my turn on watch. Still lots of rifle fire audible, though much more random than last night, and vivid green or white Very flares curving through air and giving ghostly light to everything. Also sounds of people calling to each other – hoots, whistles, and other strange noises. Presumably German paratroopers trying to join up with comrades. Could hear troop movement on road below our position but couldn't see anything. This is day when we move at last. Hope everyone ready.

06.00. Sun rising over hills towards Canea. Any other day a beautiful sight but can't dwell on it. Too much on my mind. Need to wake others to get equipment and cypher books etc in technical area ready for destruction. Have to make decisions about route to take.

First German planes heard in the distance, so expected more bombs and strafing. But only one Junkers on horizon. Headed towards Maleme airfield but, instead of dropping bombs or firing, attempted to land on western edge and miraculously made it, then immediately took off again. What was going on? All AA guns silenced? What about NZ troops around airfield? Why not trying to bring Junkers down?

08.00. Now we know. Patrol from NZ 23rd came through and told us all NZ troops withdrawn from around airfield to position behind us. This means we're isolated, in communication with Canea HQ but without any troops forward of us to protect us from German advance.

Called conference of NCOs and officers to give news. Robin, NZ platoon captain, confirmed everything. One of his blokes on recce had bumped into some Maoris sent to reinforce company around airfield but couldn't find them, so heading back to where they'd come from. Too many casualties and no water.

Jack and Eddie not impressed at being left to ourselves, without support. Ronald looking very scared, could hardly talk.

Heard another plane approaching, so rushed to top window to see what was happening. Another Junkers landed on beach just beyond Tavronitis riverbed to west of airfield and taxied to halt. Paratroopers emerging from bushes and unloading boxes of ammunition, then stretchers with wounded soldiers loaded on to plane and it took off.

That confirmed everything. Convinced that airfield lost, so sent signal back to HQ RAF Crete, then set about preparing everything for destruction and getting ourselves ready for retreat.

11.00. Small group of RAF, Fleet Air Arm and Army personnel, ground crew on Maleme airfield, came past, looking weary and wearing torn battledress. Told us Maleme definitely under German control and many taken prisoner. Parts of road to Canea under German control. Spent rest of morning supervising preparations for destruction of all equipment.

Curious lull in everything. After yesterday, expected more German action, more paratroopers, more troopships. But so far nothing. Hadn't expected to be left behind by NZ brigade, nor to be left without instructions by RAF HQ. Maybe Eddie right about top brass. Gave orders for everyone to be ready to move with water bottles, rations, ammunition and pistols.

15.00. Still no instructions but confirmation that Germans moving along road to Canea in some force, so only way out is south, over White Mountains. At conference of officers and NCOs, agreed to blow up all equipment during first bombing raid, to avoid drawing attention to position. No sooner done than first German raid arrived – some fifty or sixty Stukas and Messerschmitts dropping bombs and strafing olive groves and fields below us, around us and beyond us with machine-guns. Ordered no fire to be returned. Expected this to be softening up exercise before ground attack from paratroopers nearby but turned out to last good three parts of hour. Bombs close to our site and one gun-post wiped out, so gave orders for Receiver Van to be blown up with gun cotton and detonators.

## 22nd May

Darling Merry,

I am writing this in the early morning after the most scary day I've ever experienced. I feel a need to tell you all that happened after we left our post and I've woken earlier than the others, so I can have a little time to think of you, tired as I am from our exertions yesterday. I had intended us to set off earlier today but exhaustion has taken its toll and the others are still asleep.

It must have been mid-afternoon when we abandoned our base at Xamoudochori and set off on our flight. Just before we left, Ronald got a direct hit from bomb shrapnel which bit into his right leg and almost tore it off. I found him writhing on the ground, blood gushing from his torn leg, his rifle and glasses flung on the earth. I got a NZ Medical Orderly to move him away to somewhere under cover and wait for help. I wanted to stay with him but the others said we had to leave now. The Germans knew where we were. I didn't want to leave Ronald but another bomb landed almost on top of us. It was every man for himself.

I went back to check that the Receiver Van was fully destroyed and found the Transmitter Van burnt as well. I had to trust to luck at this point, so I made sure everyone had left the site, then set off after them. Bombers were still flying overhead, sometimes too close for comfort. I found myself in an olive grove, lying in a ditch, head covered, next to Eddie and Jack. I felt strangely protected with them.

'Best keep together,' I said.

'Too b------ right,' answered Jack, while Eddie, lying face to face with Jack, nodded.

When the bombers had passed, we rose and, stooping, ran downhill towards the next bit of cover, more olive trees, but we had been spotted, for rifle fire zinged around us as we ran. Fortunately, we all made it. There were others in that clutch of trees, some of the NZ platoon. When the next bomb landed just behind us, it created a cloud of orange dust so we all took advantage of it and broke cover for another sprint to new trees. There were soldiers everywhere now, not just from the platoon that had been guarding us but other NZs and some British who had yesterday been sent into the hills to flush out German parachutists and were now fleeing for their lives. As each bomb fell and created its own dust-cloud, we moved at pace, screaming in fear and panic, hearts throbbing, deafened by the continuous roar of the bombs and guns. I was terrified.

Eventually we found ourselves in a narrow gully, deep enough for us to advance in, as long as we stayed in a crouched position, and stay hidden from the snipers and bombers. There were five of us altogether now – Eddie, Jack, the New Zealand sergeant Carl, his lance-corporal, Jim, and another NZ sergeant called Alec, who had got detached from his outfit but had a Tommy-gun. I looked back from the gully and could see the small church I had visited on several occasions, its tower wearing a huge black hole where it had been hit by a random bomb, and below it the house that we had been billeted in until so very recently, it too scarred by the bombing.

We went up the gully cautiously, but by now I had identified our route. There was a deep ravine on the hillside that ran inland and would take us towards the distant mountains, providing good cover for us as we moved. But between it and us was a shallow valley with low-lying vineyards in it, which didn't give much cover. There was nothing for it but to wait our moment and make a dash. One at a time, when the screaming planes had passed over, we went over the top, rolling down the grassy slope into the vineyards than crawling on hands and knees through the green vines to reach another olive grove – ancient, thick, gnarled trees that offered us the best cover we had found yet.

And here we found Eleni, her son Nikos and Mr Themistocles with his shotgun, stretched out in a line in a dry ditch in the deepest part of the grove. Eleni was frightened stiff and Nikos looked bewildered, trying to reassure his mother but also unsure himself about what was happening or what was going to happen.

'Germans shoot,' Eleni said, making a gun with her index fingers.

'No,' I said, though I doubted my own words. 'Germans shoot English, not Cretans.'

'Is *kako*,' said Themistocles, waving his shotgun. 'Germans no shoot Themistocles.'

I explained through word and gesture that we were heading for the White Mountains and Themistocles nodded, indicating that this was a sensible move because he knew that there were no Germans up there yet. He wasn't asking us to take Eleni and Nikos with us now. I shook their hands and wished them well. What else could I do?

We were lucky. Soon after we found the dry bed of a stream in a valley and walked along it for several miles till dusk fell. There was no rifle fire here, no strafing and bombing airplanes. Their efforts were concentrated lower down the valley around the Maleme airfield and towards Canea itself. We had seen more parachutes falling in the late afternoon as we looked behind us but we were in no position to worry about them. Our sole purpose was survival now and the further we got away from the action, the better as far as we were all concerned.

As we clambered along this stream bed, we found water, which was a great relief for, although we had brought water bottles with us, they had soon been exhausted and it was good to taste this fresh mountain water, to soak our heads with it, and to replenish our water bottles. A little further we came upon some more Cretans, taking cover for the night away from their own village and away from the German bombers. They made a huge fuss of us, making us sit down and feeding us goat's milk, bread and feta cheese. I will never forget their generosity. From them we also learned about where there were German positions but they were, as we expected, virtually all behind us now, although they did tell us that there were stories about German mountain troops having landed that day and being marched around the western approaches to the White Mountains.

One of the villagers, an old man dressed in the same Cretan clothes as Themistocles, insisted on walking with us to the bottom of a steep track that climbed towards the base of the bare mountainside, rising steeply out of the valley below.

'*Lefka Ori,*' he said, pointing upwards to the ridge. I had heard this phrase often enough by now to know he was referring to the White Mountains. We were well on our way, or so I thought.

Eventually we reached the ridge the old man pointed us towards. It had been hard work in the darkness. The New Zealanders, Carl, Jim and Alec, had no trouble, despite all they were carrying. They are used to the outdoor life back home. But Eddie and Jack struggled, Eddie especially, not finding it easy to stretch his considerable frame from rock to rock and getting his body leaning into the wrong direction so that he stumbled. Still, in the terror of that initial bombardment, we'd promised to stick together and I wasn't going to renege on that agreement now. So I hauled him along behind me when necessary and pushed him ahead of me at other times. Jack scrambled all right, but he kept complaining that we were going in the wrong direction. He said he'd been in the Boys Brigade when he was younger and he could tell where we were and where we should be from the stars. The New Zealanders laughed when he tried to point out the Pole Star, telling him he'd got the wrong one. It was the only laugh we had all night – a sign that we were beginning to feel well away from the danger zone.

We stopped to rest for a while on a ledge, for we were still a long way from the highest point. Every time we reached a bend, there was another one ahead of us. Suddenly tinkling bells. I motioned to everyone to take cover and prime their weapons quietly. Around a corner of this ledge, which was no more than three feet wide, came a Cretan shepherd with a herd of goats and sheep, each with a bell round its neck, and a laden donkey. It turned out he was heading for a place he called Dere, a village on the way to the White Mountains, so he said we could go with him and his flock.

We walked for hours with no provisions left and our water very low. Walking without thinking now. Just keeping going automatically. At one point Jack grabbed the shepherd and swore at him for leading us the wrong way. I had to pull him off. He was just exhausted and disorientated. Not his fault. Had to calm the shepherd down. But I began to wonder if this was some sort of a trap, because we were definitely going downhill again. Then I thought I saw white houses as we rounded another bend in this interminable track, but it was nothing. Just a mirage from my dehydrated state of mind.

'Cretan b--------,' said Eddie.

'B----- Cretan b-------,' said Jack.

'Shut up, you Poms,' said Carl and Alec together. They'd become fed up with Eddie and Jack complaining.

'B------- Cretan shepherd,' said Eddie again.

The shepherd didn't understand what they were saying.

We stopped briefly under some yucca trees. Jack wanted us to sleep for a while but Carl said we ought to keep moving and reluctantly we all agreed. The shepherd had indicated that there was food and drink for us when we reached his village of Dere and we needed sustenance. Who knows what we would have been like if we'd slept through till sunrise and the baking heat that followed on?

Suddenly, we stumbled over yet another slight ridge and there in front of us was a hut in a clearing among trees. We lay down on the green grass, gratefully covering ourselves with the flea-infested blankets the shepherd gave us from his laden donkey while he went to fetch his wife to open up the shack.

Half an hour later we were wakened by the shepherd and his wife, who opened up the hut. There was a large table that three of us could lie on, while the other three could sleep on the floor. Then more villagers appeared, with bread – the last they had, they told us – hard-boiled eggs, and two bottles of red wine. And then another villager appeared, holding a cackling hen which quickly had its throat cut and its feathers removed, then it was slit open and the odds and ends which go towards forming the inside of a chicken were shaken out on to a plate. With the exception of one or two inedible organs the whole lot was placed in a frying pan – there were eggs in various stages from the size of a pinhead to a ping-pong ball, liver, heart and all the things which one gives to the cat at home. What a feast! And they would accept no payment, although we had lots of 500 drachma notes that we'd been given to speed our retreat. Finally, we thanked the villagers, they left and we took our boots off and went to sleep.

I am just so grateful still to be alive, Merry. Everything that happened yesterday is still etched vividly in my mind and I had to tell you about it. It is only thoughts of coming home to you that keep me going. I love you so much.

All my love,
Bill
x


My Darling Merry,

Second letter of the day. Another wearying day for we still had a long way to go to reach the highest point in the White Mountains before we were able to head for the sea in the southern part of Crete but we are closer to safety now. Let me tell you about it.

When everyone was finally awake, I got them into their boots, despite the moans about blisters, and was just getting ready to move, when the door of the shack opened and in came the shepherd's wife who had fed us in the very early morning hours. She was more beautiful than I remembered – long dark hair, flashing eyes and a lithe body. I could sense everyone's eyes on her. Not mine, of course, my love, for my eyes are only for you.

'*Psomi*,' she announced, holding up a loaf of bread that was clearly fresh-made. '*Eko.*'

She summoned us with her right hand to follow. And there outside was a cloth spread on the ground with bread, cheese and water laid out for us.

We couldn't help but marvel at these people. There we were, in the middle of a German invasion of their island, when their lives were threatened at every moment, when they knew that, if they were found to be helping British soldiers, they would face severe reprisals, and they were showing us this enormous kindness.

While we were eating, a small group approached us from the village. At first they were too far away to distinguish who they were but, as they came into sight, I could see that they were led by a priest in his long black surplice and distinctive stovepipe hat. He strode along the dusty path towards the shepherd's hut, his white beard riffling in the gentle breeze. Under his arm, he carried a shotgun. There were others with him, all in traditional Cretan dress. I recognised our shepherd but the other man walking with him I could not at first see, as he walked slightly behind the priest. A smaller figure trotted beside him.

Suddenly I realised who these latter two might be. The smaller figure I recognised first – it was Nikos, Eleni's son. What was he doing here inland? We'd left him with his mother back in the olive grove near their village, sheltering from the German attacks and guarded by the boy's grandfather, Mr Themistocles. But I wondered about the tall, moustachioed figure that walked beside him, resplendent in his Turkish trousers, held up with a red cummerbund, and his billowing black shirt. The glint of the knife in his cummerbund and the rifle slung over his shoulder indicated he was not to be messed with. Could this be…?

They stopped when they reached us, the priest motioning us with his shotgun to stay seated on the ground and to continue eating.

'Speak leetle English,' the priest said. Now that he stood over us, I could see he was a huge man with a large stomach, making even Eddie look undernourished by comparison. 'This Nikos, you know? This Alexandros.'

Couldn't believe it, Merry. Was this really Eleni's brother Alexandros, the Cretan *andarte* who had been living in the mountains preparing for resistance to the German invasion? If not, then what was Nikos doing here? Surely it had to be him.

The four of them sat down beside us and I offered cigarettes. Then, through the usual mixture of gesture and misunderstandings, we made sense of what they were saying. It seemed that Alexandros had gone back to Xamoudochori to check his family were safe and had moved them to a more secure spot higher in the hills. When he had heard from his father, Mr Themistocles, about us and the route we had taken, he had decided to follow us and help us. That was why he had brought Nikos, he said. He himself would lead us to the summit of the *Lefka Ori* but after that he needed to get back to his band in the hills. They had heard that German Mountain Troops were advancing from the west and he needed to be sure that they were delayed as much as possible. Nikos would show us the route after that. He knew these mountain passes as well as anyone, for before the war he had accompanied his uncle and his father on shooting expeditions there.

'Nikos good boy,' said the priest, his mighty hand patting the lad on the back so hard it almost made him choke. 'Look after.'

I wasn't clear whether this was an instruction to us or an indication of what Nikos would do. But it didn't matter. Although we protested that we didn't want to expose the boy to unnecessary danger by accompanying us, our protests were thin really, for we could see that our luck was holding. In fact, it was improving. I could almost smell the sea.

But there were still another thirty or so miles to walk, we were told, so it was best to plan another overnight stop before heading down to Suya on the southern coast of the island.

'No good road,' said the priest. 'Nikos show you path. You follow Nikos. Good boy'

We also found out from Alexandros that Maleme airfield had indeed been taken by the Germans who had cleared the runways of damaged planes and anti-aircraft weapons and were now landing aircraft regularly, bringing in more troops and equipment. Some of those troops were allegedly the Mountain Divisions that Alexandros had mentioned earlier who had been sent to approach the White Mountains from the west. There was news too of King George of the Hellenes who had indeed been on Crete but who was escaping, like us, over the White Mountains and heading down the Samarian gorge to a place called Aiya Roumeli where a Royal Navy destroyer would collect him and the rest of the royal party for withdrawal to Egypt. Alexandros reckoned they were twenty-four hours ahead of us, so there was no way we might seek escape on the same destroyer. We would have to find some other means of getting off Crete. I marvelled at how much Alexandros knew about what was happening. He and his *andartes* must have spies everywhere, I thought.

We finally took our leave of the priest and the shepherd and his lovely wife, who was crying as we set off. Our water bottles were full, we had food in our packs and we had our guides. Despite the blisters, we felt more positive than we had done the previous evening. And there were no sightings of Germans, except for occasional planes that zoomed overhead but who had no interest in our little band.

By now it was ferociously hot and, even though we kept our heads covered with the blankets the shepherd's wife insisted we take with us for protection, we could feel the sun pounding down on us as we walked along the dusty path. The track, for it was no more than a track, even though the priest had referred to it as a road, wound round hairpin bends and ever upwards. Alexandros, a rifle carried crosslike on his shoulders, marched ahead, with Nikos scampering along beside him. The heat didn't seem to bother them one bit. As the track got higher and we got closer to the last remaining snow on the mountaintops, however, it did get cooler though not any easier.

'I don't know if I'm going to make this,' puffed Eddie, as we took a particularly sharp climb. 'I'm cream crackered. Can't we stop, Skip?'

I caught up with Alexandros and indicated that Eddie was struggling.

'No stop,' said Alexandros. 'Germans.'

And he pointed to the heavens above where a Messerschmitt was sailing across the blue horizon.

'He's worried we'll be spotted,' I explained to Eddie. 'We're very exposed just here. You'll have to keep going. We'll maybe stop when we get over the top.'

'B------ hell! How far is that?' exploded Eddie.

'Don't know but look, you can see. It can't be that much further,' I answered, pointing upwards.

You know, sweetheart, that mountain tops are always much further than they look. This was no exception. The ridge fortunately was below the snowline but it was an amazing viewpoint, looking to the snow-covered heights of the *Lefka Ori* over to our left then forwards to the sea way below us. Eddie made it, though it was slow and hard work. At one point I had to carry his pack, otherwise I think we might have had to leave him. And there was no way we were going to be separated at this stage having come so far. The others helped too. Alec, the New Zealander we had collected in the gully the previous day, was especially helpful, going out of his way to encourage Eddie by telling him stories about his exploits in Cromwell, his hometown. Have got to like Alec – he's reliable, trustworthy, tough as old boots, and a really good companion. Even without the Tommy gun, he's the sort you'd want with you if you ever got into a scrape. Salt of the earth.

We said our goodbyes to Alexandros here, who stood on the ridge waving his rifle at us until we finally disappeared round yet another hairpin bend. A remarkable man. If the Germans are really on their way to winning in Crete, it will be men like Alexandros who will have to keep the flame of freedom alight. God only knows what their methods will be, but I guess they will be pretty brutal. Force will meet force. But we owe him a lot, not only for leading us over the ridge of the White Mountains but also for providing us with Nikos as our guide.

Alexandros's last words to me were:

'Nikos *pleeyo* with you.'

When I asked Nikos what *pleeyo* meant, he drew a picture in the dust of a boat. Alexandros wanted us to take Nikos with us.

I promised that I would do what he asked.

We stopped in a tiny village where there was a well. Nikos persuaded the villagers that we needed water and they reluctantly handed him the wooden bucket that drew the water up on a frayed rope from the bottom of the well. Never has water felt as deliciously cold as that. We drank and drank, till Nikos indicated that we must not deprive the villagers. We were all feeling better by now, even Eddie. Although we were tired and it was still very hot, at least we were descending now. The same pattern of deep ravines and gorges, the same hairpin bends on the red-dust track, the same sweet aroma of wild thyme, but now we were approaching greener valleys with vines and olive trees and the scent of wild flowers.

I had a long chat with Alec and Carl, the two NZ sergeants, while Eddie, Jack and Jim dozed a little in the shade of a plane tree. I told them that my understanding was that we needed to get to a village called Sphakia, where I knew there was a British military W/T station and a nearby Royal Navy unit with a frigate or a sloop of some kind stationed out at sea. These were the only British installations on the south coast of the island. I believed that, if we could get to Sphakia, I was confident we'd get a ship off Crete and on to Cairo.

'How far is this Sphakia from where this road ends, Skip?' asked Carl, chewing a stem of grass. 'Is that more walking?'

I said I didn't know how far but, from instructions we'd been given before we left the billet above Maleme, I believed we would be able to get a boat from Suya, a Greek fishing boat, with the money I'd been provided with. I knew that Nikos would be able to help with this. I pointed to the boy, who was whistling to himself and drawing patterns in the dust with a stick.

'Ya really going to take the sprog with us?' asked Carl again.

'Absolutely. We can't leave him on the island. If the Germans come across him and find he's been helping us, he's dead. Besides, I promised Alexandros. It's a matter of honour.'

'I think we might have trouble with your Royal Navy blokes,' said Alec philosophically. 'Can't see them wanting to be responsible for Greek kids, eh?'

'We'll see,' I said, though in truth I hadn't thought about this problem. 'Anyway, we've still got one hell of a journey to make before we an even think about that. So, are we ready?'

I got everyone up to their feet and set off again down the track, with Nikos leading us as usual and, just as usual, Eddie bringing up the rear, with Alec cajoling him.

The village of Aiyarini suddenly appeared below us. We could see it as the road wound down to it. Curious to see it from so far above and then to take so long to reach it. As we approached, we saw that all the old men of the village had come out to watch us. I scanned them just in case any of them had weapons but thankfully none did. So we walked openly towards them, expecting the same sort of welcome we had received in Dere the night before and that we had experienced in our time on the northern part of the island. But it was not the same. There was a sort of sullen resentment of our presence. It was not much of a village, just a few stone cottages loosely together. There was no *kafeneion* or other meeting place. We were not invited into any of the houses. We were not offered water or food. Telling them we were British didn't make any difference either. They just didn't like strangers, it seemed.

'Stone the b----- crows,' said Jack, as he sat down in front of the whitewashed church in the only patch of shade visible. 'What's up with these b-----? Don't they know we've been protecting them from the Hun?'

As if on cue, just at that moment a swarm of Messerschmitts flew across the mountains above us, heading for the action on the northern coast. Even that made no impression on these Cretan villagers of Aiyarini.

'B----- ungrateful sods,' added Eddie, whose mood has become increasingly bolshie as the journey continued.

'See it from their point of view, mate,' said Alec, always the calmer of Eddie's moodiness. 'Nobody asked us to come to their island. Nobody asked Jerry either. They probably just want to be left in peace, eh?'

Eventually, after much haggling and waving of 500 drachma notes, we got the villagers to agree to let us sleep in a ruined barn and to give us two scrawny chickens, some bread and red wine. Jim, who worked on his father's farm back home in New Zealand, wrung the chickens' necks and chucked away the bits we'd been given to eat the previous night in Dere. Alec and Jack meanwhile gathered firewood from the surrounding fields and we soon had a fire going, where we barbecued the chicken on sticks as we chewed on the stale bread and drank the red wine.

'Tomorrow the sea,' I said, lifting a glass of red wine to my mouth and pouring its contents down my throat, where its acidity burned in a strangely pleasing manner.

'The sea,' echoed Alec, raising his glass in salute. The others followed suit.

'And then what?' asked Jack.

'Then, with luck, it's a boat trip,' I replied. 'Chance to put our feet up and mend the blisters.'

'I'll b----- well drink to that,' said Jack. And we had another toast.

When the chicken was cooked, we ate it ravenously with our fingers and then drank more wine. As the fire died down and night fell, all began to get drowsy and soon everyone except me had crawled off to find a piece of hard ground to sleep on. I wondered whether it was all going to be as straightforward as I'd led them all to believe, as I got out my writing pad and kissed your photo in my wallet.

Oh Merry, I'm still finding it difficult to believe all this. It's like I'm in a nightmare. Three days ago everything seemed quite straightforward. We knew what we were supposed to do, we had a position to maintain and we were waiting for orders. Now everything is topsy-turvy. I'm just living in hope – hope that we'll get off the island, hope that we'll survive, and hope above all that I'll see you again.

Maybe tomorrow night we'll be on our way to safety at last.

All my love,

Bill

xx


### 23rd May

My Dearest Merry,

The day has not been as straightforward as I'd hoped, though we have reached the sea. At this moment it's my turn on watch by this cave in which the others are sleeping. Writing to you will keep me awake and help me think of your lovely face as I consider our predicament, for we are not yet saved. I still can't quite believe that only a few weeks ago we were together in Birmingham, you in my arms and me promising we'd get married next time I'm home on leave, and now all this! It's weird.

At dawn this morning Alec, Carl and I were up before the others, so we lit a small fire and boiled up what was left of the chicken carcases in water to make some broth to go with the bread we had saved for breakfast. Nikos heard us and came to help.

'Good walking,' he said. He's a bright boy and has already begun to pick up bits of English from accompanying us yesterday. He pointed at the pan we were boiling the broth in.

Carl offered him some soup but Nikos shook his head and moved his right arm in a sinuous manner.

'Snakes?' asked Alec. 'We have to look out for snakes, eh?'

He shook his head again.

'I think he's trying to tell us something about the route we're taking today,' I said, though I was only guessing too.

Nikos demonstrated his sinuous movement again, but this time he accompanied it with exaggerated steps, then returned to point at the pan again.

'*Farangi*,' he said. 'Good walking today.'

We were still puzzled but then Jack joined us, having been out behind the barn to relieve himself.

'Just seen where we're situated, Skip,' he announced. 'There's a b------ river bed in a gorge down in the valley. I bet it would take us to the sea.'

'*Farangi*,' nodded Nikos excitedly. 'Good walking today.'

Somehow or other I realised what he had been trying to tell us by pointing at the liquid in the pan and indicating the river's movement with his arm.

'I imagine the gorge you've seen is what Nikos is calling *farangi*,' I said. 'I think you're right, Jack. I guess the boy's taking us down to the gorge and that will lead us to the sea at Suya.'

'And then a blessed boat!' interjected Eddie, stretching himself as he joined us at the fireside. 'Roll out the barrel.'

We were glad to leave Aiyarini. There was still no response from the villagers as we packed up and prepared to leave the barn to resume our journey. Nikos went to thank the elders who had agreed to our stay there but, when he returned, he looked crestfallen too. Something strange about this place, as if it's been isolated too long.

We left down an avenue of lemon trees, which for some reason reminded me of the summer that war broke out when I worked in the hop-fields in northern Worcestershire. Did I ever tell you about it? We had so little time I probably didn't. There was an avenue of plane trees I always used to walk down to the hop-fields from the farm where I was staying, past fields of redcurrant, blackcurrant, and loganberries. There were loads of people there, most of them regulars who came from Birmingham or the Black Country every year with their families to pick the hops. We all stood around a crib of two crossed sticks at either end of a piece of sacking. The hops grew up strings supported by wires and you had to pull down the vine and then pick off the hops. From time to time the farmer would come on horseback to measure your hops with a round basket which held a bushel, and he scooped up as many bushels as were in the crib. Your card was then marked so that you could get paid for the amount of hops that you'd picked. Hop-picking was a really social event and different members of the family would be around the crib helping to pick the hops at all different times. The two eldest men from the farm that I was staying at worked in the kiln, drying the hops, and they invited me into the kiln one day. The top floor, where the men were, was covered in hops that they moved around with large wooden spades. They gave me a drink of cider out of a bottle that they had brought with them but the cider had been contaminated with the bitter taste of hops and was nothing like the sweet cider that we used to have at supper time.

Strange how that memory came flooding back to me as we walked down that avenue of trees. Maybe it was the unfriendly treatment we'd had at Aiyarini that made my mind want to think of something pleasanter. Maybe it was just the lemon trees and their aromatic blossom that reminded me of ripening fruit. Who knows? But it had certainly got me reminiscing.

It was good staying on the farm. Everyone bedded down in the outbuildings, though some families had long-standing arrangements to move into the cottages nearby. They were long days in the hop-fields but I enjoyed the physical exercise after all those years of study. Every evening on the farm we'd get the same supper – bread, cheese, as much milk as you could drink and one glass of cider, even though there were huge barrels of the stuff in the barn. Once the farmer's son had challenged me to help him milk the cows. I tried several times but I was never able to milk them using two hands. I could manage with one hand but I'd end up squirting milk at the farmer's son in the cow shed. After supper most of the men would head off down the road, through those plane trees again, to the nearby village of Knightwick, where there was a pub called The Talbot we used to frequent. We played dominoes there and shove ha'penny and darts and drank more cider, before staggering back to the farm and much-needed sleep.

From Aiyarini we walked non-stop for some distance, initially on the stony track but then, when it suddenly ended after descending into the valley, beside a riverbed. Nikos said this riverbed led to the sea. I sensed that everyone was much steadier now. They knew the end of the journey was ahead, or at least the end of the walking, we all hoped. Even I'd got blisters by now. Service-issue boots are not really designed for this kind of distance walking. They're all right for drilling maybe but for what we'd done, which I reckoned must have been the best part of thirty-five to forty miles so far, they just rubbed against all those most sensitive bits of your feet.

This was walking like hiking back home. No sense of danger at all. The Germans might as well be thousands of miles away for all we could hear or see of them today. This was a real gorge, with steep mountain slopes either side, so we walked in the shade for most of the morning. It was hard work, because there was no proper footpath, though I imagine that shepherds and their flocks used this route periodically. Once or twice we seemed to climb a little but then it was all on a gradual descent, thank God. Even those of us with bad blisters managed better today. We stopped frequently, for there were springs offering welcome ice-cool water. The first one was in the shade of some plane trees by some huge boulders that I reckon must have crashed down the mountainside many aeons ago. There were waterfalls up on those mountainsides too – white cascades, throwing their foamy liquid down the sheer drops.

Curious how vegetation grows in those barren mountainsides. Every now and again there was a cypress or a pine tree half way up the bare rock, its roots just clinging on for dear life to some tiny patch of earth. Then there were the wild flowers – I didn't recognise them but they look like the sort of rock plants we have in our garden at home, aubrietias, saxifrages, that sort of plant. And everywhere there was the wonderful smell of thyme. It was almost enough to make me forget about the war momentarily.

No one was talking much today, just tramping on, probably grateful to be in such a sheltered environment away from the hostilities and away from the mountain climbing and away from the oppressive sunshine.

About midday we stopped again at a spring. The gorge became quite narrow there and we had to wade through the shallow water. Our boots were not waterproof but so what at this stage? It was just good to have cool feet. We shared out the last of our food – bread and cheese from Aiyarini.

'How much farther d'ya think the sea is, Skip?' asked Carl, who was sitting on a rock opposite me.

'Hard to say. Nikos, *thalassa*?'

Nikos looked up from his bread and cheese.

'*Thalassa*, yes,' he nodded.

'How far?' I pressed. '*Ena, dio, tria*?'

'*Dio*,' he answered and returned to his repast.

'That's either two miles or two o'clock,' I translated, if you can call it that. 'Either way, we've just got to keep going till we get there.'

'So we can't be that far away,' said Eddie. 'Glory hallelujah! I never thought you'd get us there but you've done it. All credit to you, Skip.'

The others all muttered agreement.

I told them to thank Nikos, not me, and that we were not there yet. Whether it was two miles or two o'clock, we'd still got some walking to do. And then we had to find a caique and some Cretan willing to take us to Sphakia.

'That'll be no trouble to you, will it, Skip?' laughed Jack. 'With your command of the b----- language.'

'With my command of Nikos,' I laughed back at him. 'As long as we keep the boy happy, we've got a good chance. Without him, things might just be a bit more tricky.'

'Will they have some *raki* in Suya?' asked Eddie, licking his lips at the prospect.

'They'll have gallons of the stuff,' said Alec, 'and beer and roast beef dinners and treacle tarts.'

'You're forgetting the b----- Yorkshire puddings and the vegetables,' interjected Jack.

'And the brandy and cigars afterwards,' added Eddie.

'I say, shall we withdraw to the withdrawing room for our cigars, gentlemen?' mocked Jack in a mock posh accent, tinged with Lancashire. 'Look after the ladies, will you, Jeeves? My companions and I have some matters of great importance to discuss. Come along, chaps. To the withdrawing room, what!'

131

Everyone laughed. It was the first time we had felt relaxed enough to laugh for days. It was a sign that we were nearing the end of our trek. Or, at least, we hoped we were.

'Anyone for tennis?' asked Eddie, fastening up his belt that he'd removed while he ate.

'Afraid I have to be orf to the City,' said Jack in his la-di-dah voice. 'Come along, old bean.'

'Toodle-pip!' I added.

The New Zealanders thought we were crazy but they laughed along with us as we all set off down the gorge and towards the sea and, we hoped, salvation.

It was two o'clock that Nikos meant but no matter. We came from the rock-strewn riverbed eventually into the tiny village of Suya. Another little straggly community with a few cottages, presumably housing fishermen, for beyond the houses was this glorious wide bay with a long pebbly beach. We looked for a *kafeneion* but there was none, so we went down to the beach and found a cave in the rocks. The others sat down in there and rested, while Nikos and I went back to the village.

We were looking to find someone who would take us on their boat to Sphakia. I had made this plain to Nikos by pointing to the caiques nestling at anchor in the bay and telling him 'Sphakia'. But I think he knew anyway from what his Uncle Alexandros must have explained to him before he left us to rejoin his *andartes* in the *Lefka Ori*.

At the first cottage we came to, Nikos hammered on the old wooden door and eventually an elderly woman appeared, dressed in widow's black from head to toe, her face creased with age and sunshine, her teeth almost gone.

Nikos explained to her that we were a group of English soldiers needing to get off the island and that we needed a boat to take us to Sphakia. The old woman shook her head and went off into some long-winded response that I couldn't understand at all.

'What's she saying?' I asked Nikos.

'No boat,' he answered. 'Widow. *Andros* dead. No boat.'

'Surely she must know someone in Suya who has a boat,' I expostulated, though I was pretty sure neither Nikos nor the old lady could understand a word of what I was saying. 'Tell her we've got money to pay for the journey.'

I peeled several 500 drachma notes out of my wallet and waved them in front of her wizened face.

That seemed to do the trick. At least, it provoked some kind of response. She stepped over the threshold of the cottage, took Nikos's arm and pointed him towards another cottage about a hundred yards further down the coast.

'Kostas,' she screeched at the top of her thin voice. 'Kostas.'

When we got to Kostas's house, he was already waiting for us. Nikos explained to him what we needed, I waved the money again and we agreed a price of 2000 drachmas.

'Eksi,' he said, shaking my hand to seal the deal. And he pointed to his boat moored just out at sea in the Suya bay. 'Eksi.'

So it was to be six o'clock before we left. I guess he was wary of sailing in daylight with us, given the likelihood of German boats patrolling the waters. There was no point arguing with him, however desperate we were to get on our way. Besides we had no desire to be caught by German boats after the risky and wearisome journey we'd already undertaken. I got Nikos to buy some bread, eggs, cheese and wine from the fisherman and we took them back to the cave, where they were gratefully received by all concerned.

Six o'clock came and went and we were still in the cave, keeping out of the sun. We'd all been swimming in the late afternoon, glad to get out of our sweaty, flea-infested clothes for a short while. Then we'd lain down and slept. It was after seven thirty when the fisherman, Kostas, turned up with another man, named Yannis, and by the time we were all loaded on the boat it was almost dark. Probably safer that way. Kostas and Yannis rowed standing up, facing the way they were going, one oar each.

After an hour at sea, the wind changed direction and was driving head on at us. The waves were getting higher too and our little caique was tossing about in the stormy water. We were making little headway. It became frightening, as we sailed in and out of huge rocky outcrops that loomed overhead threatening to smash into us if we made a false move. Eventually, Kostas urged his companion to turn the boat into shore and they threaded their way through more rocks with incredible skill in the dark till we reached a huge slab of wet rock. Here we disembarked and Kostas led us over the rocks to a sandy cove with a big cave behind it. Through the usual gestures and with Nikos's help, we gathered that we were to stay the night here and resume our journey in the morning. So, wrapped up in the same blankets we were given in Dere days ago, we lay down in this cave to await better tidings in the morning. This has not been quite what we had expected.

Merry, I am weary of all this. I thought when I was given the radar training that I would be posted to a relatively safe place but this flight of ours across the mountains has been very scary and very exhausting. And we're not there yet. It's still stormy out at sea, so I don't know what the morning will bring. Sometimes I'm afraid we're not going to make it and I won't see you again. I can't bear thinking of that.

I love you so much and pray we will be together soon.

All my love,

Bill

xx

## 24th May

Dearest Merry,

I can't tell the others but I'm beginning to think we may not get out of this. I have to confide in you, even though you are thousands of miles away and even though you may never read these letters, because you are my only hope. You are the person I feel closest to in the whole world. I sometimes think in my wildest moments that you are beside me as I am thinking these thoughts, comforting me, encouraging me, giving me strength.

It's been a worse day than we'd dared imagine. Jim woke us up early. We'd taken turns on lookout duty on a higher rock above our cave and Jim had taken the last turn of the night. I went back to the wet slab of rock where the fishermen had dropped us off to look for them and their boat. What a shock! No sign of them at all. I got back to the others and explained the situation.

Carl asked if I was sure they had said they'd meet us back at that rock and I told him that as far as I could understand, that was right, but, as they didn't speak any English at all, it was difficult. Eddie wanted to know if Nikos knew more so I tried to explain our dilemma to the boy and he nodded agreement when I pointed behind me to the wet rock.

'So what do we do now?' asked Jack. 'Go looking for it? Catch a b----- London bus or something? We're right up the creek without a b------ paddle, aren't we, boys?'

I looked above where we were standing to the spur of rock where the lookouts had sat watching and beyond to the sheer face of the cliff. It looked daunting but there were cracks and fissures in it, so I thought we could probably climb up higher and maybe we'd come across a mule track or something. It was a forlorn hope, I know, but, when I looked the other way back at the sea, it was still horrendously stormy with great, white-topped breakers roaring towards the coast and breaking up on the black rocks to get within feet of where we stood.

I explained that Nikos had told me in Suya that there wasn't a road along this coast and to walk to Sphakia would take us a good twelve hours. I didn't see we had any alternative but to try walking. The boat and the fishermen were gone and the sea was no better now than it was last night.

'I guess, if we've got this far on our feet, we can do the last bit, can't we?' said Alec.

'Not more b----- walking!' said Eddie.

'Ya have a better idea?' asked Carl, looking sharply at him. 'Ya want to sit here and die? Is that what ya want? Come on, rattle your dags."

Eddie mumbled something but got to his feet anyway.

And so we set off, scrambling up the rock face, Carl in the lead with Alec and I bringing up the rear in order to push Eddie along when he got into difficulties. After about an hour we came to a sort of shelf that seemed to be heading in the direction we wanted. And there below us was the caique. It had anchored in a more sheltered spot where we couldn't see it.

'Are we going back down?' asked Jack.

'Too likely, buster,' answered Eddie. 'I've had enough of this already.'

'Hang on there,' said Alec, grabbing Eddie's arm to stop him heading straight back down the cliff face. 'Just look at the sea, will you? You really think anything's going to sail on that today, eh?'

We all looked down at the thunderous sea, roaring into the rocks. Carl didn't think that Kostas would want to move till darkness anyway, because he knew there were German ships out there and he wouldn't want to get picked up. Basically we could stay there all day, with no food or water, and hope the sea calmed down a bit by tonight or we could try walking to Sphakia and looking for some food and water on the way.

'Yeah, we're sure to find a spring somewhere, aren't we? Remember those natural springs in the gorge?' said Jim, who I was glad to have on my side. 'Come on, boys. We can crack this.'

We had a vote and it was agreed. Only Eddie dissented.

A little later we found a small spring by cypress trees with very little water coming out but enough to refresh us briefly. It was the first food or drink since the previous evening. How long can humans survive without? I wasn't sure about this. There was very little biology taught at King Edward's, so I decided to ask Alec. I set off at the back again with him, as I didn't want to get the others, especially Eddie, worried.

'The survival rule of thumb,' he answered, 'is three days without water and three weeks without food.'

'Really?'

'Yeah, a person can live without food for quite some time, usually for many weeks. The body will use its fat to help it survive. If a person has a lot of fat, I mean if he is very heavy, he'll live longer than a person who has very little fat. So how long a person can survive depends a lot on the person. Of course, if you go without food for a few weeks, you'll be very weak since you have been using your own muscles for energy,' Alec explained.

'So Eddie's got a better chance than the rest of us?'

'Theoretically, yeah. But you have to get your head round it all first, if you know what I mean. '

I nodded. We were several yards behind Eddie, walking along a flatter section briefly.

'Water is a different story,' continued Alec. 'A person will die within three to four days without water. The size of the person really doesn't make much difference.'

I needed to know.

The choice to walk may have been the wrong one. We had been moving for the best part of six hours and hardly seemed to have covered any ground. No more water was found and no food of any sort on these inhospitable cliffs. The only vegetation was dry pine trees clinging fiercely to the rocks that dropped sheer down to the sea. Every ridge we climbed took us plunging back down the other side to the base of another ridge. The only good thing was that the weather was grim – overcast grey skies threatening but not bringing rain. If only! At least there was no hot sun beating down on us, as it was when we crossed the White Mountains.

We rested by another group of cypress trees. Everyone looking exhausted. I was aware that we were living on hope and trusting in luck now. Surely there had to be a way of getting to Sphakia from where we were. Sea still thunderous.

I tried to think of a strategy. Already it was clear that Eddie was floundering. He was just too bulky for this sort of cliff walking, the constant ascent then descent, and he was moaning all the time. Alec was really good with him but I wondered if Alec might be better if I sent him on ahead to recce the route and alert us to dangers. He was clearly the fittest of us. He told me he was a keen rugby man back home and hoped to be an All Black before the war. Nikos moved like he'd lived in the mountains all his life, which I guess he had, though he didn't know this part of the island at all. Carl and Jim were okay so far. They said they were used to walking distances. They were both from farming backgrounds. Jack was doing fine too, though he looked very dry-mouthed. It seemed that some of us could summon up spittle easier than others.

Should I have sent Alec on ahead? Should we have split up and tried different routes? I couldn't believe that was wise. Sticking together had got to make more sense, hadn't it? What if I had sent Alec on ahead to try any way he wanted and look for water? Say I had given him two hours to get back to us. But then, would we really have stayed there for that time? No, that way madness lay. I'd get him to scout ahead with Nikos for the best route but no more. At this stage anyway.

It was early evening when I decided to call it a day. We were on a cliff face with some tall bushes for shelter and I didn't feel as if we'd made much progress. Everyone was complaining about the lack of food and water now but I could do nothing. I hoped it might rain – the skies were still very overcast so it was possible, maybe likely. It was much cooler by then too. Good job we kept those blankets the shepherd's wife in Dere gave us.

After I sent Alec and Nikos on ahead, I was left bringing up the rear with Eddie, moaning Eddie, complaining Eddie. I can't believe how some people are so self-absorbed. We were all exhausted, fed up, starving and thirsty but, while everyone else got on with it, Eddie preferred to grouch. I could have pushed him off the cliff at one point, just after we'd climbed yet another ridge and seen the sharp descent on the other side and he heaved himself over the top, flounced down on to the ground and said he wasn't going an inch further. How I managed to restrain myself I don't know.

I had agreed with Alec that we would keep to the same line along the cliffs, always with the sea in view, while he and Nikos tried some alternative routes, mostly by climbing higher to hunt for a better route – a donkey path, somewhere shepherds had walked, anything that might promise a more obvious journey for us. They had been right in Suya to warn us against trying to reach Sphakia on foot, we knew that now, but surely, at some point in history, some humans must have found cause to walk this way?

But Alec and Nikos had no joy. They must have climbed a good 500 feet higher than us – I could see them at one stage ahead of us and clambering strongly up what looked a sheer cliff face – but to no avail. There was nothing, Alec told us on their return. No respite. No chance. No easy salvation.

So we decided to head down to the sea-shore again to see if there was a way there of proceeding. Down we went, slithering on the dry pine needles, then squeezing between jagged rocks, on hands and knees one moment, on our backsides the next, till eventually we landed with a thud on sand. As we looked inland, we could see that this was the mouth of a stream, sadly dried up at this time of year. Carl and Jim traced its route back through the rocks but there was no water. The only water was the sea.

'Maybe we could distil the seawater,' suggested Jim, I thought half-jokingly.

'Don't be so b----- soft,' said Jack. 'How're you going to do that? And anyway, we'd be better off keeping on the move.'

Jim shrugged.

'I've heard of it being done,' he said. 'Still….'

The idea was shelved.

The inlet we'd reached offered no alternative route anyway. There were great hulking rocks to the east – the direction we needed to travel. I tried a few tentative steps but there was no way round them, except into the crashing waves. So back uphill we went, with Eddie grumbling again and everyone fed up. And we just kept on going until dusk began to fall and we decided there was no point travelling over this terrain in the darkness and we needed to rest. The last food we had was just over twenty-four hours ago back in Suya. The last water we had was at nine this morning. We were suffering.

Rain! Suddenly at last some relief. We all turned our helmets upside down to capture as much of the precious liquid as we could. And we held our hands out and licked the moisture from them and we pegged out handkerchiefs, bits of our shirts, anything we had, to catch that nectar from heaven. The rain in the helmets tasted rubbery. It was hard to extract drinking water from the wet pieces of cloth. And the rainstorm didn't last long. We went hunting for stray puddles on flat pieces of rock or gathered on the leaves of the bushes that sheltered us. It was not much but it was bliss. It eased our parched mouths and it brought back some hope that the gods were still with us.

Gradually, everyone drifted off into an uncomfortable sleep. I've opted for first watch tonight, so I can write to you about today. As I watch them, I can see Nikos's slim young body folded like a baby, Jack flat on his back with his head propped up on his arms, Carl likewise on his back with his head turned to one side, Jim curled foetally in a tight ball, Eddie flat on his back with his belt loosened and snoring.

'Penny for them, Skip.'

I looked up. Alec had been to relieve himself behind the rocks.

'Don't know what I've still got to p--- out,' he continued. 'Doubt if I took more than a few drops from that rain. You okay?'

He sat down next to me and we gazed into the darkness together.

'Concerned,' I said. 'They all expect me to come up with some magic answers, just because I had the fortune, or rather the misfortune, to be made an officer.'

'We're trained to obey,' Alec laughed. 'Basic training in the army – obey your superior officers.'

'But I'm not in the army, I'm in the RAF,' I protested. 'Besides, you guys know as much about life as me, probably a hell of a lot more. So why d'you all expect me to come up with solutions?'

'I guess it's because we've been brainwashed into believing in the superiority of the British upper class,' said Alec, chuckling again. 'Remember, you lot created the Empire. We're in awe of you really.'

'Don't be daft,' I laughed with him. 'I'm being serious, Alec. If we're going to get out of this mess, we're going to have to pool all our thinking caps and make the most sensible choices. Maybe we didn't today. Maybe we should have gone back to the boat and waited with Kostas and Yannis.'

'And then what, eh? D'you really think they'd have wanted to sail in this weather tonight?'

'But at least they could have taken us back to Suya until the weather improved. At least there was food and water there.'

'And do we know where the Germans are right now, eh? Remember, when we left the north of the island, Maleme had fallen. So the Germans had a bridgehead and they could bring in as many of their troops as they wanted. What would be the point of that parachute landing just to gain control of an airfield? Believe me, Maleme was just the start. It wouldn't surprise me if the Germans hadn't overrun the entire island of Crete by now.'

Alec was right. The lack of food and water was making my thinking awry.

'Anyway I'll leave you to your thoughts,' he said. 'I'm off for some kip. I'll relieve you in a couple of hours.'

Stocktaking time. Six men and a boy. No water. No food. Little progress. What will happen?

I've been thinking about home and you, Merry, my love. I miss you terribly. I'm glad I have this photo of you in my wallet – it keeps me going. What would you be doing now? Who knows? I don't know if the German bombers are still blitzing England.

I don't know if you're safe and well. I don't know anything. It feels like we've been out of touch with everything forever, even though it's really only a few days. I remember dancing with you, holding your warm fragrant body next to mine as we twirled around the front room of your house, listening to Glenn Miller's band. The feel of your bosom on my chest, the scent of your golden hair against my face, the pucker of your lovely lips when you laughed. And when …. Oh my, it is too much!

All my love,
Bill
xx

## 25th May

Dearest Merry,

I'm writing this to stop myself crying. You'll probably never read it because I really don't think we're going to make it now, though I'm having to pretend to the others that we will. I wish they didn't look up to me so much. I wish they didn't all expect me to be able to magic them out of this awful situation. I wish, I wish, I wish I was home with you, away from all this war. But let me tell you about the day before starvation drives all memory of it from my brain

We were up early again. There had been another light shower in the night, not enough to wake those sleeping but enough to give hope of finding water in the tin hats and on leaves or stones. Jack and Carl led the hunt, with Nikos excitedly pointing out possible sites, usually to be disappointed. Still, we all managed a few drops. Hunger pains were beginning to gnaw at my stomach and I guessed the others would be feeling the same.

We had a confab about the route. There was general agreement that we should descend again down the ravine from the bushes we had slept under to the wide valley below and decide again when we got there. Carl and Jack led off this time, closely followed by Nikos, Alec and Jim, with Eddie, muttering still, and me at the rear.

It was downhill all the way but not straightforward. There were some rocky faces to negotiate, though usually with bits of shrubs or trees to grab hold of or brace your feet against. The bigger danger was falling rocks, dislodged by one of us as we descended.

Eddie seemed to be causing more of these than anyone, so I slowed the pace at the back. That way the others in front of us wouldn't get assaulted from behind by flying rocks.

'Skip,' said Eddie, breathing heavily, as I helped him down an especially difficult bit, 'I'm not going to make this place you keep on about, Sphakia. You're going to have to leave me.'

'Nonsense, Eddie,' I said. 'No one's leaving anybody. I don't care how long it takes but we're all going to get to Sphakia. Come on, man. You can do it. We'll just go at our own pace. No need to race. The others won't get that far ahead.'

We caught up with the others, cowering under a huge pine tree because Messerchmitts were flying overhead. But they weren't interested in us, even if they had seen us. They were still flying in great swathes towards the northern coast and Maleme. I guessed that the invasion would be well under way by now. Had there been any attempt by the Allied troops to recapture the airfield? Or had the Germans got to Canea yet? It was curious to be pondering this, even to be reminded of it, in our present perilous position.

We went down into the valley at last, all looking for water, digging under plants and roots of trees, searching in nooks and crevices for any water residue, but still nothing. I had to stop a few times because of Eddie but I'd told the others to keep going and not to wait for us. Nikos came back at one point to walk with us. He's a good boy, thoughtful beyond his years. At one point he dashed into a small cave in the cliff face.

'*Nairo*,' he shouted animatedly.

We followed him into the cave, which wasn't very deep. What Nikos had found was an ice-cold, white stalactite, dripping oh so slowly. I pushed Eddie underneath it and held his head still so he could catch each precious drop. He must have sat like that for more than five minutes and all he got was a few drops. Nikos and I took shorter turns. It was something but it wasn't enough. I wondered if the others had found it too.

We couldn't see them when we came out of the small cave, so we shouted, but all we got was the echo of our voices bouncing back from the rocks. We pressed on as fast as we could, urging Eddie onwards now, as we didn't want to get permanently separated from the others. The sun was up now and blisteringly hotter than the last two days. The others had kept walking down the valley towards the sea and then, as the valley swung uphill, they had followed its line till they reached another group of pines, where they had stopped.

'You're going too quick for us,' I said when we reached them. 'Eddie's not up to all this. You know that. We ought to try to preserve energy in this heat. The quicker we walk, the more we sweat; the more we sweat, the more we burn up our energy reserves.'

I didn't really know what I was talking about but it sounded convincing. I was beginning to get worried that the group was breaking up and I didn't want that to happen. I thought we'd be better sticking together.

Alec apologised but explained he thought he had seen something white-looking a while back, a building of some sort, he thought. Even Eddie showed some enthusiasm now, as we followed Alec uphill.

There was a building – some kind of chapel, whitewashed on the outside and with curious-looking mounds on its roof. But it was empty, deserted. There was no sign of life and probably hadn't been for many years from the look and smell of it. Worse, there was no water. The view out to sea and back inland to the White Mountains was stunning but we would have swapped the view for some water.

Again, by the time we got there Eddie, Nikos and I had got separated from the others by quite a distance. I was getting concerned about this.

'Why didn't you wait?' I began. 'We decided to stick together, didn't we?'

But they had been discussing alternatives.

'Skip, we think that the best bet is for me and Alec to go up over that ridge,' announced Carl, as the three of us sat down next to them. 'Don't think we can all get up that high and maybe there's better possibilities lower down, so Jack, Jim, Eddie, Nikos and yourself ought to head down to the beach and try there.'

'Is this the most sensible idea?' I asked. 'Splitting up? Aren't we better if we stick together?'

'Think about it,' said Alec. 'All we get from sticking together is going more slowly. We have no food and no water. Effectively, we've had nothing to drink for a day and a half. That means we each can last another day and a half. Carl and I are clearly the strongest of us, so, if we press on over that ridge and whatever's beyond it, we have twenty-four hours to find water and send someone stronger back to find you.'

I asked how anyone would find us. Carl said that, when we got down to the beach, we needed to look for some shelter and then find somewhere to build a fire and collect as much wood as we could. Then, as soon as night fell we needed to keep a fire going as long as we possible. If they could reach Sphakia or anywhere else for that matter, they'd get someone in a boat to come looking for us. The local fishermen would know all the coves on the coast. They'd be bound to find us.

'Yeah, dead probably,' muttered Eddie.

'Not if we distil seawater,' interjected Jim, who had been quiet up till now. 'Jack and I have been talking about how we might do it and we think there's a real possibility.'

'So, even if we can't find a way around the shoreline,' added Jack, sounding remarkably chipper now, 'we're pretty sure we can keep alive till the bloody cavalry get here.'

I looked at Eddie, collapsed on the ground, his belt unfastened, his face bright purple from his exertions, his eyes closed. What they said made some kind of sense. Reluctant as I was to split the party up, it was true that Carl and Alec were by far the strongest of all of us. If anyone was going to get to Sphakia over these treacherous and demanding cliffs, it was them. True, I could have kept up with them and Nikos probably could have too, but none of us could think of leaving Eddie.

It seemed a crazy idea to go down to that sandy cove and wait for the unlikely arrival of help. But we were all a little crazy by now from dehydration.

'You should leave me,' offered Eddie again. 'All of you press on. Forget about me. It's okay.'

'Sorry, old mate,' said Jack. 'No can do. Churchill's orders. Every man must be saved. We're going down to that lovely beach down there, Eddie, and we're going to find a nice cosy cave for you to rest in. Then Jim and me are going to get a little fire going and, with a little help from our friends here, we're going to get ourselves some drinking water and build our strength up again. So, even if the bleeding Kiwi cavalry doesn't re-appear, we'll have had twenty-four hours more rest and be fit to go exploring again tomorrow. What d'you say, old pal?'

A wan smile crinkled Eddie's lips. I had to smile too. Jack's dry Lancashire humour did help at times.

So, it was agreed. Carl and Alec would climb up on to the ridge above us and look to continue in the direction of Sphakia, while we sought a base in the cove below to rest in, to light a fire at night in, and to try to distil seawater in.

The descent to the beach was slow with Eddie slipping and sliding all the time but finally we got there. Jack and Jim had gone ahead and, sure enough, there was a suitable cave, inland from the waterline and previously used, as the goat droppings and the remains of old fires showed us. Fishermen? Pirates? Other unfortunates like us, lost in the rocks? I hoped it was the former, for, if Alec and Carl did reach Sphakia and found fishermen to sail around the coast looking for us, this place might be known.

While Jim, Nikos and Jack collected firewood and planned their seawater-distilling experiments, I went to explore the coastline, still in a delusional state about finding a way out of this scrape. Foolish. Dehydration and hunger pangs were affecting my brain. But hope springs eternal etc. So, I clambered around the first headland beyond the cave and could see another cove some few hundred yards further on in the right direction. I tried to reach it by scrambling on hands and knees over wet rocks but got caught by a huge bow-wave and found myself knocked breathless, so I gave up that attempt.

As I crabbed my way back over the wet rocks, I got to thinking about our predicament and the choices we had made. Almost certainly we should never have left Kostas and Yannis and their caique. However long it would have taken us to get to Sphakia with them, at least we would have got there. Who knew what Royal Navy presence there was there anyway now? Who knew whether the Germans now had complete command of the island? Who knew if the rest of the Allied troops hadn't been evacuated by now? But, at least we would have been alive. At least we would have had food and, more crucially, water. Even if the Germans had reached Sphakia.

And the choice we made today to let Carl and Alec go seeking help while we waited here on this beach, what was that? Crazy. There's precious little chance of us getting rescued. I don't believe that they'll distil seawater successfully. I doubt if Carl and Alec will reach Sphakia. And, even if they do, how likely is it really that any rescue boat they might be able to commandeer might find us on this remote beach? Not very.

And why are we here? Why haven't we all gone on in hope with Alec and Carl? Because of Eddie basically. Because none of us could take the responsibility of leaving him in order to try to save our own lives. Where does all this unselfishness come from? Are we all really so altruistic that we're prepared to allow ourselves to die in this isolated spot rather than leave one of our number to die alone? Are we cowards or stupid optimists?

'Think we're getting somewhere, Skip,' said Jim excitedly from the mouth of the cave where a small fire glowed strongly. Above it they had constructed a sort of range with thick wooden branches, from which hung a tin helmet, minus its rubber casing, filled with boiling water – seawater, of course.

'Yes, I can see the boiling water but how do you purify it?'

'Well, it's the boiling that takes the salt out,' explained Jim. 'The steam is pure water.'

'But we have to find a way of cooling that b------ steam down,' said Jack. 'That's the next problem.'

I moved past them into the cave. Eddie was flat out, eyes closed, lost to the world. Exhaustion was too much for him. It was clear there was no way that he would be able to walk again, unless we got a proper supply of fresh water and maybe something to eat. Nikos was nowhere to be seen.

'Where's Nikos?' I asked the others.

'Gone foraging for wood,' explained Jim. 'There's plenty up the valley. Loads of dead trees. Maybe he'll find some berries or roots or something.'

I looked at him wryly. More crazy optimism, I thought.

I sat watching them for a while and felt a bit more solid, as they tried various ways of capturing the steam from the boiled seawater in another tin hat, only to find that the steam, when it did cool, didn't produce anything like an amount of water that could be drunk. All they got was a damp patina on the inside of the helmet which tasted of tin and didn't quench the thirst by any manner or means.

I could see these two in civvy street, working in one of our great Birmingham engineering works, coming up with novel ideas for the development of engines. They're natural scientists, curious, experimental, unwavering in their optimism. They didn't need the sort of expensive education that I'd had to prepare them for this. They just applied their knowledge of the world to the current situation and speculated on possible solutions to our predicament. But, so far, they've had no success. And I doubt whether they will. It all seems most unlikely. But it gives them hope. It gives us all hope.

I went out on to the sand, lay down as the sun was heading down on the horizon and thought of you again, my love. I took your photo out of my wallet and stared at it for a long time. I'm never going to see you again. Ever. I feel sure of that. Never going to feel your warmth against me. Never going to kiss those lovely lips. Never going to marry you and give you children. Never going to be a husband. Or a father.

Found myself crying. Couldn't stop. Mustn't let the others see.

All my love,
Bill
Xxx

### 26th May

Dearest Darling Merry,

I can almost feel you with me. Would you believe it? We've survived! We've been rescued! We are on our way to safety! We will get married after all. I just know it now. Something has been looking after us all the time. We've been tested and we've come through. I love you so so so so much.

Strange voices woke me this morning and I looked up to see two new figures flitting in and out of the cave entrance, huge figures they seemed from where I lay, black-bearded men in traditional Cretan costume. I sat up to speak.

'Water?' I croaked.

One of the Cretans turned into the cave and leant over me.

'Water,' he said with a bearded grin. '*Poli* water. *Poli* water.'

He handed me a grey goatskin and I grabbed it, forcing it to my parched lips.

'*Ligo*,' the Cretan said, taking the goatskin from me before I'd had chance to drink much. '*Ligo*.'

By now the others had woken too and were all being given water, a little at a time, to drink from the two goatskins that our rescuers had with them. Jack was on his haunches, head thrown back in exultation as the cool water trickled down his throat. Jim was licking his newly moist lips as he passed the goatskin on to Eddie, still lying on the ground but grasping at it. I suddenly realised that one of the two men was none other than Alexandros, Eleni's brother, the *andarte* captain. He came over to me, with a grinning Nikos clasped in his hand.

'Boy good,' he said. 'Boy good. *Efharisto poli*.'

I didn't know why he was thanking me. It was my stupid fault that we'd attempted this journey over the cliffs in the first place, instead of going back to Kostas and his boat and awaiting favourable conditions. I'd risked the boy's life when I'd been given responsibility for getting him off Crete and to safety.

Then I saw Alec, grinning over Alexandros's shoulder. I hadn't noticed him at first.

'Don't take too much water just yet,' Alec explained. 'Andreas is right. Your stomach won't cope and you'll get violently ill. Just a bit at a time until your belly gets attuned again. We've got some food as well.'

By now we were all sitting round the fire that Alexandros and Andreas had rebuilt in the mouth of the cave. Even Eddie had sat up. I noticed Nikos darting off to fetch wood for this fire. Odd how quickly youngsters recover, I thought. I was still feeling distinctly queasy myself but hugely relieved.

Alec opened up his bag and took out dry bread and feta cheese, which we managed to nibble at as we sipped water from the goatskins. As we ate and drank and slowly recovered some of our strength, Alec told us what had happened.

When Carl and he had left us, they had headed straight over that high crest as they had said but it was just as bad on the other side. There were more sudden drops and more sudden climbs. But they had kept going. They knew there was no way that anyone, including us, was going to get out of this alive unless they found food and water. So they had struggled on, stopping to catch their breath from time to time, but always hoping that one of the peaks they surmounted would reveal a village. They had almost given up their hopes when they suddenly stopped climbing and found themselves walking through more level territory, through a forest in fact. But then, there was still no sight of habitations. No shepherd's hut. No sign of sheep or goats. Nothing. Then suddenly they had come out of the woods and there below them was a sandy bay with a fishing village and streams running down between the houses to the sea.

'Aiya Roumeli,' said Alexandros, who had obviously been taking in some of Alec's description.

'That's what it's called,' explained Alec. 'Not Sphakia. We're still miles from there.'

They had managed to stumble down to the village and got food and water. Then by some miracle, who should appear but our friend here, Alexandros? Were they glad to see him. Seems he'd come to the village to get food for his men up in the mountains. The Germans were all over the northern side of Crete now, he had explained, so he had to come south to get support for his *andartes*. They had urged him to come with them to look for us and, when Alec told him that Nikos was with us, he was ready to move straightaway. Carl had suggested taking a boat but Andreas had said it was all but impossible to sail around the coves hereabouts. Seemed the water was very treacherous. Even the local fishermen were very wary of fishing in these waters too close to the cliffs.

'So how did you find us again?' asked Eddie, newly revived by the food and water and seemingly intent on staying alive after all.

'Didn't you hear the gunshot?' asked Jim. 'Thought you must have done.'

'What gunshot?' I asked. I'd heard nothing, so exhausted had I been.

'I took over from Jack on watch at two in the morning and about an hour later I heard a gunshot,' Jim explained. 'I was up on the rocks above the cave. So I fired my gun.'

'That was what told us where you were,' said Alec. 'We were way up above you. I only had a vague recall of the route we had taken to get to Aiya Roumeli but Alexandros and Andreas know these rocks well and, when they heard Jim's gunshot, they knew exactly where you'd be. It still took us two hours to reach you but here we are. The cavalry.'

I hugged him. I hugged Alexandros. I hugged Andreas. I was almost in tears, for I knew that, if they hadn't got to us, we were likely to have died. I wasn't sure if the others had realised that but I was fairly confident that would have been the outcome. The cave we had sheltered in might well have been littered with more bones in time – our bones.

'Gun,' said Alexandros, pointing at Jim's and my holsters.

'Oh, forgot to tell you,' said Alec, smiling wryly. 'That was part of the deal. These guys need more weapons to fight the Germans in the hills. I sort of promised them your guns if we managed to find you.'

'But we'll need them ourselves, won't we?' said Jim, clearly reluctant to part with his weapon. 'We're not home and dry yet. What if we meet up with any Germans?'

I took my pistol out of its holster and passed it over to Alexandros.

I hadn't used this yet. And I didn't think I'd be using it in future. If they hadn't come to our rescue, who knows what would have become of us? If the price of salvation was a couple of guns, it seemed little enough. Their need was greater than mine. With luck, we'd be off Crete in a day or two. Alexandros, Andreas and the rest of his *andartes* had to stay.

'You can have mine too,' said Eddie, slipping the holster and gun off his belt.

'Okay,' said Alec. 'Two guns are what I promised them. That's enough. Jim can keep his. And you, Jack. We've still got enough weapons between us.'

'What happened to Carl?' Jack asked.

Alec had left him in Aiya Roumeli to find out about how we could get off the island. There were a whole bunch of other Allied soldiers there, come down another gorge called Samaria. It seemed there'd been chaos in the north as the Germans advanced. Whole battalions had split up, with no command and no clear fallback position. So some of them had just headed over the hills and ended up in Aiya Roumeli. He hadn't had time to find out what to do next, whether the Royal Navy was close by or what, so he'd left that to Carl to find out. Finding us had been the priority.

He produced a packet of Greek cigarettes and handed them round. Never has tobacco tasted so good. It was several days since our supply had run out.

I must have dropped off after the food and water, from relief coupled with exhaustion, because the next I knew it was mid-morning. Somebody had covered me with a blanket. I noticed that Eddie, Jack and Jim had also been sleeping, though not Nikos apparently. He was sitting in the mouth of the cave, chattering away to his Uncle Alexandros and Andreas, with Alec chipping in occasionally with the bits of Greek he had picked up in their company.

'What's the plan?' I asked, crawling along the sand towards them and the white remains of the fire. 'When are we moving off?'

'As soon as you're ready,' said Alec. 'You did what I did as soon as I'd eaten – fell asleep. That's why we didn't set off earlier. I guess it's the body's way of managing. Anyway, is everyone fit now, eh?'

I looked at Jack and Jim, sipping again from the goatskins, and Eddie, looking bloated and bewildered but definitely alive.

'Can you make it, Eddie? If we take our time, Alec reckons it's a few more hours but at least we know there is a village at the end of it.'

'You bet, Skip. Don't worry about me. I'm feeling chipper now. I may not be the strongest person here but, now I know that we're near to civilization again, I'm going to get there. Lead on, MacDuff.'

I helped him up and we got ourselves ready for the trek. Sun high in the sky now. It was going to be hot and there wasn't a lot of water left in the goatskins. Alec told us to go easy on it as we still had a journey to go which involved climbing.

Mid-afternoon we finally got here to Aiya Roumeli. What a joy to find Carl, to get more food and drink, to feel safe again.

The journey from the cove was not easy. We had to climb up the pathless cliff to start with, following Alexandros who seemed to know every rock and every tree, so sure was his progress up ahead of us. We struggled in his wake, Andreas bringing up the rear and supporting Eddie when necessary. We weren't in the best physical shape, any of us after what we'd been through but we managed to keep going. I don't know how Alec managed it – this was the fourth time he'd done this journey. He's super-strong. We were lucky to have him with us. If we get back to Egypt, I'll recommend him and Carl for medals or something although I don't know how you do that, especially since they're New Zealanders and not under my command in any sense.

We stopped frequently to take water and rest. I realised what Alec had meant about being careful with the water supply. It was all too easy to want to take long draughts of the precious stuff but that wasn't a good idea. We all appreciated that. So sips only. Eddie was keeping going okay, with much puffing and panting, but not complaining like before. Jack was even telling jokes again, when we stopped to rest.

There seemed to be lots of ascents and descents, just as I remembered from the start of our trek, then eventually the ground levelled out and we were walking in the shade of the forest that Alec had mentioned. It was a bit cooler in the trees with the sunlight filtering thinly through the branches. Then at last, we reached the edge of the wood and there below was the village of Aiya Roumeli with the streams running through it, just as Alec had described it.

Alexandros guided us to the centre of the village where Carl was sitting at a *kafeneion* with some Australian and New Zealand soldiers. I recognised some of them from the platoon that had been supporting us near Maleme and wondered what route they had taken. They didn't look as haggard or drawn as us, so must have found an easier way. Carl greeted us warmly and ordered food – eggs, bread, honey, wine. I asked him to get more water first, which he did, as I was still very dry at this point.

'The Aussies say it's all up in the north,' said Carl, helping himself to a glass of wine. 'They've been on the move for the past thirty-six hours. Got split up from their commander and just headed for the hills. But they say the German advance has got as far as Canea and they're still landing more and more troops on to Maleme airfield.'

'What route did they take?' asked Jack.

'Samarian gorge,' one of the Aussies replied. 'One of our boys has a Cretan father. Knew a bit about the island from his old man. Told us about this gorge where the Cretan bandits had always hidden whenever the island got invaded. Luckily he spoke a bit of Greek too, so we got pointed in the right direction.'

'Was it hard going?' asked Jim.

'Sharp climbing, sure,' was the answer from another of the group. 'Lots of hairpin bends to get to the top then this amazing plain. He called it Omalos. It's just fantastic. You climb these great mountains and there at the very top is this long flat plain with goats being herded on it. Amazing. Then we came down into the gorge and it was a piece of p-- after that.'

'Lucky so-and-sos,' muttered Eddie.

I was anxious about how we were to get off Crete, given what the Australians and New Zealanders here were saying. I'd understood that there was a military W/T station at Sphakia and a Royal Navy presence out at sea.

'What's the prospects? Any chance of the Royal Navy getting to us here?'

'Apparently the Navy took the Greek king from here a couple of days ago,' said Carl. 'The guy in that cottage over there showed me some coins that he'd been given by one of the royal party, after they'd commandeered his fishing boat to go looking for the Navy destroyer.'

'So it's possible we might get rescued from here?'

'Not what they're all saying. Try asking yourself.'

So I contacted the Sphakia base via the local police telephone. I was warned that the line connected to the north coast, so it was probably in German hands by now but I wasn't worried. We had to chance it after what we'd gone through. I arranged for a message to HQ RAF Crete telling of our whereabouts and asking for transport from Aiya Roumeli or Sphakia and got transferred to a captain in charge of a Naval Unit, who promised to send a boat at nightfall.

We seemed to wait forever. There was a party of about thirty of us now, as more stragglers had appeared from over the hills.

Same story. Germans advancing, Allied troops in disarray. No proper command. Flight the only option. Finally, we saw a boat coming to anchor a little way offshore. A rowing boat brought the Royal Navy captain to the rudimentary jetty where we waited and told us that it had been too risky to use a Navy vessel because of the German planes overhead, so he'd commandeered a medium-sized Greek caique, big enough to take all thirty of us back to Sphakia.

Carefully and silently, a few at a time we were rowed out to the caique, where we clambered aboard and were given tins of bully beef and plenty fresh water. At last, with all aboard, we set off through the cover of darkness, expecting German blitzing at any moment, but glad to be rested and on what we hoped would be the penultimate stage of our journey to safety.

The boy Nikos is sitting next to me as I write, his head lolling on to my shoulder. He is flat out. I'd wanted him to go back with his uncle and Andreas but Alexandros insisted he was safer with us. Besides, the boy had become quite attached to us by now. And we to him.

I'm finishing this letter now, my love, thinking of you always and now I truly believe I am on my way to freedom and to being with you again some time soon in the future. If you hadn't been with me on this journey, I wouldn't have survived, I know that. You have protected me. I love you.

All my love,

Bill

xxx

## 27th May

Darling Merry,

If anything survives, it will be my letters to you. I have this desperate need to let you know all that has happened. When we get to Cairo, I'm going to post everything to you. We're nearly there now, nearer to you.

Remarkably, we reached Sphakia with no difficulty, sailing quietly through the still night on a beautifully calm sea. It was almost as if the Germans had never invaded, almost like the idyllic time before the invasion when we were providing radar cover for Maleme airfield and our pitifully few aeroplanes. Almost but not quite. For, when we reached the small jetty and disembarked from the caique, we were immediately aware that we were not the only troops in Sphakia awaiting rescue. There was a steady murmur all round the darkened quay, the sounds of men muttering quietly to themselves in the night or sharing a cigarette or even crying with the pain of wounds caused somewhere in the battles in the north of the island defending that airfield we had once watched or resisting the German advance on Canea.

I found a major from the Australian forces that had been overwhelmed near Platanias and had retreated into the hills in confusion. Just like our small band, he told me, it had been every man for himself and he had crossed the White Mountains with a small cadre of fellow-Aussies – none from his own battalion, as it turned out – intent on reaching the safety of the south coast, where, according to rumour, the Royal Navy would rescue them and take them to Cairo. He and his compatriots had been there almost two days and there was still no sign of the Navy. Even worse, however, there were now hundreds of soldiers hiding in the many caves around Sphakia waiting to be taken off.

'Canea's a goner,' he explained. 'Met up with a couple of guys from my battalion who'd just got through here last night. They said things were dreadful in and around Canea. Jerry had just had too many troops and too many guns. Once he'd got the bridgehead at the airfield, he was sending in huge numbers of troops to take the island. There was never a hope in hell of holding out.'

'So are our boys still fighting in Canea?'

'There's a force covering the withdrawal. But, from what I hear, the whole shooting match is being withdrawn back to here for disembarkation. There's a few hundred here already, mate, but you just wait – there's thousands heading over the mountains. They've already been bringing trucks from all over the island and dumping them over the cliff. If any ships from the Navy get here, we're going to aim to get on them quick. You'd best do the same, if you want my advice.'

I had gone to check out the situation after we'd found ourselves a deserted and half-ruined house on the edge of the village and bedded down there for a few hours. When the sun's heat got intense, I told the others to stay put while Alec and I, with the faithful Nikos in tow in case we met some Cretans, went to see what was what.

The muttering we'd heard on arrival was caused by little pockets of soldiers, bedraggled, exhausted, in blood-soaked and torn uniforms and with their faces empty from exhaustion and little food. Everywhere the eye could see was full of soldiers – every cave, every ruined building, every barn, every goat-stall. Those who had been unable to find that sort of shelter crouched in little groups beside stone walls or sat with their backs against plane trees. The same weariness was everywhere. There was none of the jokiness that you usually find when soldiers get together. There was no singing, no one playing a harmonica. There was only this low mutter of exhausted, defeated, frightened men.

Alec went off to search for food while I went to find a senior British officer to explain who we were and find out the situation. I had no luck. The only officers I could find were in the same state as me – and sharing the same ignorance. Alec had better luck, returning to meet me on the edge of the village, as we had agreed so as to be away from spying eyes, with two scrawny chickens, some rations, a flagon of water which he'd raised from one of the village wells and a bottle of *raki*, the Cretan firewater that we hadn't tasted for several days. Although my mission to get us taken off the island had failed, Alec's enterprise boosted morale wonderfully.

The only clear instruction I received was to lay low in daylight, in case of German planes seeing the numbers gathering in Sphakia and deciding to strafe the village. Reflecting on the last few days, I realise how lucky we have been to get this far. If Alec and Carl hadn't found their way to Aiya Roumeli, if they hadn't met up with Alexandros, if Jim hadn't heard the rifle shot and had the good sense to respond by firing his pistol, if the Navy captain hadn't been able to find a caique to take us from Aiya Roumeli to Sphakia, if.....

There are so many indeterminates in war. Chance and fortune are random, I know, even though we like to delude ourselves that we are the lucky ones, that our belief and our determination will pull us through, and that courage in the face of adversity is sufficient at all times. Isn't that which so many of our influential stories tell us? Hercules and his labours. Theseus overwhelming the minotaur. David vanquishing Goliath. Odysseus surviving so many obstacles on his way home from Troy. Those myths encourage us to believe we can survive anything and overcome any obstacle. But they're not always true. Even though they give us a sense of our own immortality, especially when we're young, reality tells us they are not true. People die in war, particularly young men.

When I look back only two days, I know we were close to not surviving. I re-read what I wrote for that day and knew the reason I had been crying. Was I afraid? Yes, but the tears were also of frustration and anger – anger that I had, or we had, got into this predicament by choosing this way of travelling from Suya over the all-but-impassable cliffs instead of going back to Kostas and his boat and waiting for the sea to change, anger that I had failed my men, for yes, I still had this romantic notion that somehow I was responsible for them, when in fact we were a motley and random group thrown together by chance in the flight from Xamoudochori.

Where did this all come from, this daft notion that, just because someone somewhere back in England had decided it, I with some rudimentary knowledge of radio and a grammar school education was fit to be an officer, fit to command other men, often older and more experienced than myself? And why did they all accept it? Eddie? Jack? Even the New Zealanders, Alec, Carl and Jim, from their more classless society? I am puzzled by all this. Armies have always had to have their ranks, of course. I think of the mighty Roman centurions and of the Greek generals but they were all men who earned their rank through previous exploits or skill. I was made a Flying Officer because of the wartime situation. Presumably the RAF needed airmen to man the AMES outfits and, by the very nature of modern fighting forces, that meant a number of airmen would have to become officers. But does my limited understanding of radio waves and an education in the Classics really prepare me to lead other men? I somehow doubt it. And yet these men have expected leadership of me. They call me 'Skip'. Even though I've tried to make every decision a collaborative one, I know they all looked at the way I was voting before committing themselves. Somehow, despite my intentions, my voice and my opinions held sway.

I am troubled by the Eddie problem. Not now. I mean, not as Eddie is now. But as he was, when he really wasn't able to move any further and wanted us to leave him. We couldn't and we didn't. And I'm proud of that, proud of myself and proud of the others. But what if Alec and Carl hadn't reached Aiya Roumeli and set about organising our rescue? What if we'd had another twenty-four hours on that beach in that cave with Jim and Jack failing to get drinkable water from their experiments with seawater? From what Alec had said, three days without water was as much as we might have hoped to survive and, apart from the odd lick here and there from rain, from stalactites, from condensed seawater, we had already been without for two days. One more and then what? Would we, any of us, have been ready at some point to ditch Eddie? To have a go at climbing up those cliffs, dehydrated and hungry as we were, in some desperate final attempt to find succour? Could we, could I, leave Eddie? Could I leave anyone?

I thought for the first time for days about Ronald at the Xamoudochori base, whose wounds prevented his setting out on this long march to safety. We had left him. I had left him. True, I'd arranged for a NZ Medical Orderly to look after him in the hope and expectation that withdrawing troops would come across them and help them on their way. But, even if they did, to where? And to what? I was damn sure that Ronald's leg was shattered so badly by the flying shrapnel that he couldn't walk unaided, even after treatment. So what would have happened to him? If the Aussie captain was right, and all the indications were that he was, as more and more weary soldiers streamed into the gulley behind the village of Sphakia during the day, then Canea had fallen and quite probably all the other towns on the north. There was no way that Ronald, even bandaged up, could have made that trek over the White Mountains. So what would have happened to him? Maybe he'd been put into an army ambulance and brought over here. Or maybe he'd have been placed in a field hospital and the Germans would have recognised it as such, so he'd have been taken as a POW.

Would it have been any different then to have left Eddie, if the worst had come to the worst? I remembered the primitive fear I had felt at the moment the bombs started exploding around us by the base and how we'd all just run for our lives. Would that same selfish survival instinct have driven me to leave Eddie to certain death? And what about Nikos? I'd become fond of the boy and he'd come to rely on us now as we had relied on him to guide us through the mountains. He had still seemed the freshest of us but Alec had said that none of us would last more than three or four days without water. Would dehydration have taken him before me? What if he had become incapable of moving while I still could walk? Would I have left him? Nikos?

War is supposed to make you impervious to all this. After all, I'd watched those German paratroopers being ripped apart by bullets as they fell from their planes and I hadn't had any squeamishness then. True, they were the enemy but they were men too, weren't they? Somebody's sons. Somebody's loved ones. They weren't just bits of ballast hanging in the air to allow our boys some target practice. But I felt nothing. Immunised, I guess, by the rhetoric of war, vaccinated against human feeling, exempted from care for my fellow men.

I look around this ruined house at my companions. They entertain themselves with card games or talk of the meals they plan to have when they get to Cairo or the women they once loved back home. Too much time spent here doing nothing has got me thinking too much.

When dusk fell, I went to look for the naval embarkation officer reported to be in Sphakia. As the light faded, the village was filling up with men, bedraggled, filthy, with several days' beard on their faces, all searching for food and filling water bottles from the wells. There were even more men here now, arriving down the gorge from their long march over the mountains. The main route from Canea, I learned, was taking troops to the east of Souda Bay then over the mountains on to the Askifou plain before reaching the village of Imbros and then the final weary trek into Sphakia.

No sign of any naval officers and no signs of any ships either but I bumped into the Australian major I'd met in the morning. His name was Freeman. John Freeman.

'It's definite,' he began, after we had exchanged greetings. 'We're pulling out of Crete. Freyberg's on his way here now and they'll get him off first, though why he deserves special treatment after the cock-up he's made of it all I don't know.'

'General Freyberg?'

'Yeah, the big cheese, the one who was supposed to be masterminding all this. Though how on earth he can hold his head up, I'm blessed if I know. Why on earth didn't he defend that airport better? And even after Jerry started landing there, he could have retaken the airfield, couldn't he? We still had more troops at that point surely.'

'I watched all of that,' I told him. 'We were in the hills just above Maleme, supposedly providing radar info. to protect the airfield, though all the planes had gone days ago. We should have been off the island then.'

'So what happened?'

'Who knows? Never got the green light to move.'

Freeman scratched a shapeless pattern in the dust.

'The sooner we get out of here the better,' he said at last. 'Story is they're going to start disembarking tomorrow. Some of the Aussies here have got Cretan women with them. They're hoping to take them too. Can't see it myself but who knows in this madness?'

We parted and I reported back to the rest in the farmhouse that tomorrow looked the likely date. That cheered them up, especially when Alec returned from a foraging expedition with three bottles of *raki*, four tins of pineapple chunks and some eggs he'd bartered off an old Cretan woman.

One more night and then.....well, let's hope this is it. Let's hope tomorrow brings the promised rescue. It all feels a bit of an anticlimax in many ways. Feel I'm closer to seeing you again, my love. And maybe even soon. Don't know why.

All my love,

Bill

xx

**28<sup>th</sup>/29<sup>th</sup> May**

Darling Merry,

I have been ill with dysentery for best part of two days. Constant vomiting and diarrhoea. Very unpleasant. Lavatory facilities, of course, non-existent so I have had to disappear regularly into the undergrowth behind the farmhouse, where the sharp stones and prickly thorn bushes add to the severe discomfort. I don't know the cause – could be the water from the well, though no one else seems to be suffering. It could be the food we had – old eggs, maybe, chicken not properly cooked, even the pineapple chunks. But again, no one else is suffering. Maybe it's just plain exhaustion – mental, physical and emotional. Surviving that horrendous journey over the White Mountains and then the frightening scramble along the cliffs from Suya, with the thoughts ever-present on that final night that we weren't going to get through and that we would perish on that lonely shore. Maybe the combination has taken its toll and my body is just reacting.

Eddie, bless him, was the one who went and found a medical orderly, who arrived and gave me medication.

He gave me a solution of glucose and salt mixed in water to replace the fluids I'd lost. Apparently I was not the only one on this beach with the problem. Conditions were ropy and he was surprised there were not more suffering.

'How long do I need to take this?'

'Until you're feeling better,' he explained. He was a short man with a West Country accent, busy in his movements and clearly harassed from his work. 'You need plenty of rest. I'd say at least a couple of days.'

'What about the disembarkation? Won't I be able to go?'

'My information is that the walking wounded and stretcher cases will be disembarked first,' he explained, as he tidied his medical kit away. 'After that, it's supposed to be an orderly evacuation. Don't worry, you should be fit to travel tomorrow. Nothing happens till nightfall anyway for fear of Jerry's planes. You should be tickety-boo by then.'

That was yesterday evening. I'd been sick all day apparently, though I don't remember the time sequence well at all. I kept being sick then needing to go outside, then coming back and falling asleep in a corner of the main room of the farmhouse which still had some roofing left. The others had made sure I was covered up, because I kept complaining of feeling cold, even though the temperature in the daytime must have been well into the eighties. Jack had volunteered, apparently, to fetch clean water and managed to persuade some officer to part with a spare three-quarter full water bottle that had not been filled from the local wells. For, though none of the others was suffering, they automatically suspected the local water which they thought might well have become infected by now with so many squaddies reaching in with any implements they could find – water bottles, tin hats, broken urns – to refresh themselves after the long march and to rehydrate themselves in the blazing heat.

Alec, unsurprisingly, had taken charge of the situation. In the last few days my regard for Alec has grown tremendously. The others too had begun to look to him as a natural leader, so it was no surprise to me that he was the one who decided what the plan of action should be. I was unaware of it at the time, of course, because I was so sick but, as soon as it became apparent that I was in no fit state to do anything, Alec called everyone together and got them to agree what they would do.

First of all, they agreed to get treatment for me. Eddie told me that they were all of the opinion that they owed me because I hadn't deserted them in the chaos at Maleme and that I had kept them going on the long flight over the mountains and along the coast. Then they had decided to find out what was happening in terms of the evacuation procedures. Alec had pointed out that it was not going to be as straightforward as they had originally hoped, because there were men arriving in hundreds down the gorge and there were going to have to be priorities decided somehow. He thought that those of us from AMES might have a better chance than the rest, because of the nature of our mission, but they needed to know for sure. Also, if I didn't recover quickly, they needed to think how they were going to manage that.

Jack had said we were going to need more rations, however long we were stuck here. And 'bloody ciggies' he had insisted. Plus fresh water. He was convinced that the well water was what had done for me, even though Carl pointed out that everyone else was okay. Alec had argued that it might only be a matter of time and that Jack was right and we needed to find a better water supply. After what they'd been through the last few days, he had said, the last thing they wanted was to die of food poisoning. So, Jack had gone to hunt for water. Carl had taken Nikos to search out some rations – steal them if necessary. Jim stayed to look after me, while Eddie had already gone to find medical assistance. Alec himself went to find out the lie of the land and see what the disembarkation situation was.

All this Carl told me much later, on the second day of my illness in fact, as I was beginning to recover and no longer felt so weak and delirious. The glucose and salt solution had had its effect. My insides were under control again – there could have been nothing left to come out – and I was beginning to be aware of my situation.

'What happened last night then?' I asked Carl, as he poured me another drink of the solution.

'It was surprisingly orderly. The order had gone out that only the walking wounded and those on stretchers were to be disembarked on to HMS Napier. Ya saw the chaos on the beach for yaself when we first got here but miraculously the arrival of the Royal Navy sorted it all. When the landing craft pulled in, there were shouts of "It's all right – the Navy's here". It was as if this was what everyone was waiting for – salvation at last. Then these two nattily dressed Royal Navy officers came on to the beach and immediately took command. They gave instructions for all the wounded to be lined up and then processed them on to the waiting landing craft.'

'Was it only the wounded?'

'Too right,' Carl grinned. 'I saw a couple of dodgers who'd put blood-soaked bandages on their heads to get into the queue but the genuine articles knew who they were and shouted out to the naval disembarkation officers. They yanked them out and booted them on to the sand.'

'Must have been a stirring sight, seeing the first to be rescued heading out to sea.'

'Strewth, it sure was, Skip, but it was heart-breaking too,' Carl continued, squatting down beside me now and offering another drink of solution. 'There were plenty guys who were walking, cheerily, as you'd expect, 'cos they were the first to get out, but there were lots of others who were in sad states. There were guys with their legs shot to pieces, guys with half their faces covered in blood and gore, guys with stumps for arms where the medics had been forced to operate quickly. It was a horrible sight really. I didn't envy them getting out first. They deserved it.'

'How many got out?'

'Hard to say,' he answered. 'Somebody told me up to a thousand but it's hard to know.'

'And what about tonight? What's the chances of our getting off? Do you know?'

'Not yet, Skip. Alec's finding out about that. He'll tell ya when he gets back.'

I glanced round our temporary base. Eddie was sitting up against a wall, his head flopped back and his eyes closed. We were all still exhausted and, whenever a chance of sleep came, we took it. Next to him sat Jack, whistling tunelessly and whittling a piece of driftwood with a knife he had found somewhere. Carl stood up from me and walked across to what had once been the doorway and looked out to the sea. Jim and Nikos had got a small fire going in the hearth and were cooking something that smelled like chicken on wooden skewers over the embers. Alec had still not returned.

An hour or so later it must have been when Alec did return and told us what he had found.

'It's hard to get any clear picture. One thing I do know is that we're quitting Crete. Freyberg's decided that we can't hold out any longer so everyone's being pulled back from the Canea front across the mountains to here for disembarkation. At the same time the Navy's disembarking the troops in Iraklion and Rethymnon. So there's thousands of personnel to be got off from Sphakia over the next few days.'

'Have they started arriving?' I asked.

'Oh, absoflippinglutely. It's chocker down there. They're arriving all the time down the gorge from Imbros. And what a bunch they are! Most of them just come along in bedraggled groups of half a dozen or more, though there's a few that have managed to stay together in platoons. But they're all shattered from the march, they're all short of food and water, they're all totally bewildered. Add to that the Aussies that are hiding up in the caves, some of them with Greek women, who've got here earlier and are still hoping for rescue and you've got a recipe for complete chaos.'

'What about us?' I pressed. 'Did you find out what kind of priority we have?'

'It was hard. No one in authority wants to talk to a non-comm like me. Specially not a colonial boy. I took your badge, Skip, hope you don't mind, and I managed to persuade a British colonel that I hadn't purloined it but that I was acting on your behalf. Explained to him about AMES and how it was important for you to be taken off the island a.s.a.p. because of your special knowledge. He promised to do what he could. So I sat on the sea wall and waited. Somebody had a radio on and I heard your Winston Churchill's voice saying "We will never desert our Cretan allies." Too late for that, I thought.'

'And when will you know?'

'Oh, he came back to find me pretty damn quick,' said Carl, smiling grimly. 'Said you were to leave tonight on the first boat out.'

'All of us?' asked Jack.

'That's where things get a bit tricky,' answered Alec. 'You, Eddie and Skip are OK. But the rest of us are going to have to wait our turn. We might still get out tonight but we might have to wait till tomorrow. We're not high priority like you blokes are.'

There was what is commonly known as a stunned silence. And stunned is the right word, because a range of emotions was playing through all of us as we took in Alec's information. Part relief, part apprehension, part regret, part uncertainty. Should we, could we, at this stage leave Alec, Carl and Jim to the vagaries of the disembarkation plan? And what about Nikos? For a moment I had forgotten him.

'What about Nikos?' I asked.

The boy looked up at the mention of his name, his frightened eyes focusing on mine.

'They say that only Greek soldiers are being allowed on board,' said Alec. 'No civilians.'

'I'm taking him with us,' I said immediately. 'How can we leave him here after all we've been through?'

I looked defiantly around the group who sat in silence, still contemplating the impact of what Alec had discovered.

'Skip, if you're well enough, you need to persuade the powers that be that we all need to be on that boat tonight,' said Eddie, scratching his belly.

I was surprised that he should show such concern.

'I wouldn't be here without what Alec and Carl did. And Jim. And Nikos. I owe them my life. And I ain't leaving without them.'

'Me neither,' said Jack, still whittling at his piece of wood. 'One for all and all for one. The seven b------ musketeers, eh?'

There was a brief snort of laughter but this wasn't really a laughing matter.

'Eddie, Jack,' I began. 'We can be on that Navy vessel tonight. Don't you want to go? Don't you want to get away? After all we've been through?'

'You bet, Skip,' said Jack. 'Can't wait. But, like Eddie said, we're not going without these boys. You'll have to talk to them down at the beach, Skip. Tell them we've given them some training in radar. Tell them anything. But they bloody come with us or we wait.'

'And what can I say about the boy?'

'If those Aussies with Cretan women up in the caves think they're going to get them out, then surely ya can find some reason for Nikos joining us,' said Carl. 'Ya promised Alexandros, remember? No going back on your word. Ya're an officer and a gentleman.'

I grinned. My strength was returning. I levered myself into an upright position.

'Okay, what time is it now?'

'Only five thirty.'

'And what time do the ships arrive?'

'Soon as night falls. About eight,' answered Alec. 'The first landing craft yesterday got into the jetty about eight.'

We agreed that we would get down to the beach for seven, so I had plenty of time to write this letter, which I hope is my last from Crete. We are all going to go together, to make it seem as if we were an organised squad, because, as Alec pointed out, only organised troops are getting through now, for the beach had been cordoned off to stop stragglers jumping the queue.

So that's how it is. The seven of us, with me at the head, are to march down in line from the farmhouse to the beach. We have done what we could to tidy ourselves up, brushing hair, fastening gaiters and tunic buttons, putting our tin hats on. Now we're ready.

It's silly, I know, but the closeness of our escape has affected me so strangely that I can almost smell your lovely perfume. I've looked again at your photograph and kissed the image. Oh Merry!

All my love,

Bill

xxx

# PART 3

# 1

After the dying of the light, we need to cling more closely to one another, in order to ease the pain and share the grief.

So it was for Tom Ennis after hearing the news of his mother's death. The stinging tears had flown quickly but that was no surprise, for he had been preparing them for many years, readying them whenever she went abroad, whenever a virus struck her down temporarily, whenever another of her contemporaries died. But later, as he had told Chantal the story as far as he knew it, a deeper emotion, a sort of long drawn-out sobbing, began to gnaw at his insides and he could feel himself becoming more and more unsteady.

'How did it happen?' Chantal had asked, after she had returned from court as quickly as she could on receiving his text message. 'How much has Ellie told you?'

Tom's rumpled face, his short-cut silver hair and his fleshy lips she had always loved looking at but his grief had made his eyes sink back into his head and his cheeks appeared to have hollowed since that morning.

'Not very much. She died in some cave in the south of Crete. She was with some old Cretan called Themis. He carried her body back to the local doctor's and they made arrangements for the funeral people in the main city, Heraklion, to collect it and keep it until someone sorted out the funeral arrangements.'

Chantal's brown eyes looked at him. She reached across for his hand.

'Tom, I'm so sorry. Your mum was a very special person. She loved you, you know.'

'I know. But what was she doing in this cave in Crete with an old Cretan bloke? It doesn't make sense, Chantal. She was supposed to be going on a cruise and Ellie was going to watch over her.'

'There's no use blaming Ellie,' she interrupted sharply. 'You know what your mum was like. She always had that feistiness in her. You couldn't always predict what she was up to, you know that, don't you?'

His shoulders sagged and his breath was laboured. His voice came reluctantly, as if he had rehearsed all these things in his head and couldn't be bothered to hear them repeated.

'Yes, I know that. But Ellie knew that too. She should have kept a closer watch.'

He wanted someone to reproach, someone other than himself, and, although he knew it was not Ellie's fault that his mother had made a deliberate escape from her watch, a bit of him still felt the need to expiate his own unnecessary sense of guilt by passing the blame.

'Come here,' she said and pulled him across to the sofa she was sitting on, where she slid her shoulders under his right arm and nestled her head on his shoulder.

Tom's crumpled body was comforted a little by her warmth.

'How did Ellie find out?' she asked, stroking his leg softly.

'The doctor who certified death contacted the police. That's apparently what they have to do with a foreign national. They quizzed this Themis fellow and he told them about the cruise ship and about Ellie. Apparently mum had told him all about her. The police traced Ellie in Heraklion and she had to go and identify the body.'

'Oh, the poor thing!' said Chantal, looking up from beneath his chin. 'It must have been an awful shock to her. How did she sound?'

He could picture his elder daughter receiving the news – the stare of disbelief, the initial shock, and then the cascade of tears.

'Dreadful. She's blaming herself, of course, though I told her not to be so silly. And I don't think she's ever seen a dead body before. She was only young when dad died.'

His whole body started to shake as he said this. The grief that had been building steadily inside him finally sought release and he could not control its expression any longer.

'My mum,' he wept uncontrollably now, his body heaving with pain. 'She's dead. And I never got chance to say goodbye.'

Chantal eased her face up from his chest till her face was against hers. She kissed his eyes, she kissed away the salt tears from his cheeks, and finally she kissed his lips, gently at first but then his response became fiercer as he sought to expunge his pain by clinging to her.

'I love you,' she said, detaching herself gently from him and standing up. 'Come. To bed. Let me hold you properly.'

*

The only plane he could get was from Gatwick to Heraklion the next day, arriving at midnight. Ellie was waiting for him, a young man in uniform at her side. Tom was immediately aware of the changed temperature. Even at midnight, the warm air hit him as he came into the airport foyer.

She ran towards him, her wavy hair falling about her face and her long Paisley-print dress flowing behind her, and flung her arms around him. They stood there in the unprepossessing entrance hall like that for several minutes, clinging to each other and weeping together, as the crowd milled past them.

'Dad, this is Mikalis,' Ellie said, as she finally disengaged herself and drew her father across to her companion. 'He's been brilliant. I couldn't have managed without him.'

Tom and Mikalis shook hands, quite formally, though the younger man smiled warmly. Tom was still adjusting to the loss of his mother, to the craziness and mystery of how it had happened, and to Crete itself, with its alien sounds and warm ambience. He had to appear in control as much as possible. It was what a father had to do.

'Mikalis is from the *Ariadne*,' she explained as they moved out to the adjacent car park. 'He's been helping me with everything. I couldn't have done it without him. He's been amazing.'

They were in the car by now, a silver Audi that Ellie had hired with Mikalis's advice. As she drove out of the crowded terminal, dodging the tooting taxis and uncertainly-driven hire cars, Tom turned to listen to what Mikalis was saying.

'Mr Ennis, I have arranged for you to have a room in the Zeus Hotel tonight,' he said, as Ellie drove into the city. 'I trust that is all right? I thought you might like a cabin on the *Ariadne* but Eleanor said you would need to be in the city in the morning, so the Zeus Hotel is best, because it is close to the British Consulate.'

Mikalis was not especially tall but he certainly was handsome, with his deeply tanned face and his blue eyes, thought Tom. He could see the physical attraction straightaway and, by the sound of it, this young man had also been very helpful to his daughter at a time and in a place where she would have probably experienced considerable difficulties dealing with matters on her own. He was glad she had had his help.

'Where is your grandmother's body?'

'There's a funeral director that the Consulate people recommended to us. They speak good English, thank God. And Mikalis has been really brilliant at explaining everything. Oh dad, I'm really sorry. I shouldn't have let her disappear like she did. It was all my fault.'

Tom reached out and touched her elbow as she drove.

'Ellie, you mustn't blame yourself. You know what your granny was like. She may have been ninety years old but she wasn't stupid,' Tom said, staring ahead at the glow of the streetlights. 'She wouldn't have gone off on her own without some plan in her mind. You know her. She'd always had that ability to be impulsive. It used to drive your granddad mad. And me sometimes. But it's also why we loved her.'

He caught his breath for a second. Already he was referring to her in the past tense. How soon his tongue had adjusted!

They pulled into a small car park in front of the Zeus Hotel, where Ellie switched the engine off after parking the car.

'Mikalis, I need to talk to my dad for a while, all right. Will you wait for me in the lobby? Can you get a drink or something?'

Inside the hotel Tom quickly checked in and, once in his room, sat down on the side of the bed and listened to Ellie's breathless explanation of events.

'I tried to call her on her mobile phone loads of times and I sent text messages all day,' she began, her eyes holding back tears, 'but she never answered. Or rather she answered twice. The first time it was on some waiter's phone and, when I called back, he just told me some story about someone taking his phone without his knowledge. I was going frantic by then. I got Mikalis to call the Greek police and they traced the call to a café in Souda Bay. When they checked, it seems that granny had been in that café with an old Cretan fellow. The waiter thought it odd two old people together like that and one of them, granny, knowing how to use a mobile phone but he had no idea who they were or where they were heading. The café's apparently near a War Cemetery or something like that. He did mention that there had been another old Cretan fellow with them and the police traced him but all he knew was that the man with granny was called Themis and he lived in a little village beyond Chania. But no one there had seen this Themis all day, so the trail went cold. I was getting really frightened by now. What was she trying to do, I wondered. Why wasn't she answering my calls or my texts? I got Mikalis to keep badgering the police but they said that, without better information, they could do nothing.'

'You and I need a drink,' Tom said, opening the minibar and taking out two small bottles of Metaxa that he proceeded to pour into two glasses. 'Here.'

They both took deep draughts of the rich brown brandy.

'What did you say about a War Cemetery?' he asked, placing his glass on the coffee table. It was all still a complete mystery. Why had his mother disappeared like that? Who was this Themis fellow? Did he have something to do with it all? And why was she visiting a War Cemetery? Was there someone buried there that one of them, maybe both of them, knew? But who? 'Where was this?'

'A place called Souda Bay. Mikalis says it is very well known in Crete. I didn't know but there was a big battle in Crete in the Second World War. German paratroopers landed somewhere over in the west and drove the British forces off the island. The War Cemetery in Souda Bay has the graves of hundreds of soldiers in it. A lot of them were Australians or New Zealanders. Did you know about it?'

Tom frowned and took another sip of his brandy.

'I seem to remember my dad, your granddad, talking about it once and mum shutting him up,' he said, pondering. 'I would only have been about eleven or twelve at the time, I think. In fact, I think it was just after I heard that I'd passed to go to King

Edward's grammar school. Mum and dad were having a bit of an argument about something and dad said something about a battle in Crete and she shut him up immediately. As if there was something she didn't want me to hear about.'

He hunted and hunted in his memory bank, trying to dredge up the snatch of conversation he had overheard between his mother and father but it was no good. It was well over fifty years ago and he could not draw any more of it back. Funny, though, that he should remember that moment all this time on.

'After you phoned me, I tried to reach her too, you know. But she didn't respond to my calls or my text message either until very late in the evening. I don't know where she was by then. All she said was 'Nearly there now'.'

'I got that one too.'

'So was she referring to this cave where she died?'

Did she know then, he wondered. Did she know that she wasn't going to make it? He'd read of cases where people foresaw their own deaths, almost prepared themselves for it, almost willed themselves to such an ending. Was that what she had been alerting them to? Or had she simply meant the cave?

'Dad, I don't know but we'll find out more in the morning. This Themis has agreed to see us. Mikalis spoke to him by phone. The police had already interviewed him, of course, but he is happy to talk to us. He specifically said he wanted to talk to you. He has something for you.'

So the mystery might be, would be, resolved in the morning. It would have to do. There was no way at this time of night that he could do anything other than try to sleep.

Ellie drained her glass and stood up.

'Dad, I'm glad you're here but it's not fair on Mikalis to keep him waiting any longer. You must be tired too, flying all that way. I suppose you had to drive to Gatwick too.'

'Chantal drove,' he said, stretching his arms. 'But you're right. Tomorrow will do. Your grandmother's not going anywhere now, is she?'

As soon as he'd said it, he regretted it. Ellie suddenly froze, then as quickly resumed her previous pose, though not without a brief question appearing in her glance.

'I'll be here early. Business starts at eight in the city.'

'Will you join me for breakfast?' Tom said, as she headed towards the door. 'And bring Mikalis. If you want to.'

*

Before meeting Themis they had to call at the British Consulate to clear up legal matters and obtain advice about getting Meredith Ennis's body flown home for burial. The consulate official who received them in his uncomfortably small office was called Webster, a large man with a florid complexion and a bald head.

'I'm terribly sorry about Mrs Ennis's death,' he began in his well-oiled voice, as he ushered the three of them to seats on the other side of his desk. 'We will, of course, do all we can to help, though you must understand HMG cannot underwrite any costs. I presume there was insurance?'

'Yes, of course,' answered Tom, reaching into his attaché case for the appropriate papers.

'No, I do not need to see those.' Webster held a hand up. 'You will need to contact the company concerned direct. Let me explain the customs in Greece.'

Tom replaced his attaché case on the floor with a weary hand, while Ellie, whose soft eyes struggled to control her tears at the reminder of her grandmother's death, reached for Mikalis's hand.

'Under Greek law, a deceased person must be buried within one month of death. However, in the case of foreign nationals the authorities will normally allow as much time as necessary. The death must, however, be registered within three days. There is no cremation in Greece and you must decide if you wish the burial to take place here or in the United Kingdom,' the official explained, as if reciting a well-worn shibboleth.

'We want her body to be flown home,' said Tom without hesitation. 'Family, friends. It's best that way.'

He had discussed it briefly with his sister Nancy by phone and they had agreed that cremation in Sutton Coldfield would be the most appropriate form of funeral. Nancy had left him to make all the appropriate arrangements.

'I'm sure you are correct, Mr Ennis. In which case your insurance company will appoint an international funeral director

177

who will liaise with the undertaker here in Heraklion, where Mrs Ennis's body currently lies, in order to arrange for repatriation. The local undertaker will embalm the remains and put them in a zinc-lined coffin. The international funeral director will need to obtain a local civil registry death certificate, the doctor's death certificate, a certificate of embalming, and a certificate for permission to transfer the remains to the UK. They are familiar with such procedures.'

'Thank you. What happens then?'

It was like watching himself going through these formal steps, he thought, while the real he felt empty with sadness and grief.

'Normally, in circumstances where a person dies suddenly, as in your mother's case, the Examining Magistrate here in Greece would order an autopsy but, because of Mrs Ennis's age, I understand that such will not be necessary.'

'Can I see her body?'

Did he want to, he asked himself. Yes, he must.

'I am sure that will cause no problem but first you must contact your insurance company and set the repatriation in motion. The Heraklion undertaker will need to be instructed about procedures to be followed, so that he is ready for your visit. If I can be of any further assistance, please get in touch. But your insurance company should take over from here.'

Back at the hotel, Tom telephoned the insurance company, explained the circumstances and gave the information required. It was all seeming rather remote now. He needed to feel it all much more personally. Perhaps talking to this old Cretan, this Themis, would do the trick.

Ellie and Mikalis were having coffee in the lobby when he came downstairs from his room.

'What time is this Themis coming?' he asked, as he sat down beside them. 'Or do we have to visit him?'

'I'm afraid we have to go to Chania to meet him,' Mikalis apologised. 'It has been a difficult time for him too, you understand. He was not prepared for all this. He does not feel able to come to Heraklion. So we must drive to Chania.'

'How far?'

'Two hours. I have spoken to Themis this morning. There is a bar by the harbour-front where he will meet us at midday. I hope that is all right?'

'Yes, of course,' Tom felt his face sagging. 'I'm sorry if I don't seem grateful. I haven't really slept.'

Ellie took his hand and squeezed it.

'We should go.'

'Yes,' Tom sighed, but stood up slowly. 'You're right. We need to know what happened from this Themis character. I can see your grandmother at the funeral parlour when I come back. Do you want to come too, love?'

'I don't know.' Her face went even paler than it had been. 'I've seen her once. When I had to do the identification.'

'Of course, I understand. See what you feel when you come back.'

*

Themis was sitting on a cushioned bamboo chair at a restaurant just beyond the white-domed Turkish Mosque on the waterfront of the old Venetian harbour in Chania, staring out at the minaret-style lighthouse on the end of the sweep of sea wall opposite. He was wearing a blue jacket over his shirt as protection against the mild breeze that blew from the sea. His orange worry beads sat loosely in his left hand. His grizzled old face, with a day's growth of silver beard, looked up at their approach and he stood up.

'*Kalimera*,' he growled. 'I am Themis. I am very sorry about Mrs Ennis. She was a very special lady. Please, will you join me? Drinks? Sandwich? Something else?'

They shook hands quite formally and took places around the table on which his emptied cup of Greek coffee sat.

'I'd like a beer,' said Tom, indicating the bright sun high in the sky now. 'It's warm.'

'I'll have the same,' said Ellie.

'*Kafe ellenikos*,' said Mikalis, smiling his thanks.

'I did not know that she was acting secretly,' began Themis, as the drinks were being fetched. While he spoke, he twitched his worry beads back and forth over his hand. 'She never mentioned that. When she spoke to me on the phone, she said that she was coming to Crete on a cruise and was it possible for me to meet her. I did not know about not telling her granddaughter until we had reached Souda Bay.'

'But why was she being so secretive?' asked Tom, still puzzled about his mother's reasons for meeting up with this old Cretan. 'What did she ask you to show her that she didn't want Ellie to know about? How did she know who you were? What's the big secret?'

Themis looked at Tom through his narrowed eyes, then at Ellie beside him, both leaning slightly towards him now, as if awaiting some revelation.

'Didn't you know about your father's brother?' Themis began again. 'Bill Ennis? Flying Officer Bill Ennis? Your uncle?'

There was a photograph. It stood on top of the china cabinet at his mother's house. A tall thin man in Royal Air Force uniform with dark hair, a slight smile on his lips and a pencil moustache. It had been there since time immemorial. It was his uncle, his father's brother. He had died in the war. But he was never spoken about. There was never any mention of him.

'My uncle was in the Royal Air Force. He died in the war. I always presumed his plane was shot down,' Tom said, still mystified. How did this old Cretan Themis know about his uncle? And what did it all have to do with his mother and her death?

'No. Bill Ennis died here in Crete. He did not fly planes. He was in charge of a radar post just a few miles from here before and during the Battle of Crete in May 1941. The Germans invaded the island by air, dropping large numbers of paratroopers in order to establish a bridgehead at the airfield of Maleme. Hundreds of young Germans were shot down as they came down through the air but thousands more landed. Within a few days, they had driven the Allied forces out of the north of the island. Those that survived escaped over the *Lefka Ori*, the White Mountains you can see behind you, to reach a place on the south coast called Hora Sfakion where the Royal Navy rescued many of them. Some were marched back over the mountains by the Germans and sent into Prisoner-of-War Camps. Some died. Your uncle was one of those.'

Tom didn't know what to feel most – sorrow, certainly, but also curiosity and a tinge of anger. The feelings kept shuffling around in his head, each as if seeking dominance.

'But why was my mother out here? What did she want you to show her? And why didn't she tell anybody?' he demanded testily.

'I can answer some of your questions,' said Themis, gazing into the depths of the harbour. 'Others you will have to find for yourself.'

A waiter arrived with their drinks, which he placed on the table, breaking for a moment the tension that had been building up. Ellie looked at Mikalis, who made a *moue* with his lips and shrugged lightly, and at her father who was staring fiercely at the ancient Cretan sat beside them.

'Your mother first phoned me from England,' Themis resumed, toying with his worry beads. 'She said she was coming to Crete and wanted me to take her to places where Bill had been. So I took her to Souda Bay, where his remains are probably buried, though in an unmarked grave. Then we went to the place where the radar had been set up and then we followed the route over the mountains until we reached Hora Sfakion.'

'But why you. Why did she contact you? What had you got to do with all this?'

'I was a young boy at the time,' replied Themis, his old eyes moistening now as memories of those days came clear again. 'Bill and his crew had their radar post in my home village of Xamoudochori. I was their guide over the mountains to Hora Sfakion.'

Tom sucked in his breath. Things were beginning to click into place now.

'So you took her over the mountains to this place you've been talking about and then what happened? Is that where she died?'

Themis coughed and then resumed.

'Bill Ennis was one of the bravest men I have known. He saved my life and lost his own doing so. When the Royal Navy ships came to rescue people at Hora Sfakion, Bill would not go aboard unless I went too. The Naval officer refused permission, so Bill and a New Zealand soldier called Alec Bryce and I hid in a cave until the next night. We were going then to swim out to the ships and hope they wouldn't throw us back in the sea.

Bill died during the day before he could attempt this. Alec and I survived by sticking to the plan.'

'Gosh!' said Ellie. 'A hero in the family!'

'Your grandmother wanted to see the cave where we had been together. That is where I took her. And that is where she simply stopped breathing. I am sorry.'

Tom looked at his daughter, at Mikalis, then back at Themis. He was bewildered still. It was all very interesting to find out about how his Uncle Bill had died but he didn't really feel any connection with him. There was just that photograph and that snatch of remembered argument between his mother and father. But why had she come all this way at her advanced age just to see where he had died?

'But why all the secrecy?' he expostulated. 'I still don't understand why she didn't tell anyone?'

Themis reached under the table for a multicoloured woven Greek bag and pulled out a large manila envelope stuffed with papers.

'These are for you,' he said, handing them over. 'I promised your mother that I would give them to you personally. She said your father would have wanted you to have them. The answers to the remainder of your questions are in there. But you must forgive me now. It has been a difficult two days for me as well. I need to return to my home for some rest. Goodbye.'

# 2

The room was warm and comfortable, not as he had expected. It was more like the lounge of someone's house, with its leather armchairs and sofa, coffee table and long beige drapes tied back. Through the French windows he could see a verdant lawn stretching away with borders of blue and pink flowers and a weeping willow tree. There was a bowl of white pebbles on the coffee table and a tall vase filled with pink gladioli stood on the hearth.

'Let's just remind ourselves where we got to last week, shall we, Tom? You have recently found out that the person you thought was your father was in fact your uncle. Your biological father died in the war before you were born and your mother married his brother, yes? Your mother kept this information from you all her life and she has recently died. And it was on her death that you found all this out, yes?'

Tom Ennis, sitting in the firm leather chair opposite the black-suited and white-bloused Dr Stephanie Barrett, nodded.

'Would you just like to go over again how you found everything out?'

Tom sipped from the ice-cold water she had given him, placed the glass back on the marbled surface of the coffee table and reached for the large manila envelope he had brought with him. Why do I have to go through all this again, he thought to himself. He'd explained it all the previous week. She seemed a sensible woman, not the sort that wouldn't be listening, not some quack. He'd never been for counselling before. Was it always like this?

'It's all in here,' he said wearily. 'You can read it all if you want. I've read it enough times now to know it by heart.'

He held the envelope half across to her but she didn't take it, sitting quite still in her chair, her chin angled sharply from her high-necked white blouse.

'I'd rather you told me yourself, Tom. Take your time. Just tell me in your own words.'

Tom sighed. He had indeed been wading through the papers his mother had asked Themis to pass on to him for the best part of four weeks and it still didn't make sense. He needed someone to help him make that sense. It was Chantal, his wife, who had urged him after the funeral had taken place to seek counselling. He had pooh-poohed the idea. Mumbo-jumbo it all was, as far as he was concerned. Never been proved scientifically. Mumbo-jumbo. Chantal had persisted. She knew of several of her past clients who had benefited enormously from professional help. Rape victims. People whose children had died in accidents. Wives of murderers. I'm not in that category, he had protested. Not like people like that. It's not the same. It's not as serious. But then why are you grieving so much, she had pressed. Why don't you just try it?

'Okay, but I don't want to go over all this again' he replied to Stephanie Barrett's question. 'I need to find how to move on. Isn't that what I'm here for?'

Stephanie Barrett crossed her legs and reached for her glass from the table. They were all like this to start with, she thought. All wrecks. All protesting weariness. All wanting instant solutions. None of them prepared to work through their pain. All the same. Even the intelligent ones, like Tom here.

'Yes but, Tom, it takes time. We need to be patient. Please.'

Tom sighed then began, reciting the story as if it were a mantra. As if I'm at Alcoholics Anonymous, he thought to himself.

'My mother died in Crete just over four weeks ago. She was ninety. She died in a cave on the south of the island where an elderly Cretan gentleman called Themistocles had taken her. She asked him to give me this envelope, in which there is a war diary and letters written by the man I thought was my father's brother together with a letter from him to her and a note from my mother that says 'Your father would have wanted you to have these'. I didn't understand. Then I read the letter which was clearly addressed to her. And most of what was supposed to be a diary consists of letters to her and he refers to her as his sweetheart. And then I realised what she meant. The person who had written that letter and kept that diary was not the person I thought was my father but his brother Bill. *He* was my blood father. He died in Crete during a major World War Two battle and that's why my mother went there, to see the places where he had been and where he had died. And she never told me or anyone, as far as I can tell. It was a huge family secret. I'm sixty-five years old and just discovering that my father is not the person I thought he was and I will never see my real father.'

That's better, she thought. Started him off anyway. Now press on to his emotional state.

'And how did you feel when you realised that?'

He hadn't believed it at first, had thought there must have been a mistake. He had read all of it again and again, wanting to believe that it wasn't true, that maybe his mother and this Bill had been sweethearts once but that it had ended and then she had taken up with his father Bert. But the dates didn't fit. He had had to check his birth certificate and his parents' wedding certificate. His mother and father – Bert – had married in July 1941. This Bill character had been writing to his mother calling her his sweetheart in May 1941. And he was born in November of that year. There could have been no mistake.

'I knew that I had been conceived before the wedding but I was in my twenties when I discovered that and I just put it down to all the movement that must have been going on because of the war. I never really gave it much thought. But now I realise that mum must have got pregnant through my real father and then, when he was killed, married his brother, the man I called my father. I can only guess this was done out of some confused sense that it would be the best for me.'

Interesting. He was beginning to apply some logic to the situation but, of course, that wouldn't help. He needed to get in touch with his emotional side. Probably hadn't been in touch for years, maybe for most of his life.

'So what do you think about that decision?'

There was a momentary pause but then Tom replied, the volume of his voice noticeably louder.

'Just now I'm totally confused as to who I am. Three weeks ago I thought I was one person. Now I think I'm someone else. I can't sleep for thinking about it. For sixty-five years I've been one person, the son of these two people I called my mum and dad, inheriting their genetic behaviours and learning their rules for life, and for the next however many years I've got left I am someone else, someone with the genes of someone I never knew and can never know. It's just mind-blowing. I feel completely and utterly lost.'

'Are you angry with someone because of this?'

Tom looked sharply across at Dr Stephanie Barrett, his counsellor. Of course, he was angry. Wouldn't you be, he wanted to say? And, of course, he wasn't comfortable with that. Hadn't his whole life been about being logical and keeping control of his feelings? Wasn't that the best way for humans to behave? Well, wasn't it? Why was she pressing him about his anger?

'Yes, I'm angry with my mother for withholding this from me all my life. I'm angry with my father, who's dead now, I mean the person I thought was my father, for not telling me but also for marrying my mum in the first place when presumably he knew she was expecting and knew that it wasn't his child. And I'm angry with my real father, this Bill, for dying like that and leaving my mother in the lurch.'

She replaced her glass on the table before resuming.

'Would you like to talk about the person you thought was your father, the one who brought you up?'

He hadn't expected that. He'd expected to talk about his mother. Bert was dead, had been for many years. Besides, they had never been that close. Still, if she thought it might help.

'We were never really close. He died twenty years ago. I have to say I never really missed him that much. It was strange really because I was working in the factory with him for his last few years and we got on fine then, but it was like as a couple of colleagues, you know what I mean? It wasn't like father and son. When I was younger, I talked to a few of my contemporaries about this and we all felt it was a lot to do with the war. Our dads weren't here in the first few years of our life, so we never really bonded with them. Besides that, it wasn't expected for men to look after children in the nineteen-forties and -fifties, was it? My

186

mother brought us up. That was her full-time job. Dad ran the business and that was his job. Wasn't that normal?'

'A lot of men were emotionally damaged by the war, that's true. It was very common for men not to talk about their experiences.'

He was dredging back in his memory bank now, recalling what he knew about his father's – Bert's – war.

He had been in prisoner-of-war camp. He knew that, because his mother had told him. He had been captured in Italy and sent to a camp in Austria. He had worked on a farm there from what he could recall. At the end of the war, he and some others had walked out of the camp and somehow or other got back to Britain. He had never talked about it though. He had asked him once, when he was nine or ten. He'd been looking for something in the spider-webbed loft of the house and had came across his creased army cap. He had taken it down the loft ladder and asked him which regiment he'd been in. He had said it was the Sherwood Foresters and he had asked him what it had been like in the army. He'd been brought up on those comics, *The Wizard* and *Hotspur*, and had read nearly all the Biggles books so he had been expecting something about fighting the Germans but he had just said it was nothing like you read in the comics, nothing like that at all. Then his mother appeared and, when she saw that he'd got his old army cap, she had told him to go and do his homework because 'We don't want to go over that old stuff, do we, dad?' And that was it. He had never mentioned it again. Neither of them ever had, now he came to think of it.

And now I can see why, he thought to himself. Neither of them wanted to talk about the war in case something was said about my real dad and about how he died and about how they got married so soon afterwards. That was why there was this stifling cloak of silence. It wasn't just the war they were avoiding talking about, it was those first few years of my existence, because that might have triggered mention of my real father and the reasons for their marriage.

'Do you remember any particular times when your relationship was especially strained?'

'How d'you mean?'

'Such as arguments, rows, maybe physical violence?'

Tom shook his head.

No, not really. Certainly there was never anything physical. There had never been any physical violence, although, come to think of it, there was never very much physical affection either. But again, those were the times they had lived in, weren't they? Men didn't show affection publicly, did they? Tom himself had had to learn to do it late in life. When men began to change because women forced them to.

'Oh, we had our rows, of course we did. When I was in my teens, I remember walking home at about midnight from some girlfriend's house and his car pulling up alongside me. He'd been sent out by my mother to look for me because she was worried I'd been murdered or something. He didn't say anything all the way home but I was aware of this icy silence. When we got back, they both had a go at me for being so late, how they'd been worried sick, didn't I ever think of their feelings, who was this girl anyway, why hadn't I telephoned to say I'd be late, et cetera, et cetera. Although, when I think about it now, it's my mother's face I can see, it's my mother's voice I can hear. Dad – Bert – just sat there nodding agreement with everything she said.'

'So would you say he was a good father to you?'

Was he? Certainly he was a steady presence in the family, solid, reliable, hard-working. In fact, so hard working that he spent more time at the factory than he did at home. But, when he was at home, he had been a proper father, hadn't he? Then again, what is – or what was, for times change, don't they – a proper father? He had nothing to measure him against. He was there, on Sundays, at Christmas, on birthdays, on family holidays. Tom could remember his presence then as he was growing up. Other than that, Bert had spent a lot of time smoking then falling asleep in front of the television.

'Yes, I suppose he was, within his limitations. I think he was a decent man. I think he was good to my mother. I suppose his marrying her in the first place was a pretty special thing to do in the circumstances. I suppose that was maybe the reason why she kept it quiet all her life, because of what he had done in becoming my father. He was very fond of Nancy, that's my sister, when she was growing up, I do remember that. He showed her much more affection than he showed me but I just thought that

188

was because she was a girl. It never occurred to me that there might be any other reason. But yes, he was a good father. He kept a roof over our heads, he fed and clothed us, he paid for my education. He even took me in to run the factory eventually. Yes, you could say he was a decent father. You see, I've never known any other so I can't compare him with anyone else. You don't see other people's relationships much, do you? I mean, when I went to play at any of my pals' houses when I was young, I don't remember anything different about the way their fathers treated them. That was just the way it was in those days. It's different now, of course, isn't it?'

She watched his face as the memories trickled across his brain. This line of approach wasn't stirring anything dramatic. She needed to press the bigger button, the emotional heart button.

'What about your mother then? Would you like to talk about her?'

Tom could feel a double jolt occurring inside his mind, like two bombs exploding simultaneously. One part of this was the enormously warm affection he felt for his mother, an affection that had lasted over all those years of his life, even when they had had cross words, and which was still controlling the grief he felt at her recent death. But the other part was a hurt, a deep and currently all-invasive hurt, that she should have kept the knowledge of who his real father was to herself all his life, that she had kept this secret, this most important, this vital secret from him.

'I've always loved my mother. Always. When she died, even though she was ninety, it was a great grief to me. I miss her still. She could be a funny old stick, with her odd ways, but that's what made her tick. She took up yoga in her seventies, you know. Said she was bored and needed something to occupy her mind. She'd trained herself as a fashion designer earlier too. After my sister and I had left home, she took over all the designing at the factory. Said she needed to keep busy now we'd left. I bet Dad – Bert – was glad to have her there, because she drove the business into new areas. By the time I joined it, we were already a brand name and operating in several key world markets. That was my mother's doing. It was her designs that transformed the business, I know. Dad – Bert – recognised that. So I wasn't surprised when she came up with this notion of a Mediterranean cruise for her ninetieth birthday. It was just the sort of thing she'd been doing all her life. She went off to Spain once with a friend of hers and they hired bicycles and rode everywhere in the resort. She was about my age then, can you imagine? When she was younger and had become the chief designer at the firm, she used to go off to Paris for fashion shows on her own. And she could hold her own with all those high-powered fashion people there. There was one chap she got on especially well with, called Pierre. I met him once when I went to London with her for some fashion event or other. Funny bloke. But that was the sort of thing she would do – pal up with the most outrageous people, even though she'd come from quite a sheltered background in Birmingham.'

'And how do you feel about her now?'

He paused and thought but in truth he couldn't pin down his exact feelings – they were still too jumbled up.

'I don't know. Angry. Hurt. Let down. Confused. I can't think why she never told me. Why would she keep it all secret? Yes, I can understand when I was growing up that it would have been problematic but surely not later. I was at school with someone who was adopted and his parents told him when he was ten years old. It was no big deal. He'd come to terms with it. You can find out who your birth parents are now, can't you, if you were adopted?'

'Yes, the law was changed some years ago. People who were adopted have a right now to find who their birth parents were. It was very common in the past for such matters to be hushed up. Do you blame your mother?'

He looked across at her. Where was all this going? He didn't feel any better now than he had done when he first came to visit her a week ago. Was it all worth the bother? And it wasn't cheap, as he kept telling Chantal, not cheap at all. But she had told him he mustn't think like this, he had to give it time.

'Yes, I do. Yes, I suppose I do blame her. Not just for what happened all those years ago but for not telling me and for making my dad – Bert – keep quiet about it too. And then to let me find out like this, after she's died. I feel like a fool. I never suspected anything like this. She's been carrying this secret for sixty-five years and then she lets me find out this way, after her death, so I can't ask her about it all. And there's no one else to ask.'

That was what was annoying him most, he realised. She wasn't there for him to ask, for him to argue with, for him to really ever find out the reason for the secrecy. It wasn't so much the realisation of his paternity as the deliberate secrecy. That was what was hurting most. And he would never know its rationale.

'Can you recall any times when she might have tried telling you but then not been able to?'

Tom screwed his face up, as if trying to recall.

He could remember, at his grandfather's funeral – his mother's father, Granddad Wilson – his grandmother and his mother had been talking afterwards back at their house. He must have been nine or ten at the time. He had really missed his grandfather when he died. He had been a very special person. He had loved going to their house because he always had some new treasure to show me. The house was an old one with a cellar where he had a workshop and he used to show him how to make dovetail joints and mortise and tenon joints. He had helped him once to make a bread tray for his mother's birthday. And he always had a new book for him to read.

'After my grandfather's funeral, I overheard my mother and grandmother talking in hushed voices. I wanted something, I can't remember what it was, but I went over to where they were and, as I approached, I heard my grandmother say "Are you going to tell Tom soon?" They were both looking very anxious as they spoke but I thought this was because my grandfather had died. I said, "Are you going to tell me what?" "Nothing dear," said my mother. "Nothing for you to worry about." Maybe that was what they were talking about, who my real father was and whether I should be told. Who knows? It's all such a long time ago.'

'No other occasions?'

He dredged back in his memory again.

'When my sister Nancy got married to Len, there was a bit of a kerfuffle, I remember. I never understood it at the time. My

191

first-born, Ellie, was only a few months old and she was a bit of a handful on the day because she was teething so most of our attention, that's my first wife Julia and me, was on her. But at the wedding reception, my father – Bert – got rather drunk and, when he got drunk, which wasn't very often, to be fair to him, his voice got louder and his face got much redder. Anyway, I could hear his voice from where we were sitting with our baby and he seemed to be boasting about something to my mother. I couldn't make out most of it but I do remember him saying "He'll never be able to give a daughter away, will he? Just as well a son doesn't require the same thing." It didn't mean a thing to me at the time but it struck me as an odd thing to say, which is probably why I've remembered it. I guess, from what I now know, he was probably talking about my real father, Bill.'

There was a lengthy silence as Tom took in the significance of what he had just recalled for Dr Barrett. She watched his face as it first of all contorted then relaxed, as the painful memory slotted into place in the narrative that was still unfolding for him.

'Tom, I think we've done enough for this week. I'll see you same time next week, all right?'

*

'Are you jealous of your sister, Tom?'

It was three weeks later, in the same room, but the gladioli had been replaced with yellow orchids. They hadn't, in his view, got any further in the intervening weeks. Merely gone over the same ground. And he'd had to get back to the factory to deal with the backlog of correspondence and bills. He was finding it hard to concentrate on work but at least some of the time it helped to occupy his mind.

'What d'you mean?'

What was she asking him now? What could Nancy have to do with all this? He'd only mentioned her briefly when he'd told about that incident at her wedding. Was this really important?

'I mean, do you think that your sister got a better deal because she was the child of both the people you called your parents?

Tom thought hard, rehearsing all the moments of shared growing up he could remember and the subsequent coolness between Nancy and himself after they had both left home.

'I don't think so. We fought as children, sure, but I think most children fight, don't they? Isn't that part of the growing up process? My two, Ellie and Will, certainly did, I know that. I think Nancy and I got on just fine through our childhoods. I don't think dad – Bert – excessively favoured her or anything like that. Yes, he was certainly more affectionate towards her when she was a child, I can remember that but I can't remember resenting any of it. It just struck me as what happened if you were a girl. She was a girly girl, if you know what I mean. I don't mean she couldn't enjoy rough and tumble games or playing out in the street or any of those sorts of things but she always liked dressing up. Especially for birthday parties or when we went out to visit or when we went to the pantomime at the Hippodrome every year.'

Funny how that stuck in his mind but he could remember those annual pantomime visits as if they were yesterday. *Aladdin, Cinderella, Sinbad*, all of the traditional shows. And Nancy always got really dressed up. But that was common in those days. He just sort of wore his best school clothes but she always had to have a special dress for the occasion. But that may have been mum's idea more than hers. Maybe she just came to expect it? They weren't the same nowadays, those annual events that you used to look forward to as a kid, but he could remember the big fuss that was made when the new season's Jersey potatoes arrived or when it was blackberry picking time and they'd pick pounds of them and his mum would turn them into loads of jars of jam. It wasn't like that now, was it, because you could get everything all through the year, couldn't you, in the supermarkets.

'You were talking about the differences between Nancy and yourself.' She softly interrupted his reminiscing.

Tom looked across at her. She was an attractive woman. Aged about forty, he thought. Slim figure, hair pulled back from her forehead and fastened at the back with a comb. Blue jumper and black trousers. He'd never really noticed her as a woman before. Was this a sign that he was getting better, that this counselling was helping him and making a difference?

'Oh yes, well, I don't think we were treated any differently really. I think she was just treated like a girl, that's all. Like every girl was in those days. Or at least the girls that I knew where we were growing up.'

'And are you close now?'

Nancy and Len lived in north Staffordshire and he rarely saw them these days. They had their work and he had the business. To be truthful, he didn't really think they had approved of his divorce from Julia, even though they had accepted Chantal. Yes, they kept in touch, in a desultory fashion – occasional phone calls and even more occasional visits – but nothing much more. There were several years between them after all. It was simply that they lived separate lives.

'Not especially. There's no great rift or anything like that. I can see where you're pointing me but it's nothing like that. Nancy was never as good at school as I was so university was never an option for her. She went into nursing and made a successful career out of it. Give her credit, she made a great success out of it. After her son started school, she went back to work and she eventually became a nursing manager. She was helping with the nurse training at Keele University in the last few years before she retired.'

'But you're not that close?'

'I suppose not, no.'

Yes, they had spent time as a family at Christmas and at birthdays, the sort of thing that most families did. And they'd had to be close again recently, of course, because of their mother's death, getting the body back to England and all the funeral arrangements. Nancy had found it tough too, even though, like him, she'd been half-expecting it for years. She'd lived a long life had their mother.

'How has she reacted to the knowledge that Bert wasn't your father?'

Nancy had thrown up her hands in horror, proclaiming herself aghast at this new knowledge, he recalled. 'Typical,' she had said. 'Just like mum to do something like this on us. Won't she ever give us peace?' But that was just Nancy's theatrical stuff. She didn't mean it. She had always done this kind of over-the-top emotional reaction as a kind of protective blanket against revealing her true feelings. But what those were, who knew? Probably her husband Len was the only one.

194

'I don't really know how she feels about it all deep down. I mean, we talked a bit about it at the funeral and afterwards and she was just as shocked as I was, especially about the way it had all come out through Themis and all that. But we haven't really talked about it all since then. She knows I'm having counselling, so maybe she feels she shouldn't intrude. She talks to Chantal more than she talks to me. Surprising really. I never thought they'd get on that well together.'

That had been a surprise. He hadn't thought they had that much in common. Maybe they talked about him?

'Do you feel differently about her now than you did before your discovery? Now you know that you had different fathers?'

Did he? Did he? He supposed deep down he did, though he couldn't really explain how. And the most important factor, the central factor he would call it, was their mother. She had been the dominant parent for both of them. They had had a shared childhood in a home where their mother ruled the roost. He didn't mean bossily. What he meant was that it was she who had created that warm sense of homeliness. It was hard to explain but they had both loved their home life. They'd always share that.

'I don't know if I really feel any differently about Nancy now. As I said, our lives are so different and distant from each other – and they have been like that for a long time – that it's hard to conjure up something that may not be there. Nancy is my sister, always has been, always will be. I don't know how you're supposed to get on with your sister but I think we get on fine.'

There was a pause, as Stephanie Barrett prepared her next line of probing and Tom reflected on why he and Nancy were not that close and whether it mattered.

'I'd just like to clarify something before we finish for today,' she said, easing herself back in her chair. 'Your real father, Bill Ennis, you really didn't know anything about him until you received those papers on your mother's death?'

Tom looked up at her. He had been lost in thoughts and memories of Nancy and of their shared childhood. He sighed, as he realised again how much he had been duped over the sixty-five years of his life so far.

'There was a photograph of him in his RAF uniform on my mother's china cabinet. It was always there, next to her wedding photograph. At some point, and I really can't remember when, though I've been casting about in my memory to find the moment, I was told it was dad's brother, my uncle, and he had died in the war. I was never told anything else and, since I'd obviously never seen him, I just accepted the fact that he was dead. I never had any feelings about that. How could I? I didn't know him.'

He had that photograph at home now. It was the only picture he had of his real father. He looked at it all the time, trying to imagine what he was like, what he thought, what he felt. He had tried to picture him in Crete, on that tortuous escape he and his men embarked on across the mountains to reach the place where the Royal Navy could take them off the island. And that incredible act of bravado that he chose in order to save Themis. And how he died.

She waited for him to continue. There was a minute or so of silence.

'He was awarded a medal, you know, for that act of bravery. Distinguished Service Order. My mother had it in her handbag when she died. He called her Merry, you know. Nobody ever called her that to the best of my knowledge. Dad – Bert – called her Meredith. That was her proper name. *He* called her Merry. It's in his last letter to her and in all those letters in his diary. It's hard to think of her as a young girl in love, being called Merry by a dashing RAF airman on his way to be a hero.'

'Do you think you would have liked him if he had lived?'

How could he know that? How could he know what his father was really like? He was barely more than a boy himself when he died. Not much older than Tom when he left Oxford. Did he know then what he was doing? Was his character etched already on his face? The child may be father to the man but accidents happen and people get driven off course. That tall thin man in the photograph with the dark hair, the half-smile and the tiny moustache was his father. That's all he knew.

Of course, he was a war hero, wasn't he? He had been brought up on all that tosh about war heroism. He would have loved having a dad who'd got a medal. It would have given him quite some status amongst his mates at school, wouldn't it?

But he just didn't know. He couldn't tell from that photograph what he was really like. His diary showed him to be a thoughtful person, someone who cared for others and someone who took his responsibilities seriously. But how could he know what he would have been like as a father? As his father? It was just so infuriating.

'I can't get to grips with it all. I keep going round and round in circles, thinking what if this and what if that. But it's no good. It's not getting me anywhere. I really want to get to grips with all this and to feel settled in my head. I thought you were supposed to be helping me to do that?'

She smiled lightly at him. Although he didn't realise it, he was making good progress. Getting him to articulate his feelings was the first and most important stage. He had almost certainly never talked like this to anyone else. No one else would have, or could have, challenged him like this.

'I think we might be ready for that very soon. But not just yet. Go away and reflect on all we've talked about today and we'll see where we get to next week. All right?'

*

Stephanie Barrett ushered Tom to his seat and held up a bottle of *Marques de Caceres*.

'I thought we might celebrate the fact that you've been coming here for ten weeks now with a little something. Are you okay with red wine? D'you like *rioja*? This is one of my favourites.'

Tom Ennis sat down on the armchair and took the glass she offered him, holding it steady while she poured.

'Thanks. Cheers.'

'Your very good health. And I mean that truly. I think we've covered a lot of ground in the past few weeks. I know you must feel at times that you've been going over the same territory time and time again but I do hope you also appreciate that each time you reveal something more about your feelings at different moments in your life. Do you feel you've benefited from our sessions?'

He sipped at his wine thoughtfully. These meetings had become important to him, more so than he could have anticipated given his initial ambivalence. He had confided as much to Chantal who had smiled knowingly. 'Up there with the rape victims then?' she had teased him and he had smiled, recognising the obduracy that had initially made him resist her suggestion. Yes, it had been good to talk about all these things in the confidentiality of Dr Barrett's room. Yes, it had been surprisingly useful to actually get some of his feelings towards his family out in the semi-open.

'I suppose yes, I have to confess it's been much better than I originally thought.'

'What did you expect?'

'Oh, I don't know. I suppose I half expected some sort of Freudian analysis of my dreams, something like that.'

She smoothed her skirt with her left hand and smiled.

'There are different forms of counselling. I prefer to let the patient focus on what matters to them and try to help them to come to terms with whatever it is that is causing them distress.'

It didn't feel to Tom as if he had actually come to terms with anything yet. He was still floundering in the wake of this so recently imparted knowledge about who his real father was and of his mother's death.

'So do you think I've got to that point?'

'No, but I do think we're closer to it than perhaps you think you are. I think you are ready to confront your *daemon* now.'

Tom laughed lightly. It was a strange phrase she had used.

'What is my demon then?'

'I said *daemon* and I meant *daemon*. It's originally an ancient Greek word and it meant spirit or genius. Its connotation with evil occurred later. What I mean by the word is the essential being of a person, their core of belief if you like. I think you are ready to confront yours honestly now.'

Tom looked across at her. For the first time in their meetings she was animated. A slightly pink blush suffused her cheeks as she lent partially toward him. He noticed the V-necked cerise blouse, the black skirt, the sharp heels.

'Sorry, you've lost me.'

'Tom, I need you to think very carefully before you answer my next question. If you are going to deal with the distress in your life, you are going to have to be absolutely and resolutely honest, not just with me but with yourself.'

'Okay, but I still don't see what all the great drama is about.'

'All right, Tom. I want you simply to tell me what difference it would have made to your life if you had known about your real father earlier.'

He gulped. He hadn't expected that. He reached for the wine glass and steadied himself with a good mouthful of the rich ruby wine. Would it have made any difference? Yes, of course. But what difference? Maybe he ought to think about when it would have made a difference. If he had known as a young child, what then? Maybe it would have helped explain why he and Bert were never that close although he had never really felt troubled by all that. He still thought that was more to do with the times they lived in, expectations of male behaviour just after the war and all that.

What if he'd found out later? At King Edward's? What difference would that have made? There were boys in his class who were adopted – at least one that he could recall, Snowy Davies. There were boys whose fathers had died in the war and were being brought up by their mothers. None of that really mattered. What mattered were the joys of algebra, knowing the periodic table backwards, whether you could get full marks in your homework and how good you were at football. Those were the things that mattered. And later on it was whether you could get an attractive girl-friend, one with long legs and a slim waist you could put your arm around, one who'd let you kiss with your tongue in her mouth. No, it probably wouldn't have made much difference then. He would still have argued with his parents, because that's what adolescence was all about. It would have merely given him an extra reason for his arguing.

At Oxford perhaps? Would it have made any difference to be told then? Unlikely then too. That was too much about finding his own identity in the maelstrom of changing fashion, changing ideas and revolution in youth culture that was dominating the landscape in those days. So he'd arrived in a blazer and flannels but left in jeans and a leather jacket. He'd started as a believer in opportunities for the brightest and best, which was what he'd been encouraged to believe his grammar school had provided, but left to the cries of equal rights for all. And, of course, Oxford was where he spent huge amounts of time chasing women, downing large amounts of alcohol and playing football. He barely had time for his parents at all while he was there and, when he did come home for the university holidays, he found home stifling and boring and he longed to get back. Often he would go and spend time with one or other of his new friends at their homes in Leeds or Bristol or Manchester, anywhere that they could recapture the essence of their lives at Oxford, aided by copious amounts of alcohol naturally. One summer, he even took a part-time job as a park-keeper in Oxford in order to remain there rather than go home, although he got the sack after one week for refusing to scoop up the dog muck in the park.

So when would the knowledge of who his real father was have made a difference? At his marriage? At either of his marriages in fact? At his first wedding to Julia, would it have made any difference to know that the genial clown who had drunk too much at the wedding reception was not his real father, who was dead, but his father's brother Bert, who had married Tom's mother in order to provide him with a father? Almost certainly not. And Bert was dead himself by the time Tom married Chantal. Maybe at the births of the two children? Maybe it would have been good for them to grow up in the knowledge that Bert wasn't their actual grandfather but was their step-grandfather. But what difference could that possibly have made? And at what point in their lives would he have told them anyway? When would they have been able to understand the fact and the consequences of that fact? And what were the consequences anyway? Merely a different name on a piece of paper. It wasn't as if they were being cruelly treated by some wicked grandfather who beat them at every opportunity. Quite the opposite, in fact, Bert was a good grandfather, kindly, thoughtful, patient, always ready to listen to his grandchildren's stories. When he was there, that is, for more often than not he was at the Enniswear factory whenever Tom, Julia and the children came to visit them in Sutton Coldfield.

'I don't know,' he said at last. 'I really don't know. I've just been thinking about what you said about confronting my *daemon*. I think I see what you mean. It wouldn't have made any difference, would it? I couldn't have had a happier upbringing. I couldn't have wished for a better mother. The things that have happened to me, the emotional crises, have been my own doing, haven't they? It was my fault that my marriage to Julia broke down. I've always known that, though I suppose I've tried to rationalise it by telling myself that we'd drifted apart anyway and were really leading separate lives in the same household. Giving up teaching wasn't such a big problem, because I knew I was struggling by then, and I was glad to get out, if the truth is told. As for meeting Chantal and marrying her, that was probably the best thing I've ever done. She is my rock.'

'So is the cloud beginning to lift now? Are you still angry with your mother?'

Was he? Was he still? He searched through the layers in his brain, as if hunting down that elusive single atom that contained his ultimate feeling for his mother. But it was not that simple. If only it were.

'I don't know. I still feel kind of resentful of her for not telling me the truth.'

'Even though you could have done nothing to change that truth?'

'I know. It's illogical really. But I still feel a bit angry.'

'Are your feelings for your mother more of love than of anger?'

He paused, sensing the warmth of her memory flooding his body, much stronger than that irritation that still lurked in the depth of his mind.

'Yes, definitely. That's never been in doubt. She was a wonderful mother.'

'So, Tom, knowing all you now know, can you forgive your mother for not telling you who your real father was?'

Tom Ennis took a deep breath, narrowed his eyes and looked across at the attractive woman sitting opposite him, the woman who had steered him these past weeks through exploration of his feelings towards his family, and in particular his parents.

'Yes,' he said simply. 'Yes, I can.'

# 3

Will Ennis had been entrusted with making the arrangements, while his father was undergoing counselling. There weren't many perks these days for young journalists but a good address book was still an essential tool for his work and in recent years he had made contacts at Birmingham Airport through anxieties about airport security in the light of the terrorist threat and about the contentious planned expansion of the airport to produce a third runway. One of those contacts had been able to advise him on the best means to fly to Crete in the early autumn, since most of the charter flights had ceased for the winter. There were three possibilities – taking a cheap flight to Athens and then using either Aegean or Olympic Airways to get a direct flight to Chania, taking a more expensive direct flight to Heraklion, or finding a last-minute package on one of the few charter flights still operating in late September. The direct flight from Gatwick was the only real option, Will decided, so that's what it had to be, though his contact did manage to get a small reduction on their tickets.

The plan was for four of them to go – Tom, Chantal, Ellie and Will. His Aunt Nancy had declined the proposed trip.

'I went to the funeral, didn't I?' she had argued. 'I don't think I could face any more. Besides, it's your father who has to come to terms with it all, isn't it?'

What she meant, Will had come to realise, as the story of Bill Ennis had emerged and as his father had come to terms with who his real father was, was that she, Nancy, was the actual child of Bert and Meredith, as she had always believed. For Nancy, shocking though her mother's secrecy over the years had been, there was no confusion about her own identity. Mother, father, they were as they had always been. And now she had laid them both to rest. End of story. Well, if not quite end of story, at least end of that particular chapter. Dealing with her mother's ghost might prove as difficult as dealing with her mother had been in real life but that was for the future.

'So thanks, Will, but no thanks,' she had said, when he rang her up with the idea that he and Ellie had first mooted. 'I never was that keen on flying anyway and I don't think this trip is absolutely necessary. As I say, I've seen my mother's coffin being dispatched. That's sufficient.'

It was Ellie who had first suggested it. She and Will had gone for a *balti* in Adil's in King's Heath soon after their grandmother's funeral in Sutton Coldfield.

'You can fill me in properly now, El,' he had said, as he tore a chunk of hot *naan* bread and prepared to scoop a mouthful of curried chicken from the black *balti* bowl with it. He leaned forward to avoid splashing on to his new trousers and to absorb the aromatic herb smells from the newly-prepared dish. 'What was Granny up to in Crete really?'

Ellie, dressed simply in jeans and sweater, her hair tied back with a large comb, had looked across at her dark-haired brother.

'You know, Will, I can see the resemblance,' she had begun, cocking her head to examine him. 'I've been looking at the that photo of Bill – our grandfather. What do we call him – Granddad Bill? As opposed to Granddad Bert? Anyway, I can see the resemblance. You've got the same nose and chin as he had. And the hair. His was that colour.'

Will had grinned impishly and his dark hair had flopped over his right eye.

'So?'

'So I'm just saying, that's all. You look like him. Like Granddad Bill.'

Just from that photograph? How could she tell?

'Okay, so I know all the business about his time in Crete and where he died. And I know, obviously, about Granny keeping it all quiet from us all and escaping from your clutches to meet this Themis character. But what was she hoping to find there? She knew he'd been dead over sixty years, so what was…?'

The remainder of his sentence had been drowned out by shrieks of laughter from a group of students sitting at the long table next to them.

Ellie had chewed thoughtfully on her prawn *balti* and let the disturbance subside.

'You've read the diary, haven't you? All of it?'

'Yeah.'

'So you know about the journey he took. Did you know Granny only got the diary a few years ago?'

'No.'

Will had looked up, his right eyebrow raised. He hadn't been party to this bit of information. Ellie, reaching to pour herself a glass of red wine, had explained.

'Dad told me about how this punk woman had come to her house once with this diary. Said she was the granddaughter of one of the airmen that was with Granddad Bill – it still sounds funny saying that. D'you remember that one he called Eddie? The fat one?'

Will had nodded, while helping himself to some *tarka dall*.

'The one who couldn't keep up? Who wanted them to leave him to die? That one?'

'Yes, him. Granny told dad and Aunt Nancy about this punk woman visiting her but she never mentioned the diary. Themis told us about where it came from. Well, that must have set her off thinking about visiting Crete to see where he died and to visit the places he'd been to.'

'So you think she'd been planning this jaunt for some time?'

'Oh yes, absolutely.'

'The whole journey?'

'Not quite. But, I think, once dad and Aunt Nancy had agreed to pay for her Mediterranean cruise, she started planning it. Some of it was Themis's idea. All she knew was that Bill had died in Crete and his body was buried in a War Cemetery near Chania. A place called Souda Bay. Funny thing is that's where she texted me the first time to tell me not to worry.'

Ellie had recalled the scare she had had when she had first realised her grandmother had gone missing, the panic as she had chased around Heraklion with Mikalis trying to get the police or the British Consulate or anybody to take an interest and to go looking for her, and then the first text message from Souda Bay which turned out to be a red herring but did at least reassure her that her grandmother was alive. She had shuddered momentarily.

'The crafty old devil! So how did Themis fit into the plan?'

'You know who he was, don't you? He was the boy who guided them over the mountains, who Granddad Bill died protecting. Well, he told Granny that he would take her to this cave which was the last place he was known to be alive. He decided to take her on the route that Granddad Bill and his men travelled.'

'So that was why she wanted to find him.' Will had sat back, eyes wide open in surprise. He had not previously made the connection.

'It was all your fault, stupid!' she had laughed, her white teeth gleaming in the dimly-lit restaurant. 'You showed her how to Google on your laptop. That was how she found Themis in the Greek phone directory online and traced him. Miraculously he was still alive and in the same village where he was born. He told me all that.'

Ellie had laughed again as Will pulled a face.

'Don't beat yourself up. Granny would never do what she was told, remember? That's one of the reasons we loved her so much. She was a character. She lived life to the full and she lived a long time. And I think she died where she wanted to be, near where our Granddad Bill died.'

As Will was wiping up the remnants of his meal with another chunk of *naan* bread, she had made the suggestion.

'So that's where we ought to take her ashes. To Crete. That would be fitting. She would have appreciated that, wouldn't she?'

'To that cave?'

'No, stupid, to the War Cemetery. That's where we think he was buried. So that's where we should scatter her ashes.'

It was lucky, Will had thought at the time, that no decision had yet been made about the ashes. His father had still been in a state of shock at the funeral and, when pressed by the funeral director, had prevaricated, saying they all needed time to think what was the most appropriate place, given the new knowledge that all now shared.

So, Souda Bay it was to be. Their father, Tom, still receiving counselling, agreed without really listening to them, while Chantal said it was a really good idea. Will had spoken to someone at the War Graves Commission to see if there was any protocol that needed to be observed before their planned visit to scatter Meredith's ashes at the Allied War Cemetery and had been told that it was best to get in touch with the local curator, whose contact details he had been given. There were no formalities that had to be observed, he was informed, though it would be appreciated if the time and date were notified to the curator in order to ensure that there was no clash with any other activity at the cemetery.

So, time and date having been agreed, Will had organised the purchase of flight tickets, car parking at Gatwick Airport and car hire in Heraklion.

'Next Wednesday,' he told, first Chantal and his father, then his sister Ellie. 'I'll pick you up.'

\*

In the interim Will did some exploring on the Internet. First, he found a map of Crete and traced the journey that Themis and his grandmother must have traversed from Heraklion (Iraklion in Granddad Bill's diary) to Souda Bay to Xamoudochori to Deres (Dere) then over the White Mountains or *Lefka Ori*, as he was beginning to call them himself, to Agia Ireni (Aiyireni) to Sougia (Suya) to Agia Roumeli (Aiya Roumeli) to Hora Sfakion (Sphakia). One day, he thought, it would be interesting to do that journey himself. But not this trip. It could wait.

He found an account of the Battle of Crete and read how Maleme airfield could have been recaptured if the Allied commanders, in particular General Freyberg, had fully appreciated the situation on the ground and sent reinforcements to retake the airfield after the New Zealand battalion defending it had mistakenly withdrawn on the first night before the Germans had secured it. That explained how Granddad Bill and his men had been left exposed and why they had been forced to flee so precipitously. He also discovered how the German invasion of Crete was the first time their troops experienced massive civil resistance from women, children and the elderly, who were the bulk of the population. That helped to explain the role of Alexandros, the *andarte*, and Nikos, or Themis as he had come to think of him now, in helping the British and New Zealand troops to escape and the callous murder of Themis's family.

He had also found about the Souda Bay Cemetery and how it was the last resting place for over fifteen hundred of those from the British Commonwealth who died between May 20th and 31st 1941 in the Battle of Crete. Almost half of the graves were unmarked, he had read, and those unidentified graves were marked only with 'KNOWN UNTO GOD'. Was his Granddad Bill in such a grave? He did not know. No one had asked that question. He telephoned the War Graves Commission to find out and was told there was no record of a William Ennis in a marked grave at Souda Bay. Useful to know that, he thought. At least he could prepare the others. They would have to decide where the most fitting spot for the ashes would be, perhaps only when they reached the cemetery.

Then he had hunted for information about AMES, found it stood for Air Ministry Experimental Station and was the name given to RAF units using the recently invented Radio Direction Finding devices to plot the incoming flights of German bombers in the early years of World War Two. These devices, later known as radar, he discovered, were unknown to the Germans and those personnel trained to operate them had to swear an oath of secrecy and were told that, if they ever breathed one word of the operation they were involved in, they would be shot. So that was the outfit that Granddad Bill had been responsible for! Amazing to think he must have been a sort of secret agent. That hadn't been obvious from his diary. He obviously had only seen himself as doing a job that had to be done. Indeed, so much of his diary revealed him to be rather unsure of his own abilities, particularly in leading others. And yet clearly he was a natural leader. His success in guiding his men across Crete under such extreme conditions showed that.

He found a RAF veterans' site and posted a note asking if anyone still alive had known Flying Officer William Ennis, DSO, who served with AMES in Crete but there was no response. Probably everyone who might have been around at that time was now dead, he thought. He followed his grandmother's strategy and tried tracing Alec Bryce in New Zealand through phone directories and made contact with his eldest son, who explained that his father had died some years previously but that he had mentioned Bill Ennis several times in conversation as one of the bravest men he had known. They all knew the story of how their father had escaped from Crete with the young Cretan boy and how Bill had died. But that was all. There were no other mementoes. Just stories handed down over the years within families. As this one would be in time, Will thought.

Tom Ennis, his father, decided to sell the Enniswear factory. Neither Ellie nor Will had ever shown any interest in the business, although he had tried to persuade them that they could have run it between them. He had always talked about the premise as his pension fund, if the family didn't want it, and he was being offered a good price for the site, which was in an area undergoing considerable regeneration. Will had spent some time tracing articles about Enniswear and E.J. Ennis & Sons, as it had previously been known, in the *Birmingham Post* where he was working at the time. He had put these together in a leather cover and given it to his father as a memento. He had kept a loosely bound copy for himself. He had looked at it again, as he prepared for their journey, and saw in its pages his grandmother aging from young married mother, proudly standing beside Granddad Bert at the factory gates with the first bras that the company had manufactured, through middle-aged matron, by now chief designer showing off their latest range of products, to the sprightly seventy-year-old retiring from the business to 'do other things with her life'.

And what other things, he had thought. Especially this final thing, this secret visit to be where the father of her son, the man she had loved, had died, this closing of the circle.

And Will had looked at the photograph again and again of Granddad Bill, as he now thought of him, of that young man in his RAF uniform with his dark hair and thin face. Did he really look like him? And what else had he inherited?

*

The late September sun was still blazing down when they finally reached the olive-tree grove that is the car park for the Allied War Cemetery in Souda Bay. Sweaters and jackets worn in England's cooler climate had already been discarded as soon as they emerged from the Nikos Kazantzakis airport at Heraklion and secured their hire car for the two-hour westwards journey on the National Road. Climbing out of the car, they gazed through the metal gateway at the white-marbled forecourt and the lines of white headstones stretching between lush grass either side of it and beyond to the depths of the blue Aegean Sea.

'Wow!' said Will, in awe at the sight. 'This is really something, isn't it?'

'It makes you want to be quiet,' said Chantal, holding Tom's hand supportively. 'Just remembering.'

Ellie, in a simple black skirt and white blouse, led the way through the gate and past the white-marbled shelter towards the tall, centrally placed Cross of Sacrifice. Will, similarly dressed in white and black, went into the shelter to see what was there, for he'd read on the Commonwealth War Graves website about the Cemetery Register. Tom in crumpled linen trousers and shirt and Chantal in well-cut grey skirt and cream blouse followed behind, pausing at the first row of headstones to read the inscriptions.

'How many did you say are buried here, Will?' called Chantal, gazing at one of the unmarked graves.

'Over fifteen hundred. Half of them are unmarked though.'

'Poor, poor boys. That's all they were. Look at the ages of so many of them, Tom. Twenty. Twenty-two. Nineteen. Just boys. It is awful.'

Tom was looking especially hard at one grave dedicated to 'An Airman of the 1939-1945 War'.

'What are you thinking?' she asked, squeezing his hand.

'That's what I used to think he was, an airman. I mean, I never gave him much thought, if I'm honest, but that photograph was always there and I just imagined that he'd died in an aeroplane. I never knew about radar and all that sort of thing being part of the RAF. Too much time reading Biggles, I suppose.'

He smiled wryly to himself, though his heart still felt heavy.

'This one is different,' Chantal said, steering him further along the line of graves. 'Look, it has Royal Air Force added.'

'And that phrase 'KNOWN UNTO GOD'.'

She looked at him.

'I never thought you were religious, darling.'

'I'm not. Nor was my mother and I don't think my father was either, from what his diary showed. But he did go into a chapel when he was stationed near here and leave some coins, even though he wasn't a believer. It's in his diary, remember? I guess I just feel something of the same here. This is a special place. Not just for me, I know, but for hundreds of others as well. And it must have been especially so for mum.'

He glanced down at the small brown cardboard box in his left hand in which was the metal urn containing her ashes, as Will appeared at their side. Yes, he could forgive now.

'I think it's time now,' he said, moving towards Ellie by the Cross of Sacrifice with Will following behind them.

Ellie turned as they approached.

'It's hard to understand it all. This is where Granddad Bill is buried but we don't know which grave. After suddenly finding about his existence, we still can't find a place that we can say was his last resting place.'

'Ellie, love, we know enough,' Tom said. 'And your granny knew enough. That's why we are here to unite them at last. Come.'

And he led them to the end of the grassed pathway to the very edge of the cemetery where it tipped over towards the Aegean Sea.

'This is where we say our last goodbyes,' said Tom. 'Remember, we each say what we have to say. You first, Will.'

Will scratched his right ear and screwed up his face.

'Is this really necessary, dad? I mean, I know we agreed and everything but isn't this just a bit embarrassing, standing here and mouthing off? Do I really have to?'

'It was what my counsellor said would be a great way of making our peace and saying goodbye simultaneously,' answered Tom, removing the black metal urn from its box.

'And I think she was right,' interjected Chantal. She knew, from carefully negotiating her relationships with Tom's two children over the years, what she could and could not say to them and one thing she could do was be firmer than Tom himself was at times. She knew Will in particular would not choose an argument with her, when he might with his father over the same issue. 'I'll go first.'

She reached into her trouser pocket and pulled out a sheet of paper to read from.

'This is from the bible. I know you are all heathens and you know I am not a churchgoer. But I grew up in a family who found great comfort in the bible. My mother especially would read from the bible at times of distress and I learned from her that, whatever one's belief system, there are words from the past that echo our feelings today and have an eternal strength to them. So this is from Ecclesiastes.'

She stepped slightly away from Tom to read.

'To everything there is a season, and a time to every purpose under the heaven. A time to be born, and a time to die; a time to plant, and a time to pluck up that which is planted. A time to kill, and a time to heal; a time to break down, and a time to build up. A time to weep, and a time to laugh; a time to mourn, and a time to dance. A time to cast away stones, and a time to gather stones together; a time to embrace, and a time to refrain from embracing. A time to get, and a time to lose; a time to keep, and a time to cast away. A time to rend, and a time to sew; a time to keep silence, and a time to speak. A time to love, and a time to hate; a time of war, and a time of peace.'

'Good grief, Chantal, you sound like a preacher,' said Will, in mixed admiration and awkwardness.

She gave him a light smile and folded the paper away into her pocket.

'Thank you, I take that as a compliment. My mother would have appreciated your saying that. Now you, Will.'

Will scratched his ear again in embarrassment.

'Okay, I've not brought anything to read. I did look for stuff on the Internet but I couldn't find anything that I thought was either appropriate or that I could manage. Most of it is just so sentimental. And Granny wasn't sentimental. That's what I remember about her more than anything. She hated all that false emotional stuff, all that gushing at weddings, all that mass hysteria over Princess Di's death, all that crying over trivial matters. I don't mean she was hard. We all know she was the kindest and most generous person you could wish to know. But she just could never go along with phoney emotionalism. That's all I can call it. That's how I will remember her chiefly. That's what she has meant to me. I remember, when we were kids, Thatcher deciding to retake the Falklands and all that jingoistic flag-waving when the Task Force ships were setting out from Portsmouth. We were watching it all at Granny's house and she said that all that cheering would soon turn to weeping when they found what going to war really meant. I was only eight at the time and I didn't really understand what she meant but I learned later. And now I really know what she meant. That's how I will remember her.'

Tom and Chantal stood in silence, heads bowed, as he spoke. From time to time one or other would nod briefly in agreement and recognition. Ellie's eyes moistened as she listened and as she then also recalled their childhood and the importance of Meredith Ennis, their Granny, in their growing up.

'I want to talk about Gladly,' she began, sniffling. 'I know it might sound silly but it means a lot to me. You know how Granny used to take me for picnics in the Botanical Gardens and how she told me this story about Gladly the cross-eyed bear that was once housed there. I know now that was a true story because one of the ceramicists we funded through the Arts Council a couple of years ago was commissioned to produce pottery pieces for display in their gallery and he was told the story. But what I never found out for many years, me and my naïve trustfulness, was that the treats I always got as I left the gardens were not from Gladly but from Granny. I think I must have been seven or eight before I realised that. Maybe even nine. Granny gave me the power to believe in a good future. I know it's maybe made me too trusting but rather that than being cynical. I shall remember her most for her boundless faith in life.'

Chantal took Ellie's arm and squeezed it.

'Thank you, Ellie. I didn't know about Gladly. But it all makes sense. Thank you.'

And now it was Tom's turn. He had been preparing for it for some time in his head, ever since his counsellor, Dr Stephanie Barrett, had helped him to work through his anger at his mother's deception. Now he stepped forward.

'I have known for many years that I would have to say something at my mother's funeral. Ever since my stepfather, as I now know him to be, your Granddad Bert, died and I listened to that vicar none of us knew mouthing off platitudes about him, I knew that I couldn't allow that to happen at mum's death. And I've had a long time to prepare, haven't I? Who could have guessed that she would live to such an age, ninety years of life? And who could have guessed in their wildest dreams that her end would come as it did? And so, despite my years of expecting and preparing, when it came to the funeral, I just wasn't ready to speak. That's why, as you know, we got that Humanist woman to lead the ceremony. Now I can speak but what should I say?'

He paused and looked at the others, who were gazing at him in support and shared sorrow.

'How long is a person's life? Bill Ennis died in 1941, sixty-five years ago, my age. And yet he lived in mum's heart until she died and he lives in each of us. We are the harvest of the love that he and mum, Bill and Merry, as he called her, shared so fleetingly so many years ago. Without the seed that was planted then, I would not exist and nor would Ellie or Will. And so I would never have met Chantal.'

He smiled warmly at his wife and she reached out her hand to touch his arm.

'How long is a person's life? It's only a few months since mum died and we all still carry her memory inside us. We remember passing moments with her, we remember her idiosyncrasies, we remember her strength, we remember her determination, we remember her stubbornness. And now we know of her love, the love for Bill she bore in her heart for so many years, the love she gave to Bert for so many years, and the love she gave to each of us for always.'

He looked at his children, their eyes cast down as they thought about her, and at Chantal who was smiling encouragement at him.

'So how long is a person's life? We do not know. But we shall carry your granny, Bill's Merry, my mum inside us as long as we live.'

Tom took the lid off the urn, turned it upside down and Meredith Ennis's ashes drifted down to the seashore, as all four wept in the afternoon sun. And, as they wept, a mild breeze arose and seemed to carry a tune in it, a tune played on a Cretan *lyra*, though there was no one else in the cemetery, only the rows of graves, only those restless souls 'KNOWN UNTO GOD'.

# Acknowledgements

The central section of the book, Bill Ennis's 'Cretan Diary', draws extensively on the experiences in Crete of the late Professor James Britton, as described in his memoir *Record and Recall*. I am very grateful to his daughters, Celia and Alison Britton, for permission to use this material. Antony Beevor's book *Crete: The Battle and the Resistance* is a goldmine of information about the Battle of Crete.

I am also grateful to Nik and Emma Perkins, Angel Scott, Alastair West and John Rowe who read earlier versions of this book and made helpful suggestions. Above all I want to thank my wife Enid for her constant support and her interest in my Cretan research.